THE CITY OF Bordeleaux, in the ancient land of Bretonnia, is having to put up with the loveable rogues Florin and Lorenzo. Fresh from their adventures in the Ogre Kingdoms, Florin and his companion are quickly burning through their new-found wealth and making enemies left, right and centre.

Having returned with them from the land of the ogres, Katerina is having difficulty shedding her savage nature and acting like a young lady. And the in-laws are not too impressed with her…

When her husband is murdered, Katerina responds the only way she knows how, going on a feral rampage throughout the city. Can Florin and Lorenzo stop her before Bordeleaux becomes a savage city?

More Florin & Lorenzo from Robert Earl

**THE BURNING SHORE
WILD KINGDOMS**

A WARHAMMER NOVEL

SAVAGE CITY

Robert Earl

A BLACK LIBRARY PUBLICATION

First published in Great Britain in 2005 by
BL Publishing,
Games Workshop Ltd.,
Willow Road, Nottingham,
NG7 2WS, UK

10 9 8 7 6 5 4 3 2 1

Cover illustration by Ralph Horsley
Map by Nuala Kinrade.

© Games Workshop Limited 2005. All rights reserved.

Black Library, the Black Library logo, Black Flame, BL Publishing, Games Workshop, the Games Workshop logo and all associated marks, names, characters, illustrations and images from the Warhammer universe are either ®, TM and/or © Games Workshop Ltd 2000-2005, variably registered in the UK and other countries around the world. All rights reserved.

A CIP record for this book is available from the British Library

ISBN13: 978 1 84416 198 0
ISBN 10: 1 84416 198 6

Distributed in the US by Simon & Schuster
1230 Avenue of the Americas, New York, NY 10020, US.

Printed and bound in Great Britain by
Bookmarque, Surrey, UK.

No part of this publication may be reproduced, stored in a retrieval system, or transmitted in any form or by any means, electronic, mechanical, photocopying, recording or otherwise, without the prior permission of the publishers.

This is a work of fiction. All the characters and events portrayed in this book are fictional, and any resemblance to real people or incidents is purely coincidental.

See the Black Library on the Internet at
www.blacklibrary.com

Find out more about Games Workshop
and the world of Warhammer at
www.games-workshop.com

THIS IS A DARK age, a bloody age, an age of daemons and of sorcery. It is an age of battle and death, and of the world's ending. Amidst all of the fire, flame and fury it is a time, too, of mighty heroes, of bold deeds and great courage.

AT THE HEART of the Old World sprawls the Empire, the largest and most powerful of the human realms. Known for its engineers, sorcerers, traders and soldiers, it is a land of great mountains, mighty rivers, dark forests and vast cities. And from his throne in Altdorf reigns the Emperor Karl-Franz, sacred descendent of the founder of these lands, Sigmar, and wielder of his magical warhammer.

BUT THESE ARE far from civilised times. Across the length and breadth of the Old World, from the knightly palaces of Bretonnia to ice-bound Kislev in the far north, come rumblings of war. In the towering World's Edge Mountains, the orc tribes are gathering for another assault. Bandits and renegades harry the wild southern lands of the Border Princes. There are rumours of rat-things, the skaven, emerging from the sewers and swamps across the land. And from the northern wilder-nesses there is the ever-present threat of Chaos, of daemons and beastmen corrupted by the foul powers of the Dark Gods. As the time of battle draws ever near, the Empire needs heroes like never before.

For Clara

*Unexpectable, spectaculous
and very lovely*

PROLOGUE

'You. Stop dragging the chain.' Gul's captor didn't bother to raise his voice. Instead, he let his whip speak for him. The blur of it snapped through the darkness to bite into flesh.

A line of white-hot pain scribbled itself across Gul's back. He stumbled forward clumsily, tripping on the rough stone floor of the tunnel that he was being herded down. The captive manacled to the chain gang ahead of him broke his fall. She whimpered miserably beneath the impact and his muttered apology brought another blow stinging out of the darkness.

'No talking,' his captor mumbled, his voice as soft as his whip was sharp.

Gul still had no idea how he had come to be here. The last thing he could remember before waking up in this terrible underworld was the fog. It had come rolling in off the sea, the vaporous depths of it creeping through the crumbling docks of Bordeleaux with the slow menace of a malignant disease. Its tendrils, thick as gruel, had reached everywhere.

The fog had brought its own distinctive smell with it, too. A smell almost thick enough to taste. It had combined rotten seaweed with dead fish, mildewed slime with drowned meat.

It was perhaps the most disgusting thing Gul had ever smelt.

That was why he had burrowed deep within a coil of ropes, his blanket over his head. But then, suddenly, the blanket had been torn away and the smell of the fog had been replaced with something else, something like burning straw.

A second later and there had been nothing.

Ahead, the tunnel twisted deeper into the living rock, the narrow passage winding through the granite like a wormhole through an apple. Gul listened to the chink of chains and heard a curse as another of the captives stumbled. Behind him somebody vomited. The retching and the splatter did little to help Gul, who had felt as sick as a potcheen drinker ever since he'd woken up.

Through the nausea he began to wonder if this was indeed a punishment of the gods.

But no. Despite his throbbing head he didn't think so. Although their faces were no more than black holes beneath their hoods, Gul was sure that his captors were mortal men. What was more, the air which chilled this dank labyrinth was tinged with the familiar scent of brine, and his grandmother had been quite definite about daemons breathing sulphur.

Slightly reassured, Gul concentrated on keeping his feet. The stone underfoot had become treacherous and he edged his way forward with practiced care.

After perhaps an hour a sound began to whisper along the passageway. It throbbed like the heart of some great and slumbering beast, a low, hungry murmur that sent an edge of panic racing through the captives' veins.

Gul realised, however, that this was no monster. It was just the sea, her waves washing up against some hidden shoreline. Shale began to crunch beneath his bare feet as the tunnel widened and gradually flared open into a natural cave. Beyond it, framed by an arc of stone like the stage of a moonlit theatre, lay a beach.

The score of chained captives stumbled out into the pale light, their manacles glinting like silver in the luminescence. Granite heights towered up all around them, dizzying ramparts that crowded out the sky on all sides apart from the west. Here, the sea held sway, the rolling beat of its restless immensity sending phosphorescent waves spuming upwards towards the stars.

'Stop.'

The chain gang staggered to a ragged halt. Gul shivered, his nerves combining with the chill sea breeze to send a sudden spasm through his body.

'No moving,' a guard said, and snapped his whip with lazy sadism.

More pain. This time, though, it served Gul well. The sting of the blow served to cut through the dizziness that had been with him since he'd woken. Shaking in cold and fear, he peered into the shadows of the imprisoning cliffs, studying the cove for any chance of escape. What he saw instead was the first movement from the men who had been lurking there.

'Welcome, my old friends.' The voice which oiled out from the darkness was as smooth as a viper. 'It is a joy to behold you once more. And in such good health!'

'Likewise,' one of Gul's captors said and paced warily towards the hidden speaker. Although he wore the same shapeless robes as his fellows, this man was clearly their leader. Everything from the tone of his voice to the set of his shoulders marked him out as such.

For a moment, the captain stood alone on the sand, his hood giving him a monstrous appearance in the moonlight.

'Come, my old friend,' he said, speaking with the careful insouciance of a man who knows the danger of sounding afraid. 'Let us embrace. For old times' sake.'

'Of course,' the voice from the shadows said and, moving with a reluctance which was strangely at odds with the honey of his words, the lurker waddled out onto the sand.

Despite the high dome of his helmet he was as short and round as a barrel. He wheezed as he paced through the sand, his chest heaving as he threw back his robes and spread his arms wide open. The gesture of trust was belied by the flash of burnished steel that armoured the roll of his stomach, but Gul was no longer paying attention to these details.

Instead, all his attention was focused on the thing that had lumbered out of the shadows after the fat man.

It was like something from a nightmare. Although vaguely human in shape, the thing was at least twice the size of any man Gul had ever seen. Its black silhouette loomed up into the night as it advanced, the elephantine thud of its feet flattening the sand.

In the gloom its head was as featureless as a boulder, but Gul could make out the pinpricks of its eyes. They gleamed with an animal intelligence as the beast studied the chain of captives. To Gul, the gleam seemed horribly hungry.

As it drew nearer, a chorus of moans and sobs rose up from the captives. They shifted, and for a moment it looked as if the whole chained line was about to stampede.

The guards had obviously been expecting this moment.

'Stay still,' they chorused. Whips hissed gleefully, snapping against bruised flesh as the captives were herded back into a straight line. More than one of them was weeping with pure terror as the thing from the darkness ground to a halt behind its master, its silvered eyes never leaving the prisoners.

The fat man giggled in delight.

'Ah, I see that my bodyguard is creating his usual impression,' he said smugly, and quickly embraced the other man.

'That and the magnificence of your presence, of course.'

'Magnificence, yes.' An invisible smile was evident in the fat man's voice. 'I just wish that I could pay your merchandise here the same compliment.'

Gul's captor barked, an explosion of humourless laughter.

'Don't worry about that, my old friend, because your customers certainly will. Once this consignment is cleaned and rested you will see they are the best yet.'

The fat man waved a plump hand through the air, as if to brush the claim away.

'Oh no,' he said. 'Please don't denigrate yourself. The last consignment was much better.'

'For field slaves, perhaps. But this time we have rarer goods. See here.'

So saying, the hooded merchant led his client towards the line, which shifted uneasily as the fat man's monstrous bodyguard drew nearer.

Gul, sweating despite the shivers which racked his scrawny body, felt his throat tightening with terror. A splash of moonlight illuminated the monster's smashed visage, revealing a ravenous leer.

So great was his terror that he barely noticed the two slavers that had strolled over to stand in front of him.

'Now look at this one,' the hooded man said, and waved a hand in Gul's direction. For a moment he thought that it was him that the man was singling out. Then he realised that it was the girl beside him.

'Exactly. You can see what I mean,' the shorter man said, pretending not to catch the other's meaning. 'She's so thin that she'll hardly be of use in the fields, let alone the lapis mines.'

Again, Gul's captor choked on the attempt at laughter.

'Here, you,' he called out to one of his men. 'Bring that lantern over here so that I and my old friend can see the mistake he has made.'

The man hurried over, lantern raised, spilling a wash of golden light across the captives.

Squinting against the sudden brightness, Gul looked across at his fellow prisoner and the breath caught in his throat.

For one heart-stopping moment he was sure that she was Maria, his childhood sweetheart. Her button-nosed profile, still sweet despite the glistening of tears; the sweep of her corn-silk hair was tangled after her ordeal. Even the way she hugged herself against the cold, arms clasped over the torn cloth of her tunic. These and a dozen other details filled Gul with dumb-witted amazement. But then his eyes cleared and so did his wits. Although she could have been her twin, the girl who was chained next to him wasn't Maria. He felt slightly guilty at the disappointment he felt.

'Now look at her properly,' Gul's captor told the merchant. 'See the colour of her hair? It's so yellow it's almost white. And look at the shape of her. She's skinny all right, but only in the right places!'

'Hmm,' the fat man rumbled, his face remaining impassive. He reached out a podgy hand towards the girl and, as casually as a man examining a horse, he tilted her head to examine the roots of her hair. When she pulled away he slapped her, hard across the face.

Gul's face twisted into an unconscious snarl.

'I suppose she might have some value,' the fat man admitted, dropping his hand to the girl's shoulder and turning her around. She stumbled and he slapped her again, this time across the back of her head.

'Stand still you silly–' he began to complain.

Suddenly, to his own surprise, Gul found himself speaking. 'Leave her alone, you bloated toad!' he spat, his clenched fists raised as high as the manacles would allow.

Despite the fact that his challenger remained shackled, the merchant sprang backwards with a squeal of alarm. 'Bran,' he squeaked, scrabbling around the hulking monster who waited behind him. 'Help!'

After a second of confusion, the thing shrugged and lumbered forward. As the great slabs of its hands reached towards him Gul began to realise what a mistake he'd made.

'No, wait,' he cried. His rage had deserted him now, scoured away by the molten intensity of those inhuman eyes. He tried to pull back, but the pressure of the other captives in the chain gang held him as fast as a fly in a spider's web. Before he could struggle further, hands as big as hams seized him with bone-snapping strength. The gristle in his skinny shoulders crunched and he screamed in pain as he was lifted from the ground. For a moment the great beast held him close, the stench of its breath strong enough to make his eyes water.

'Well, go on then,' its master said with a vindictive whine.

Through a prism of tears, Gul snatched a last glance at the girl who was cowering on the shale of the beach.

Oh Lady, he thought, as a gaping maw of blunted teeth descended on him. Why couldn't I have been born one of the duke's oxen? And with that thought, the jaws closed and his short, hard life was over.

THE CHIEF SLAVER watched the last of the longboats pulling away through the surf. The vessel sliced easily through the rolling waves, her prow lifted high by the weight of the ogre in the stern. Beyond this boat lay half a dozen more, and beyond them the three-masted silhouette of the merchant's ship waited on the dark horizon.

The captives' journey, the slaver knew, had only just begun.

A sudden memory of what the ogre had done to the boldest of them flashed through his thoughts, and a smile crept across his features. It usually took hours for these damned Arabyans to get to the point, but the revolting spectacle of the ogre devouring its victim had lent a rare urgency to the proceedings.

'Ready when you are.'

The slaver turned and found his men waiting for him, their backs bent beneath the empty chains they had to carry back. Behind them, a broken shape lay on the sand, little more than a smear in the moonlight.

His partner followed his gaze. 'Shall we bury him?'

'No,' he decided. 'Why bother? We'll leave him for the crabs.'

And so saying he turned and led the way back into the tunnel, eager to start celebrating yet another successful business transaction.

CHAPTER ONE

THE HERRING BOAT was perfectly built for the job she had been designed for. Most of her twenty-two feet was sharply angled for maximum speed, essential when chasing the great spring shoals. Beneath these sleek lines, though, her bottom was as wide and plump as a matron's. However rich the sea, she could comfortably hold the biggest of catches.

Like every boat in Bretonnia, she had an effigy of the Lady fastened to her prow. The goddess's wooden eyes gazed sightlessly into whatever future lay ahead of the vessel. Her blindness was perhaps fortunate, for without it she would never have been able to look so serene.

By contrast to the Lady's expression, the man who clung to the pinnace above her looked anything but serene.

That was understandable. Florin d'Artaud was a newcomer to this profession. The unbroken lines of his well-proportioned face, the unblemished smoothness of skin, the windblown tangle of fashionably shoulder length hair – these and a dozen other details marked him out from the grizzled hands that usually sailed this boat.

He'd bought her a fortnight ago, and he'd only learnt to sail her a week after that. Perhaps that was why the wildness of his windswept hair was matched by the wildness in his eyes, and the anxiety was apparent beneath the commanding bark of his voice.

'Take her to starboard,' he called back, raising his voice against the snap of the sliver of canvas they were using.

At the other end of the boat, Lorenzo, who was at least grizzled enough to look the part of a sailor, heaved on the tiller. He cursed as he did so, and the wiry muscles in his arms bunched as he struggled against the current.

It was a struggle he won, and a moment later the boat wallowed ponderously to the right.

Florin grunted with satisfaction and looked ahead once more. His eyes narrowed against the spray that exploded up from beneath him, although it had already glued the shirt to his body, he barely noticed it. He was too busy concentrating on the rolling depths below, and the occasional dark patches that marred the lighter blue.

'Shit!' he swore suddenly as one such dark patch raced towards him. 'Port. Go to port!'

Lorenzo hesitated for a moment, his face contorted in thought, and then hurled himself against the tiller. As he did so his cursing grew louder, and he spat his complaints into the quickening wind. 'Why don't you just say left and right?' he snapped as the boat veered away from a fist of submerged rocks.

'What?' Florin shouted without turning his head.

'I said, why don't you speak Bretonnian?' the older man yelled back. 'Port and starboard. Why not left and right?'

'It's so nobody gets confused,' Florin bellowed, raising his voice above a sudden snap and billow of the sail.

Lorenzo rolled his eyes and, deciding not to distract the lookout any further, contented himself with muttering. After all, this was no place to be distracting anybody.

Known as the Bite, this was one of the most lethal stretches of water around Bordeleaux. On one side the coast reared up in tiers of cliffs; a black rock anvil whose tiny coves were littered with the bones of countless wrecks. On the other side lay a scattering of tiny islands, barren except for the bleached guano of the birds that nested upon them.

And in between these two jaws, lying in terrible predatory wait beneath the cover of the sea, were the Bite's granite teeth.

Florin glanced across as the last of the tiny islets slipped by to starboard and breathed a small sigh of relief. According to the real fishermen he'd bought this boat from, this marked the end of the Bite and the beginning of clear water. Unwilling to take any chances, he stayed at his post anyway, content to leave the sail half furled and Lorenzo at the tiller.

Only when the last of the islands was far behind them did he shin his way back down the pinnace, stretch the cramp out of his muscles, and clamber along the deck to where his old comrade waited.

'What time do you think it is?' he asked as he took his shirt off and wrung it out.

Lorenzo shrugged. 'I'm not sure, but it must be well after noon by now.'

'Then they should be there,' Florin said, pulling his shirt back on and taking the bandolier Lorenzo handed to him. He checked that the sword was secure in its scabbard before dropping it over his head. Then, after tightening the shoulder buckle, he retrieved his hat. The dull grey of the moleskin was brightened by the metallic sheen of a peacock feather and the silver of the brooch upon which it was fastened.

'Tell me again,' Lorenzo said, looking at his friend with a jaundiced eye. 'What do we say if a customs boat stops us?'

'We tell 'em we're herring fishermen,' Florin reminded him as he fastened a silk cape around his throat, 'who haven't caught any... ah. I see what you mean.'

Lorenzo smiled.

'Well, never mind,' Florin decided. 'As long as I get back into costume after we take delivery.'

'Speaking of which,' his friend said, nodding towards the headland that was pushing out to sea in front of them, 'isn't that the one?'

The two men studied the outcrop. The broken shape of a ruined tower jutted up towards the sky. To Lorenzo, the finger of blackened stone looked like an obscene gesture, but to Florin it seemed to beckon.

'That's the one.' Florin nodded, and felt a faint rush of excitement. This deal had been a long time in the planning. It had been a delicate matter, too. The Tileans were a notoriously jumpy people, especially when it came to risking their business. Only Florin's family name had earned him the introduction to their agents, and only the fact that he'd been recognised as one of the great Castavelli's followers had clinched the deal.

Castavelli, Florin had learned, had become one of Tilea's most celebrated heroes since his return from the green hell of Lustria. Florin wasn't surprised. All the men who'd returned from that particular fiasco had gloried in their new reputations. What had surprised Florin was learning that, according to the Tilean version of events, Castavelli had been the leader of the expedition. His courage had inspired everybody else.

Apparently, he'd even saved Florin's life.

Not pointing out that things had in fact been the other way around, had been one of the hardest things Florin had ever done. But now, as they rounded the headland and the Tilean merchant vessel edged into view, he began to realise that it had probably all been worth it.

Lorenzo whistled through a gap in his two front teeth as he saw the ship. He had expected some greyhound slip of a boat, all sprung sails and nervous energy. But the ship that awaited them looked built for nothing but business, regardless of how competitive that business got.

'It must take a lot of men to sail a ship like that,' Lorenzo observed thoughtfully as his eyes slid along the fortress lines of her hull.

'Must take a lot of men to defend it, too. Even the gold of her figurehead looks worth stealing.'

Lorenzo chewed his lip thoughtfully. 'Of course, they might not just defend her. What if they decide they'd rather rob us than trade?'

'That wouldn't make much sense.' Florin frowned. 'Why jeopardise their business like that?'

'Greed?' Lorenzo offered.

Florin nodded and his frown turned into a sudden, wild smile. 'You might be right,' he allowed. 'But to the hells with it. It's too late to turn back now.'

Lorenzo shrugged and checked the knife that lay hidden along the small of his back. The weight of it, snug against his spine, lent him a reassurance that Florin's blind confidence could not.

And anyway, the older man thought, at least he knew how to swim.

One of the Tilean lookouts saw their approach and waved. Florin slipped off his cloak and waved it back, letting the blue material stream out in the pre-arranged signal.

Now they were near enough to see the crossbowmen who lined the ship's gunwales. There were perhaps a dozen of them, their faces suspicious and their armour black with the tar that protected it against the sea air. The only bright things about them were their weapons. The sprung steel arms of their crossbows glinted with the dull menace that was the only insurance available in this trade.

'Three hundred crowns,' muttered Lorenzo, dragging the tiller to one side as they slipped into the ship's shadow.

'And tonight it will be three thousand,' Florin said, then leapt forward to grab the rope ladder that one of the Tileans dropped down.

'Want me to come with you?'

'No, I'll be all right,' Florin told him and, making sure that his hat was safely crammed down onto his head, he began to shin his way up the rope.

Above him the crossbowmen waited as patiently as hangmen by a scaffold.

'Gods damn it,' Lorenzo muttered again, and tied off on the rope. 'We should have just bought wine from the guild like everybody else.'

'YOU MUST LISTEN to reason, my dear,' the lawyer said, his face wrinkling into an understanding smile beneath the grey mop of his hair. 'You're obviously an intelligent girl. We can all see that. And your sentimentality is certainly to your credit. But you must realise that this marriage isn't a real one.'

Katerina said nothing. Instead she just watched the lawyer with bored indifference. Her mother had led him into her quarters over an hour ago, and ever since then he'd been smiling and wheedling as desperately as a starving gnoblar.

The man's avuncular smile began to fade beneath Katerina's unblinking gaze. Somehow, the fact that she was wearing little more than a sword belt and a smock made her icy appraisal even more unnerving. He wasn't used to dealing with ladies who dressed in such clothes.

Or rather, in such a lack of them.

The lawyer looked at the girl's mother for reassurance, but Comtesse Hansebourg's own icy stare was scarcely more pleasant than her daughter's.

'The thing is,' he hurried on, 'because you were married on a ship, it probably doesn't count…'

'Probably!' the older woman snapped. 'What do you mean, probably? The whole thing was meaningless.'

'Well, quite,' the lawyer hurriedly agreed. 'None of the Hansebourgs have been married at sea before, so it goes against all family custom. More important is the fact that you'd already been promised to Monsieur Mordicio. He had a prior claim that no mere ship's captain had the right to overturn.'

'Exactly,' the comtesse said. 'How dare he try to break the deal we had with Monsieur Mordicio? Mercenary swine!'

Katerina ignored her and waited until the first bead of sweat appeared on the lawyer's forehead before replying.

'The ship's captain had the right, regardless of my family's name,' she told him, green eyes never leaving his. 'Just as I had the right to choose my own husband. Which is why I am married to Sergei.'

The lawyer pursed his lips and silently cursed. Her mother had led him to expect that this girl was an illiterate savage, but she seemed to have as keen a grasp on Bordeleaux's tangled marriage arrangements as any gold-digging professional.

'Well, my dear, even if the ship's captain did have the right, and he probably didn't, it still wouldn't be legal.'

He waited for Katerina to ask him why. When she didn't, he told her anyway.

'The thing is, you need witnesses of good standing for a marriage to be legal. And by good standing we mean respectable burghers, not sailors and mercenaries.'

'Are you suggesting that the d'Artaud family is not of good standing?' Katerina purred.

The comtesse barked with sarcastic laughter, but the lawyer looked suddenly wary. There were rumours about the youngest of the d'Artauds; the sort of rumours that meant that he was, if not respectable, then at least respected. Or, if not respected, then certainly feared.

'Ah, the d'Artauds,' he said, clearing his throat and looking away. 'I see. Well, all of this is academic anyway. Without a signed document this marriage is, to all intents and purposes, null and void.'

Katerina smiled for the first time and, like a gambler revealing an ace, she lifted her smock and pulled a roll of parchment from beneath her garter belt. The lawyer swallowed. Katerina dropped her skirt back down and he managed to drag his eyes away from her legs to study the document she threw at him.

'Here,' she said. 'Florin got it for me.'

'Florin!' cried her mother, her voice shrill with outrage. 'I might have known. He's a terrible influence. I forbid you to see him again!'

For the first time, Katerina deigned to look at the older woman. 'Just try,' she said, and the two of them locked eyes.

'Well, yes, anyway...' the lawyer murmured, seizing upon the distraction. 'I can see you two want to be left alone. I'll just get my things and—'

'Stay where you are,' the comtesse snapped, turning on him.

He sighed and sank back down into his chair. 'Very well,' he said. 'Although I don't see what more I can do.'

'Do it anyway.'

He pulled at the tip of his nose, his mind racing. The Hansebourgs were a powerful family. If they decided that one of their women wasn't married, then, in the normal run of things, she wouldn't be. Add to that the involvement of that old gangster, Mordicio, and her marriage didn't stand a chance. If only he could persuade the girl herself of that.

'I know,' he said, face lighting up as inspiration struck. 'Non-consummation. You haven't had any children, have you?'

Katerina shook her head. 'What does non-consummation mean?'

The lawyer's mouth fell open and he started to blush. She was beginning to see why the ogres who had raised her had held her fellow humans in such contempt.

'Well, erm, it means... Well, you know about the breeding pens for the bullrings? It's sort of like that. Consummation, I mean. As opposed to, erm...'

Katerina constructed an expression of perfect innocence and shook her head.

'I still don't understand...' She shrugged, and bit back her laughter as his cheeks darkened from red to purple. By now he was squirming so much that he might have been sitting on a nest of fire ants instead of a cushioned chair. He looked desperately towards the comtesse.

For once, she showed him some mercy. 'What this old fool is trying to say,' she said, 'is that because you haven't slept with Sergei your marriage doesn't count.'

'But I sleep with him every night.'

The comtesse tutted impatiently. 'You know perfectly well what I mean. You haven't produced any heirs.'

'Oh well, if that's the only problem,' Katerina said, suddenly tiring of the game, 'we'll go and get right back to it.' She rolled to her feet with a fluid grace and made for the door.

'Sit back down,' her mother shouted, but Katerina's only response was to veer towards the lawyer. 'Thanks for the advice,' she breathed and flashed him a wink before padding out of the drawing room.

'Well, well, well,' the lawyer croaked, wiping the sweat from his forehead. 'Modern girls, eh, comtesse? Very independent.'

The comtesse shot him a glance and he shut up.

'You'll have to do better than that,' his client declared. 'Monsieur Mordicio is a patient man, but he's already waited six months. Whatever Katerina says, she belongs to him. We made the agreement years ago.'

While his client paced up and down, the lawyer noted that she was quite a beautiful woman. Well, handsome, perhaps, rather than beautiful, with gorgeous sea-blue eyes. She was quite a wealthy widow, too, he surmised, as he studied the generous swell of her body beneath her clothes.

'Well?' she asked, her raised eyebrow a question mark.

For one panicky moment, the lawyer thought that she'd noticed his ungentlemanly appraisal, but he soon recovered his wits.

'To be honest with you, comtesse,' he said, 'if neither the young lady nor her husband want an annulment, there isn't very much the law can do. But I wonder...' He trailed off, until his client tutted impatiently.

'Ahem, I wonder if the young man in question might be induced, for a certain financial consideration, to realise that an annulment would be in Katerina's best interests? I was given to understand that he was from a fairly impecunious background?'

'Pay him off, you mean.' The comtesse shook her head. 'No. Her uncles have already tried. They were quite generous in their offer, too, but you know how ungrateful these strigany are. He wouldn't even consider it.'

'I see. Well then, the only other way is by order of the duke. And to be honest, comtesse, by the time you receive an audience, old age will probably have dissolved the marriage anyway.' He chuckled good-humouredly. The comtesse didn't join in.

'So, you're saying that the only way to annul this marriage is for that damned strigany to die?'

The lawyer stopped chuckling.

'Well… yes,' he admitted, a troubled frown creasing his forehead. 'But I wouldn't advise… I mean, now that he's married to a Hansebourg, the duke would punish anybody who had a hand in his death. Even a fellow Hansebourg. If you get my meaning.'

'Yes, I do,' the comtesse said and smiled for the first time since they entered the room. It was a radiant expression and for a moment she looked almost as beautiful as her daughter. 'Now, if you will excuse me, I have things to arrange.'

'Yes, yes, of course,' the lawyer said, gratitude evident in his voice. He gathered up his papers and, with a quick bow, he turned and hurried from the room.

He wanted to make sure that she couldn't tell him what arrangements she was suddenly so keen to make.

BY NOW, ANY doubts that Florin had had about the transaction were long gone. It wasn't just that the barrels of Tilean wine he'd bought had all been tested and safely stowed on his own boat, although that had certainly helped. No, what lent him such an air of confidence was the fact that the wine tasting had been going on for more than an hour. That and the lying.

It seemed that the captain of this ship, a Signor Ballideci, was a distant cousin of the hero Castavelli, which meant that he couldn't hear enough about his illustrious relative's heroics. And, despite the egotistical pang Florin had first felt upon hearing the Tilean version of the events in Lustria, he was happy enough to lie on Castavelli's account. After all, although hardly the hero his countrymen thought him to be, the mercenary had been a friend and a comrade.

'So there we were,' Florin said, accepting yet another goblet of the finest wine the Old World had ever produced. 'There were no more than a hundred of us and out there, as far as the eye could see, was a vast horde of monsters. Horrible they were. The smallest was twice the size of a man and they had scales harder than any armour.'

'You must have been terrified,' Ballideci said in the rolling dialect of Tilea.

Florin agreed. 'We were. We were all terrified. In fact, many of us wanted to run. But then Captain Castavelli leapt up onto the pyramid and said… and said…' He trailed off, his imagination failing him despite the wine, but Ballideci was there with the words.

'He said, "Have faith, my brothers. The work ahead may be bloody, and some of us might fall. But in days to come, in every taverna in the land, men will say, "I wish I'd been there"'.'

'Um, yes. That's right,' Florin said and Bellideci smiled proudly.

'I learned the words of the play by heart,' he explained.

'And then,' another of the crew chipped in, 'Castavelli led the cavalry charge.'

'Yes, I was just getting to that,' Florin said, desperately trying to guess what his former comrade had said about a cavalry charge. It wasn't as if they'd even had any horses. But before he could continue the story, a cry from the crow's nest brought the party to a sudden halt.

'Doganale! Ufficio doganale!'

The crowd that had gathered around Florin exploded outwards, the men running like hares from a wolf. Although the deck was crowded and snared with hawsers and tackle, the crew moved with a practiced ease, scuttling to their positions and leaving Florin standing alone and confused. Captain Ballideci, remembering his guest, paused as he followed them. He turned back to slap him on the back and grinned enormously.

'It was very nice to see you. I tell my cousin we meet back in Tilea. Ciao.'

'What's the rush?' Florin called after him, but the only reply the captain could spare was 'Ufficio doganale.'

Florin dodged through a group of hurrying sailors to peer over the gunwale at Lorenzo. 'Get a move on,' the older man shouted up at him. 'Didn't you hear what they said? A customs boat is coming.'

'Damn!' Florin swore. With a last swig he emptied his goblet and vaulted over the side of the ship, sliding back down the mooring rope with palm-blistering speed.

'The wind's against us, so we're going to have to tack,' Lorenzo told him, already untying the rope and pushing away from the side of the ship. Florin cursed again. The run in had been relatively easy; with the wind behind them they had been able to ride before it and steer with the tiller. Now, though, with the wind against them, they would have to tack, to use the angles of the sail to zigzag into it.

But first they would have to row clear of the Tileans.

'Right then, on three,' Florin said as he seized hold of his oar. He had a sudden flashback to Lustria, and the days they'd spent on her malarial waterways, but then all of his thoughts snapped back to the task at hand.

'One, two, three!'

The herring boat was designed for sailing, not rowing, and she moved with a ponderous reluctance against the current. Undeterred, the two men hurled themselves against their oars and, gradually, they began to nose their way out of the larger ship's shadow.

Florin waited until they were two lengths away before stowing his oar and racing forward to unfurl the sail. It snapped eagerly in the breeze as he did so, and the boat rolled alarmingly as the material billowed around a bellyful of air. For once, Lorenzo was too busy to complain. He'd just unhitched the ropes that controlled the boom, and now he heaved on one of them. The sail swung round in response, belching out the air and slicing neatly into the wind. Florin, ducking beneath the swinging boom with perfect timing, rolled back to seize the tiller. As he pulled on it, he could see that the Tileans were also on the move. Even as some of their crew dragged the ship's anchor up from the depths, her sails were filling.

The Bretonnian watched anxiously as the larger vessel overtook them, her wake setting his own boat rolling from side to side. The Tileans turned, and for one terrifying moment it seemed that the two vessels would collide. But then the Tileans were in front of them and, with a surge of white water that soaked Lorenzo with brine, they were past them and heading out to sea.

Captain Ballideci, seeming not to hear Lorenzo's curses, waved his hat over the side and yelled 'Ciao!'

But Florin didn't return the gesture. He'd just seen how close the customs cutter was.

He would have spotted it before had it not been coming straight for them. As it was, the pale billow of its canvas had blended in with a skyful of white clouds, and the sharp angle of its prow had been lost against the rolling expanse of the ocean beyond. The predatory shape grew larger even as Florin watched, and, to his surprise, he saw the Tileans steer straight towards her. The sea curled up beneath their hull like soil beneath a plough as the southlanders turned, and for a moment the customs ship was eclipsed by her gilded stern.

'What are they doing that for?' Florin yelled to Lorenzo as the two ships drew nearer. 'They look as though they're going to meet.'

The older man twisted the sail into a new angle before replying. 'Treachery?' he suggested as they cut back into the wind.

Florin spat the suddenly sour taste of wine out of his mouth, his attention torn between the two ships and the sea ahead. The customs men had come from the clear ocean which didn't leave him with many options. If the Tileans were in league with the enemy then they wouldn't be drawing them away, and if they didn't draw them away then he and Lorenzo would be faced with a lethal choice.

They'd either have to surrender or risk tacking back through the Bite. A sudden image sprang unbidden into

Florin's mind. It was of his boat's hull being torn out from under her, her timbers splintered into matchsticks by the gnashing granite teeth of the reef. The vision was horribly realistic, right down to the way he and Lorenzo were pitched into the sea.

Another man might have taken it as an omen, but not Florin d'Artaud. To the hells with it, he decided in a flash of alcohol-fuelled boldness. After all, it was me that held things together in Lustria, not Castavelli. It was me who discovered the Ogre Kingdoms… And it was me who rescued Katerina Hansebourg.

The thought of what Katerina might say if he did surrender squared his jaw with fresh determination, and he scowled across at the customs ship.

By now the Tilean was almost upon her and Florin suddenly realised that this was no pre-arranged meeting. Far from it. The smuggler's sails remained as fat as an ogre's gut, and her helmsman had kept her arrowing towards the exciseman as straight as a battering ram.

'What's he doing?' Florin shouted to Lorenzo, surprise edging his voice.

'Ramming her, it looks like,' Lorenzo replied, sounding surprised himself.

'That's insane. They'll both go down.'

But that didn't seem to bother the Tileans. When the customs cutter turned to circle around them, the southlanders turned too, keeping their ship aimed at their enemy with a lethal, suicidal precision.

Again, the cutter turned, and again the Tileans turned with her.

'They're going to do it,' Florin breathed into the wind, his voice hushed with respect. 'The lunatics are actually going to ram her.'

And, right up until the point where the ships were barely a length apart, it seemed that they would do just that. It was only when the collision became inevitable that the Tileans made their move.

It was the most incredible display of seamanship Florin had ever seen. The way that the Tilean's three sails shortened, then swung around like three perfect mirror images. The way that every man on the ship leapt over the gunwales to hang from her side like so much moveable ballast. The way in which the weight of her anchor was harnessed to pull her tiller with a superhuman speed – these and a hundred other perfectly synchronised manoeuvres sent the fifty tons of merchantship slipping past the customs boat with barely a foot to spare.

Amidst the desperate ballet of his men only Captain Ballideci remained still, the swirl of his cape marking him out amongst the sweating crew. He didn't move until he was level with the deck of the customs cutter, and even then it was only to lean over and wave a horned fist towards the pale faces of the excise men.

Florin found himself cheering. Even Lorenzo cackled as the Tileans slid past their nemesis, some of them finding the time to jeer at her terrified crew as they raced to reset their sails. Before the customs ship had a chance to recover, the smugglers were scudding away to the south, sprinting before the wind that would take them back to the safety of their own waters.

'What an escape!' Florin exulted. 'What a nerve! That Ballideci is a hero even if his cousin isn't.'

The customs boat had put out more sail, her crew struggling to pick up speed, but Florin wasn't concerned. The Tileans were well clear and opening up their lead by the minute.

But then the cutter turned and something hit Florin like a punch in the stomach. It was the realisation that the ship wasn't even going to try to catch the Tileans.

It was going to pursue them instead.

'I told you we should have just bought wine from the guild,' Lorenzo grumbled as the same realisation hit him too. For a split second the two men hesitated. They could surrender. They'd lose the boat and the cargo but at least they'd be safe.

They exchanged a glance and, with a burst of desperate activity, started to angle their boat back towards the hungry jaws of the Bite.

CHAPTER TWO

SERGEI WIPED THE sweat off his forehead. It was pink with blood from the cut he'd taken, but he smiled anyway. He was enjoying himself.

And so, to his own surprise, was his instructor, Monsieur Dodieu.

The two men circled each other, their steps soft on the sand floor of Dodieu's practice chamber. This was an expensive building to be used as a fencing school, but Dodieu could afford it. For the past thirty years, the swordsman had made a living by teaching the sons of nobles and merchants this aristocratic art, and it was a job he was good at.

The son of a ruined nobleman himself, he never overestimated the martial ability of his equals, contenting himself with teaching them a dozen or so moves, simple formulas that he beat into them with constant repetition and the occasional nip of steel.

Although the students he instructed would never be real masters of the art, Dodieu had no qualms about the exorbitant fees he charged. After all, the only foes they would be likely to fight would be fellow merchants or other commoners, and in those contests the basic skills he taught provided a lethal edge.

Not that they'd be much use against the young man that now stood in front of him, Dodieu thought with a wry smile.

'If you're trying to provoke me with that expression,' Sergei told him as he took a step backwards, 'it won't work.'

Dodieu laughed. 'I'm just smiling at your attempt to keep your guard up,' he said, and when Sergei started to reply he lunged forward.

Steel flashed like lightning as the strigany slashed at his instructor's blade. There was a hiss as the two swords slid against each other and a grunt as the two men met, shoulder to shoulder. Sergei, forgetting himself, hooked upwards with his left fist and Dodieu spun away from the blow.

'I didn't teach you to do that,' he accused.

Sergei grinned. 'No.'

Dodieu's eyes gleamed with pleasure. It had been years, perhaps even decades, since he'd found such an interesting opponent. Although the lad held his sword gracelessly, he had the sinewy form and animal reflexes of a true swordsman.

He had the instinctive aggression too.

Dodieu watched the youngster advance and just managed to duck out of the way as he stabbed forward. He twisted to one side as he moved, then slashed back to nick Sergei across the tip of his nose with the point of his blade.

Despite the fact that the injury must have hurt, the youngster didn't flinch, even for a moment. Instead he remembered to lift his guard. Dodieu felt a moment's satisfaction. He was learning. He was just about to test how well his pupil could maintain this poise when the door to the chamber swung open and some sort of mastiff padded in.

Dodieu scowled into the gloom at the end of the room, then raised his hand to finish the practice session.

'Excuse me,' he said, keeping his voice polite as he addressed the figure that followed the animal into the chamber. For all he knew this might be another wealthy client. 'We don't allow animals into… into…'

The sword master trailed off as the animal moved into the light. Now that he could see it clearly, Dodieu realised that this was no mastiff. Not only was it bigger, but its half-ton of graceful weight was all feline. From the banded twitch of its sinuous tail to the green patience of its eyes, the big cat prowled towards Dodieu and his pupil like an old tom approaching a pair of mice.

Not that an old tom would be sporting anything like that array of teeth. In fact, the beast's canines looked as long and as sharp as the sword master's own blade.

His surprise vanished as quickly as it had come. This must be some sort of assassination attempt, he realised. This wasn't the first time somebody had tried to kill one of his students during the distractions of training. Dodieu hadn't let it happen before and he was damned if he'd let it happen now.

'Sergei,' he said, voice as level as the dagger that had suddenly appeared in his left hand, 'stand behind me.'

'What?'

'Stand behind me.' There was a snap in Dodieu's voice. The beast was almost within pouncing distance and the master adopted a stance that would have earned a nip of steel for any of his students. Arms open, feet level, torso exposed – everything about him suggested unpreparedness. It had been a suggestion that several men had been fool enough to take over the years. None of them had lived to regret their mistake. Unfortunately, this daemonic feline was unwilling to take the bait. It stopped when it was barely a dozen steps away from the man, its emerald eyes narrowing with suspicion. Then it seemed to lose all interest in him and, sinking back onto its haunches, started to lick its paws.

Dodieu's brows creased in puzzlement as, from behind the animal, its handler burst into a peal of delighted laughter. He frowned even deeper when the girl stepped into the light.

Although dressed in the high boots and belted tunic of a young squire, she was certainly not that. From the animal grace of her walk to the sparkle of green laughter in her eyes, Katerina seemed more akin to the beast before her than any of Dodieu's pasty-faced apprentices.

'Did you think she was going to eat you?' she asked as she ran her fingers through the big cat's fur. It purred at her touch, its eyes closing with pleasure. Sergei, his own pleasure at seeing the girl equally apparent, walked towards her.

'Wait a minute,' Dodieu said, gesturing for him to stay still. 'You mean to tell me that that thing is yours?'

'Oh, Tabby isn't anybody's,' Katerina answered.

It was scant reassurance but Dodieu dropped his guard anyway. He liked cats, and even with a monster like this one he could tell when they were too contented to hunt.

'Master Dodieu.' Sergei turned to him, suddenly remembering his manners. 'Permission to leave the floor?'

'Yes, certainly,' his tutor said, eyes never leaving the sabretusk. 'I wonder if you'd consider selling her to me?' he asked. 'She'd make a fantastic mascot. I'd treat her well, too. A warm bed. Meat every day. The occasional student.'

Katerina sniggered at the joke but shook her head. 'No, I'll never sell her. She's my friend.'

'Yes, I can see. If you ever change your mind, though, the offer will always stand.'

'Thanks anyway,' Sergei said as, arm in arm, he, Katerina and Tabby made their way back out to the teeming streets beyond.

After the cool space of the fencing chamber, Bordeleaux's streets reminded Sergei of the stinking labyrinth where he had first found his beloved. Still, at least he and Katerina had the luxury of the space that opened up around Tabby. Everybody else had to fight their way through this sharp-elbowed stew of humanity, struggling past their fellows as they went about their lives.

With some, their business was easier to guess than with others. The girls who hung out of the street corner windows, for instance. They surely hadn't stripped to their bodices because of the heat of the day. And the porters who struggled past, bent double beneath their massive loads, weren't doing it for fun.

Others, their wares draped around their necks or displayed on portable wooden trays, might have been honest merchants had it not been for the children that skulked around them. These youngsters lurked in the shadows beneath the overhanging upper storeys, their malnourished faces alert for the wink that would send them after a likely mark.

Even as Sergei watched, one of them dodged forward and thrust his hand into a drunken porter's belt purse. But the victim obviously wasn't as drunk as he seemed. Without breaking his stride he slapped the hand away and gave the child a whack that knocked him to the ground.

'Reminds me of when I was young,' Sergei smiled nostalgically as the child rolled back to his feet and scuttled away.

'Reminds me of home,' Katerina said.

'Home?'

'Skabrand, I mean,' Katerina corrected herself. 'Skabrand. Not our home.'

Sergei pursed his lips thoughtfully and slipped an arm around her waist.

'If you want to go back, we can,' he told her as she leaned into him. 'We can go with one of the caravans. Jarmoosh would be happy to see you again. So would the rhinoxen. In fact,' he lied, 'I would like to go back there. We could go hunting every day. And I know how to make wine from berries.'

Katerina sighed happily. Sergei was so wonderful.

'No, we'll stay here for a while,' she decided. 'It's not all bad. Tabby likes it, too, the lazy thing. She doesn't have to chase her prey any more.'

The cat's ears twitched at the mention of her name and Katerina sighed again.

With these two beside her, she didn't care where she was. After the lonely lifetime she'd spent in the wilds of the east, every day with Sergei was a bonus. Everything else was unimportant.

'I've got an idea,' Sergei said as the walls of the Hansebourg mansion appeared around a corner. 'Let's go hunting. Just the three of us. We can take horses and go to the forest for a few days. Remember your uncle's friend said we could hunt deer there? We'll take Tabby and have some real sport.'

'Good idea,' said Katerina, and looked adoringly at the handsome lines of her husband's broken nose and scarred jaw. Good looking *and* sensitive, she thought happily, and squeezed him.

FLORIN HAD THOUGHT the customs men would have had more sense than to follow them into the Bite. After all, tacking through the submerged hazards was dangerous enough for the small boat that he and Lorenzo were struggling in. For a three-masted cutter, the risk of hitting a reef was a dozen times greater.

Unfortunately, it transpired this was a risk that the pursuing captain was prepared to take. He seemed confident in his knowledge of these waters, even risking a full topsail.

Or perhaps, Florin thought, it wasn't confidence that drew him on. Perhaps it was rage. Perhaps, after the way in which the Tileans had escaped, the pursuing captain was just desperate to capture anybody, and Florin and Lorenzo were the only anybodies left.

To make matters even worse, the wind had picked up. Even with their sail half furled, manoeuvring it was exhausting work, and Florin's muscles were already burning beneath his sodden shirt. He grimaced with pain as they veered once more to the portside and considered swapping back with Lorenzo. Then he thought better of it. The older man was struggling enough with the tiller. They couldn't really spare the seconds it would take to swap positions either. By now their pursuers were so close that he could see the way that the wind plastered their pilot's moustache back across his cheeks.

Twenty feet in front of them, a telltale spume of white water leapt up and, with a warning cry to Lorenzo, Florin heaved the sail to the right. Barely a minute later they were slipping past the granite outcrop, so close that their wake washed against it. As it disappeared to the stern, Florin realised how close these evasions had taken them to the jagged walls of the cliffs. They loomed above, the rotting hull of an ancient wreck lying wedged between two outcrops like a morsel between a giant's teeth. Florin, feeling the beginnings of panic in his chest, swore loudly and adjusted the sail.

Between this, the strain of looking for the next hazard and the serpents of agony which twisted through his arms, he wasn't paying much attention to the cries of the pursuers. Maybe if the wind hadn't smeared them into one many-voiced wail he would have noticed how shrill it had become. As it was, it took the *boom* of an exploding hull to snatch his attention back from the elements.

It was a terrible, apocalyptic sound. Even against the whine of the wind the splintering timbers sounded incredibly loud. As the Bite's stone teeth punched through them the frame of the ship started to give way, the great beams that lined the hull snapping as loudly as bones. For a moment, Florin thought that these sounds were coming from his own boat and the panic that had been growing in his chest flared brightly. But even as he summoned up the determination to take control of this lethal situation he realised, with a surge of almost ecstatic relief, that it wasn't his boat that was doomed. It was the customs ship.

Lorenzo was shouting something at him but Florin ignored him as he quickly furled the sail. Now that they were no longer being pursued they didn't need to risk the speed of the chase. Better to crawl their way home yard by patient yard.

From behind them there was a long, drawn out screech, followed by a deep boom of displaced water. The smugglers' boat rocked as a sudden swell of water hit it, then settled back down into the gentler roll of the waves.

Florin tied off all the sail apart from a single thin strip, then turned back to Lorenzo. 'Made it,' he exulted, a wild smile on his face. But despite their escape his comrade obviously didn't share his joy. As Florin followed his gaze he could see why.

The death of a ship, he realised, was a terrible thing to witness.

In the moments it had taken him to react, the cutter's sleek, predatory lines had been reduced to a broken tangle of snared rigging and shattered wood. One of her masts was already gone, torn free by the brine that washed over her. The other two, meanwhile, had fallen against each other to form a sagging cross. But all of this ruin was as nothing compared to the damage to her hull. Once as sleek and solid as a tree trunk, it had burst open like a rotten barrel. Even as he watched, Florin could see that the ocean was completing what the rocks had begun, and tearing the ship's body in half. She groaned as she was dismembered, and white surf sprayed up from beneath the crashing timbers like blood from wounds.

Caught between the currents and the rocks, the crew didn't stand a chance. Some of them still held to the disintegrating ruin of their vessel, clinging to her with the mindless faith of a babe for its mother. Others, either braver or more foolish, hurled themselves into the foam and clung to pieces of flotsam. Florin and Lorenzo watched them, their faces drawn as they looked at men struggling against their doom.

Florin was the first to speak. 'We should save them,' he announced.

Lorenzo watched a lad of about fifteen struggling to crawl onto a barrel as it bobbed through the waves. Every time he got to the top it rolled, pitching him back into the sea. In another place, the spectacle would have been funny.

'We won't have room for them with the hold full.'

With a sudden screech, the cutter's two remaining masts collapsed, crashing down onto the deck like the blades of a guillotine. A chorus of screams rose up from beneath them, before being snatched away by the wind.

The two smugglers looked at each other.

'Well then,' Florin said, with a manufactured shrug. 'The first ones we rescue can throw the barrels overboard.'

Lorenzo's thoughts turned to the quality of the wine they carried. Then, damn the quality, he thought about the price. And how it would have been almost pure profit.

'Are you crying?' Florin asked, but the older man just shook his head.

'No, no. Let's just get it over with,' he spat and, with the expression of a condemned man, he turned back to the sail.

'We'll take her in to about thirty feet,' he said bitterly. 'Then I'll hold her in position while you drag them in.'

'Thirty feet's a long way to swim against the current.'

'Use a rope,' Lorenzo told him, and grabbed the tiller as tightly as if it was the neck of one of those damn fool customs men.

Moments later, Florin dragged the first of the sailors out of the waves. He was a grizzled old rascal, and tough. He barely paused long enough to slap his thanks into Florin's arm before shaking himself off and taking a fistful of the rope. The next one to struggle over the side was the youngster that had been trying to climb onto the barrel. He coughed and spluttered on the floor of the herring boat like a landed fish, and would have continued to lie there had his mate not kicked him into action.

Half a dozen more men soon followed, and then Lorenzo had to turn away. He was unable to watch as, at Florin's instruction, they rolled the first of the wine barrels overboard to make room for the rest.

Why did I ever team up with this young lunatic? Lorenzo asked himself, and tried to ignore the dangerous feeling of pride he felt as more of the customs men were dragged from the sea's lethal embrace.

CHAPTER THREE

Buried below Bordeleaux's moonlit streets, as deep down as the guilt within a hellbound heart, there was a chamber. In the chamber was a man, swaddled in a pair of winter cloaks.

It had been the same the last time he'd been down here. The crumbling brickwork and roughly hewn granite seemed to radiate cold.

As he warmed his bony fingers against his lantern, the possibility of manufacturing ice here floated through his mind. Perhaps he could find some mage with the ability to lower the temperature a couple more degrees?

His dark eyes gleamed hungrily as he thought of the money an ice merchant could make in the streets above. Maybe he should try. After all, he needed to keep body and soul together. Who didn't? And he was not a rich man.

Well, not rich enough.

No, better to keep this chamber a secret. As far as he knew, only he and his... partners... knew about it. The fact that he could reach the subterranean confines of this meeting point from his own counting house was what made it so valuable. That and the fact that his partners could also reach it without exposing themselves.

There was a suggestion of movement from one of the tunnels that led even deeper, followed by a sudden draught of stinking air. The man drew the lead box he'd brought closer to his bony chest, though the stuff that was sealed into the box wasn't something that any sane man would treasure.

There was another movement from the tunnel beyond, and the *clink* of steel on stone. The man lifted his lantern and peered into the receding darkness of the tunnel.

'Hello?' he called softly. 'Is that you, Skrit?'

The answer came from behind him.

The man shrieked and spun around, but even as his pulse accelerated the shadows flickered and moved, and a squat shape was belched out from the darkness.

It detached itself from the wall, its crooked limbs twisting as it scuttled into the cone of light. The twin chisels of its teeth gleamed with reflected flames, and its eyes narrowed as it chittered something in its inhuman language.

'Ah, there you are,' the man said as the sharp snout of the thing's face appeared from beneath its hood. The horrible intelligence that glimmered within its eyes made the verminous slope of its head even more horrible.

The man felt relief flood through him as he recognised his partner.

'You almost gave me a heart attack,' he said, pulling at his wild beard to hide the shaking of his hands. 'You shouldn't sneak up on me like that, my boy.'

'Sneaking,' the creature squeaked. 'Sneaking and killing. Yes. Now give me the stone, quick, or I show you how.'

Almost coincidentally the scaly length of its tail lashed forward. The curved blade it held glowed with a sickly green phosphorescence in the gloom, and even though the light it cast was faint, it left black spots dancing in the human's eyes.

He looked away and blinked, then smiled a smile that seemed almost genuine.

'Skrit, my old friend,' he said, shifting the lead box from one hand to another. 'Nothing will make me happier than to give you this. But first I need to know that you understand about the target.'

The bestial thing writhed, caught between the instinct to murder this frail old creature and the knowledge that to do so would mean no more warpstone.

The man, guessing his partner's impatience, hurried on. He'd already explained what he wanted to one of its messengers. He'd explained it a dozen times. He'd even given it two different locks of hair to make doubly sure there was no confusion.

But even so, he needed to be certain that the assassin understood.

'Remember, don't harm the girl. Only kill the man.'

The beast squirmed, its poisoned knife blurring as its tail lashed back and forth. Hatred, terrifying in its intensity, sweated from every pore of the assassin's flea-ridden body.

'If you harm the girl,' he pressed on, ignoring the creature's agitation and speaking slowly and clearly, 'then I won't pay you. I will also never give you any more warpstone. Never. No more.'

The assassin's eyes narrowed into vicious slits and a frightening stillness came over it. For a moment, the man was sure that it was going to snap and attack him, but even so he met the madness of its gaze with an icy calm.

'Do you understand?' he asked.

With a screech of irritation, Skrit replied. 'Yes,' he shrilled, voice sharper than claws on slate. 'Now give me stone quick-quick or I cut out your glands.'

The man handed over the lead box and retreated. The assassin pounced upon it, forgetting him entirely as it hurriedly prised open the lid and peered inside. The green glow that throbbed from within lit up an almost human expression of greed on its bestial face.

It chittered excitedly as it reached inside to touch its prize. When its paws brushed against the treasure, a spurt of musk sprayed out from beneath its tail, an unconscious reaction of unholy ecstasy.

It took some minutes before it could finally bring itself to close the box and by that time the frail old human had gone.

Skrit knew his mission would provide plenty of opportunity for fun. Chittering with excitement, the assassin wrapped the warpstone fragment in its tattered rags and scuttled away into the darkness. There was much to prepare.

THE OAKS WHISPERED together, their boughs gesticulating in the summer breeze. The sounds of the city, softened by distance, drifted through the warm air, the far-off noises as soothing as the hum of the bees. Occasionally, a flight of sparrows would land to chatter for a while before flitting off to swallow more flies.

After the uproar of Bordeleaux's crowded streets the lands beyond her walls were almost eerily quiet.

Not that Katerina or Sergei noticed. As they rode along the narrowing tracks they had eyes only for each other. Their horses dawdled along lazily, their suspicious eyes never leaving Tabby's low, loping silhouette for a moment, and the mule that followed them trudged along beneath the supplies and stowed weapons.

'How long since we saw the last riders?' Katerina asked, closing her eyes and turning her face to the sun. She smiled in the heat and Sergei, seeing the happiness on her face, smiled too.

'Maybe an hour,' he replied. 'Maybe more.'

'I can't believe how empty this land is.'

'You're turning into a real city girl,' Sergei teased her.

She punched him playfully and he laughed.

'Remember the wastes around Skabrand?' he went on. 'They make this land look like a tavern.'

'Or a bedroom,' Katerina said.

Sergei's heavy brows creased in puzzlement. 'How do you mean?'

Katerina leant over in her saddle and whispered into her husband's ear. 'We could tie up the horses by those olive trees,' she told him, 'and I'll show you.'

An hour later they brushed the leaves off each other and climbed back into their clothes. By now, the sun had sunk low, and the heavy shadows of late afternoon stretched across the track and the fields that lay beyond it. In the distance, the squat huts of a peasant village clustered together like piglets in a sty, and even as the two travellers watched, the first hints of smoke from cooking fires began to float up towards the sky.

Katerina felt her mouth water as she imagined what they might be cooking. Since her return to civilization, she had learned to enjoy the rich flavours of Bretonnian cooking. The thick wine sauces, the spicy venison marinades, the honey and cream delights of Bordeleaux's cake shops – these and a dozen other dishes had gradually softened the hard lines of her scrawny frame and made her curves even curvier.

'I wonder what's cooking?' Sergei echoed her thoughts.

'Whatever it is, I'll eat it,' Katerina decided happily. 'You gave me an appetite.'

Sergei chuckled and ran a hand across the stubble on his head. Katerina was delighted to see a touch of embarrassment on his face. He was so sweet!

'I'm sure they'll be happy to sell us some.' Her husband changed the subject. 'And maybe a couple of chickens for Tabby.'

Katerina nodded, a look of proprietorial smugness on her face.

'She is very intelligent. Tabby. Tabby! Get behind us. Behind.' She gestured and the big cat, with a look of perfect nonchalance on her face, circled back past the nervous horses and fell in behind the pack mule. 'It's best if the villagers see us first,' she explained. 'Some people are so silly when it comes to her. Just because she's bigger than normal cats.'

By about half a ton, Sergei thought affectionately. His wife somehow never seemed to understand why most people regarded the razor-fanged predator as anything more than a kitten.

'What do you fancy to eat?' he asked after a few moments of companionable silence.

'Veal,' Katerina decided. 'With mushrooms and onion gravy.'

'Or how about carp baked in cream?'

'Mmmm. Or lizard legs fried in breadcrumbs.'

'With baked apples afterwards?'

This happy conversation lasted until the sun sank below the trees and, their stomachs rumbling, they reached the village of Regout. It consisted of maybe a score of wattle huts arranged in a rough circle, their crude walls sagging beneath their roofs.

Although the air was piquant with the smell of wood smoke, there seemed to be nobody in the village. The doors of the hovels remained closed and not even a hen moved amongst the dirt.

'Hello?' Sergei called, raising his voice. 'We'd like to buy some food.'

There was no reply.

Katerina scowled. 'Hey, open up!' she ordered. 'Don't be so rude. We're not bandits.'

Sergei smiled fondly at his wife's attempt at diplomacy and dismounted. There was still no sign of life; the hovels were silent. Ignoring a sudden feeling of unease, Sergei walked over to the nearest of them, arranged the battered contours of his face into what he hoped was a friendly smile, and knocked on the frame of the reed door. There was a scuffle of movement inside followed by a muffled voice.

'I know someone's in there,' Sergei told the door. 'Come on, don't be unfriendly. We only want to buy some food.'

For a moment, he could hear a muted conversation from within the hut. Then, reluctantly, the door opened and several figures came cautiously out.

Sergei had never been the best of actors. What he saw wiped the smile off his face and replaced it with an expression first of confusion, then of horror.

Katerina's reaction was even more forthright.

'Ranald's left ball,' she cursed, eyes widening at the children who staggered out into the light. 'What's wrong with them? Is it a plague?'

'No.' Sergei shook his head. 'Not the plague.'

He'd remembered where he'd seen such living skeletons before. He remembered the sunken eyes, dark pits that seemed little more than the sockets of a skull. He remembered the distended stomachs, too, the bellies as bloated as a corpse's after a week in the sun.

'What is it, then?' Katerina demanded as she swung off her horse to stand next to him. The woman who had emerged after the youngsters, her own frame as wasted as theirs, stumbled into a door frame at her approach, her eyes wide with what looked like fear or perhaps just desperation.

'Hunger,' Sergei told her.

'Hunger?' Katerina repeated, her voice edged with disbelief. 'No. The fields are full of crops. How can there be hunger in this land?'

Which was when the mother of this starving family started to cry. 'The baron,' she wailed, as if this were the name of some particularly bloodthirsty daemon. 'Lord Greville takes all our grain.'

Katerina looked from the blubbering woman to her famished children and then back again. From the corner of her eye she could see that other doors were opening in this silent village. Curiosity, she supposed, had finally got the better of them.

'But where are your menfolk?' she asked, still confused by the situation. The woman responded to the question with a fresh torrent of grief.

'Working in the slate mines,' she sobbed. 'Lord Greville said they had to work there until the winter planting. It's for his lordship's new castle.'

By now the children had joined in with their mother's tears, and Katerina looked at them disapprovingly. Some of them looked at least ten which was, she considered, far too old for this sort of thing.

'What I mean is, if this Greville took all of your food, why didn't your men kill him?'

Suddenly the woman's grief was gone. In its place was an expression of sheer terror.

'Inside,' she whispered, grabbing the nearest of her children and edging back into the hovel. 'Inside, I said!'

'What did I say?' Katerina asked as, behind her, other doors started to slam shut. Sergei just shrugged as the woman they'd spoken to closed the door on them, her terrified eyes the last thing he saw before the frail structure was jammed shut.

'Well, my darling,' he said, turning back to the horses. 'Looks like we'll be cooking our own food.' But Katerina didn't move. Sergei turned back to find her staring at the closed door, the finely sculpted arches of her eyebrows furrowed in thought.

'What is it?' he asked.

She frowned. 'Some of those youngsters reminded me of my gnoblars,' she said, her voice soft with nostalgia. 'Although they were a bit whinier. Still, I suppose they don't know any better.'

'I suppose so. Your gnoblars were a lot healthier, too,' Sergei complimented her. And so they had been, he thought. Vicious little monsters could have been the death of us all.

Katerina nodded as if reaching a sudden decision.

'Yes, you're right. Come on.'

Sergei wondered what he'd been right about as he followed her back to the horses. When she unhitched their bag of dried provisions from the mule he was surprised, but only for a moment. His beloved was nothing if not sentimental.

With a thud, she dropped the sack onto the dirt.

'Have our food, you useless creatures,' she called out to the closed doors. 'Although you should be out fighting for your own.'

When there was no response, Katerina grunted with disgust.

'Gnoblars,' she muttered and swung back into the saddle.

By the time the peasants re-emerged, she and her husband were no more than dots on the horizon.

CHAPTER FOUR

Skrit hated moving in the daylight. The brightness made his eyes sting and water just when he needed them most. Everything was awake, that was the problem. Awake and aware. Each movement had to be taken carefully, lest it alert the man-things that ruled the day.

They wouldn't always rule it, of course. Every skaven knew that. Eventually, the Horned Rat would lead skavenkind to the dominion that was their destiny.

Unfortunately that day was strangely slow in arriving.

The sunlight filled Skrit with a constant, gnawing anxiety. The filthy hairs that furred his back bristled and he bared his teeth in a silent snarl of agitation. Behind him, the scurrying mass of his followers froze as they sensed his sudden change of mood. By the time he turned back to them they had already blended into the undergrowth. Skrit hunched his shoulders and tried to look meek, an attempt to lure one of them into a challenge.

When none came, he sprayed the ground with disgust and turned back to the trail they'd been following. The scent of it was fresh, especially that of the monster. Skrit had found some of its footprints earlier, the deep blackberry shapes mixed in with the hoofprints of his prey. Once again he thrilled at his genius in bringing so many of his followers. His mood lifted slightly and, with a twitch of his tail, he scurried forward. A moment later and he found an overgrown ditch that ran along the side of the track. It was half full of mud and dead, rotting things. Skrit felt his mood lift even more as he slithered along it, writhing through the filth like an eel.

Soon find them, he thought happily.

Very soon.

THE STAG CRASHED through the undergrowth, his great fetlocks tearing through the brambles as he fled. In front of him a stream gurgled through the forest, the path of it a deep, ankle-breaking trench.

Without a second's hesitation the stag's muscles bunched and he hurled himself across the water and onto the other bank. His hooves thudded onto hard soil and he lurched forward, nostrils flaring with exertion as he pushed himself onwards.

A dozen paces later and the undergrowth cleared enough for him to break into a gallop. He dodged between the tree trunks like the world's biggest hare, his great chest swelling as he sucked in huge lungfuls of air. Broken beams of sunlight rippled across his back like shoals of fish, and his hooves blurred with speed.

And yet, despite all of this, the smell of predator grew stronger behind him. The stag wasn't sure exactly what sort of predator it was. Its scent was new to him and he had only caught a single glimpse of it between the trees. That glimpse had been all he'd needed, however. Everything about the strange animal, from the long blades of its teeth to the impatient twitch of its tail, had screamed danger.

There were other scents on the wind now but the stag paid them no heed. Whatever lay ahead could surely be no worse than that which was pursuing him.

The trees began to thin and, just ahead, the gloom of the forest gave way to the molten copper tones of a stripped wheatfield. The stag, loath to go so close to settled lands, veered away to the left.

A moment later and he staggered to a terrified stop. A fresh wash of adrenaline fizzed through his veins as the predator appeared in front of him. With a panicked volte-face he turned and raced back towards the fields. The fear of humanity was quite forgotten now that he knew how close the predator was.

His chest was burning with exhaustion when the two archers appeared. They seemed to spring up from the very ground beneath his feet.

This time he had no time to react. Even as he tried to turn the hum of their bowstrings surged into a scream of agony that shot through his body. He fell, his powerful legs thrashing in instinctive defence as he collapsed forward.

But there was no defence now. Before he could even think about struggling back to his feet, one of the hunters, her hair flaming as brightly as the blood which pulsed from his punctured heart, leapt upon him. There was a blinding flash of steel, an instant of burning pain, and then nothing.

Nothing at all.

'Well done, my love,' Sergei laughed as he rushed over to join his wife. She grinned back at him and then bent to complete her butchery. Her thighs wrapped around the still warm body of the stag as she deftly tied off the artery she'd just cut. There was no point in wasting good blood. Then, content with her handiwork, she stood back to examine their kill.

'He's a big one,' she said. 'Look at how many points his antlers have.'

When Tabby loped into the clearing, the two of them were wrestling playfully across the stiffening carcass of the stag.

The big cat watched them disdainfully before prowling over and opening up her prey's belly with a single swipe of her claws.

The smell of intestines brought Katerina and Sergei back to their feet.

'We'll leave her the innards,' Katerina decided, 'and hang the rest from a tree.'

'It looks too heavy to lift. Maybe we should have brought the horses.'

'No, the smell of them would have frightened him. That's why me and Tabby never used rhinoxen to hunt back ho… I mean, in the ogres' lands.'

Sergei shrugged. 'Well, no matter. There's plenty of wood. I'll show you how to make a hoist.'

'A hoist?' Katerina asked, all innocence. 'Is that something from the book that Lorenzo gave you? The one with all the woodcuts in it?'

Sergei cleared his throat and hastened away to start looking for the right sort of branches. He selected three of the strongest, hacked them down, then lashed them together into a single length.

Leaving Tabby to gorge on the stinking stew of their kill's innards, he selected a pair of trees with boughs that were roughly similar. He passed the hoist over one of them so that it became a long lever, then tied the stag's antlers to the far end. Then, throwing his weight on the opposite end, he lifted the carcass high enough for Katerina to tie its antlers against the opposite tree.

'Nicely done,' Katerina told him as they admired the hanging deer.

Sergei looked at the red meat that glistened within the fur and felt his mouth starting to water. He had eaten nothing but berries since Katerina had given their supplies to the villagers the day before.

'I'll go and get the horses,' he decided. 'Then we can start cooking.'

'I'll come with you,' Katerina said. 'We can wash together in that stream.'

'Sounds good.'

Tabby watched them trudging away and stretched. She purred with the sheer pleasure of laziness, then turned back to the bloody mess of her feast.

She had almost finished when, deep within the bushes behind her, something stirred. Her ears swivelled as she turned to face the sound, and her blood-soaked muzzle wrinkled as she sniffed at the air. The movement stopped. For a long, breathless moment the bushes remained silent apart from the rustling of the wind.

Fighting the soporific effects of a bloated stomach, the big cat got to her feet and padded towards the place where she'd heard the sound.

Green eyes glittering, Tabby thrust her nose towards the undergrowth. Something was hidden there, she could tell. Something that smelt unpleasantly alive and possibly edible.

Her whiskers were almost touching the thorns when, with a sudden panicked energy, two blurred shapes exploded from the bushes.

Tabby sprang back in surprise, her razored claws unsheathing themselves in an instinctive reaction. She watched the pheasants flutter upwards, their wings beating frantically as they fought for altitude. Then she licked her lips, and the taste of blood reminded her of the giblets that still remained uneaten. The subsequent surge of greed ended her interest in the undergrowth as suddenly as it had begun.

Her stomach rumbling, Tabby turned and went back to feed.

SKRIT WAITED UNTIL the monster had reburied its head in a string of intestines. He waited until he could hear the slurp and rip of it feeding. Then he waited some more.

His followers skulked nervously around him. Skrit could barely contain the shivers of rage that wracked him. Not only had one of these worthless underlings almost ruined his plan, but it had actually had the nerve to put him, its master, in personal danger.

Not that Skrit was afraid of the great purring beast that had almost found them. No, not at all. Not a bit of it. Not him.

Unfortunately, he didn't know which of his miserable slaves had attracted the cat's attention. But that hardly mattered. It was all of their faults for not watching each other.

Warmed by this logic, the assassin amused himself by planning the punishments he would inflict back in the burrows. These happy thoughts helped to soothe him as he waited patiently for the big cat to roll over and fall into a glutted sleep.

Only then did he deign to move. Gradually, each and every movement a study in caution, he wormed his way through the mulch of the forest floor. Only when he was sure that he was out of sight of the big cat did he raise himself up and scuttle away after the humans.

He had wanted to wait until nightfall before tackling them but this was too good an opportunity to miss. The very thought of facing their animal had dampened his hind legs with the musk of fear. But now, it seemed, he wouldn't have to. He wouldn't even have to risk his followers against it.

Skrit bared his incisors in a grin of vicious delight. Up ahead, the trees began to thin into open country but that was no problem. The lands here were cut through with countless irrigation trenches and drains. Skrit regarded them as a gift from the Horned Rat himself, and he and his followers had spent the last few days squirming through these slimy tunnels as happily as maggots through a corpse.

Now they did the same again as, yard by silent yard, they closed in on their victims.

AFTER THE HEAT of the day, the water felt like liquid ice. It flowed over a wide, shallow bed of black polished pebbles. Tiny silvered fish usually darted amongst them but this afternoon they were gone, hiding in the roots of the willows that lined the banks.

Not that the green-shaded currents of the river were empty. Far from it. Even as the fish slunk nervously through the reeds the gurgle of its flow was drowned beneath Katerina's shrieks of delight and the splashing of the water.

Two horses and a mule looked on as their masters chased each other through the freezing shallows. If they were embarrassed by the humans' nakedness they gave no sign. When they did begin to whinny it was with anxiety, and it was because of what they smelt, not what they saw.

'Wait a minute,' Katerina gasped, holding up her hand as Sergei closed in on her.

'Ah, surrendering?' he asked, lowering his numbed hands to scoop up another splash of water.

Katerina tossed back the sodden tails of her hair as proudly as a lion with its mane.

'Not likely,' she said. 'But look at the horses. See the way their ears are laid back? I think they've smelled something.'

Sergei looked at them for a moment before looking back at Katerina. By Loki, she's wonderful, he thought. He let his eyes slide down the damp curves of her body, lingering on the heavy rounds of her breasts. Although she was as naked as the day she was born there wasn't a trace of self-consciousness about her. Quite the opposite. She stood with an animal poise.

Even now, Katerina looked more dignified than the most perfumed and bejewelled of aristocrats. Not for the first time, Sergei thanked the gods that had gifted her to him. He had never even suspected that the happiness he had known with her could actually exist in this world.

Oblivious to his appraisal, Katerina turned and took a step towards the horses. They had begun to pull at their tethers, and Sergei realised for the first time how agitated they had become. He moved to follow Katerina to them but then, suddenly, he froze.

In the shadows that swathed the far bank something had moved. Something almost man-sized. Sergei squinted into the gloom, silently cursing the sunlight that he had been so enjoying a minute before.

Behind him one of the horses screamed.

The noise was greeted with more scurrying on the far bank.

'Damn,' Sergei cursed as he realised how far away his weapons were. He was turning to get them when the attack came.

The first Sergei knew about it was when the gloaming light splintered into a dozen blurred stars. They came spinning towards him, the jagged edges of the throwing stars spitting poison as they flew towards his throat.

Had the skaven been worse shots he would have died there and then. As it was, all twelve of the poisoned blades passed in a tight cluster through the space where he had been standing seconds before. He screamed a warning towards Katerina as he rolled to one side and plunged into the water.

Ignoring the pain that the submerged pebbles bruised into his shoulder, the strigany flipped back to his feet. He blinked the water from his eyes in time to see the first of the assassins emerging from the darkness and his heart skipped a beat. It was horrible. Despite the semblance of humanity that lurked in the thing's malformed body it seemed more rat than man, and more nightmare than either. Behind it, more of its fellows pushed forward. The sight of their yellowed fangs and silvered blades snapped Sergei back into action. Whipping his arm back, he hurled the stone he had picked up at the first of the things. It shrieked as the pebble bounced off it, but Sergei didn't wait to see how much damage his improvised weapon had done. He was too busy ploughing through the water towards Katerina and their mounts.

'Unhitch the horses!' he yelled at her as he stumbled onto the bank. But it wasn't the tethers she was fumbling with. It was the bundle which held their weapons.

'No time for that,' she yelled back and threw him his sword.

He saw that she was right. In the seconds since the first attack, the assassins had almost closed with them. Their twisted shapes had danced through the water and the reeds as easily as wind blown leaves, and they were already so close that he could see the poison that smeared their knives.

He wanted to tell Katerina to hide behind him. He wanted to tell her to run. But instead of wasting his breath he just unsheathed his sword and leapt forward.

The first of the assassins, its snout wrinkled in a vicious leer, realised too late how far ahead of the pack it had come. It hesitated as it waited for them to catch up, but in that very moment Sergei struck. Stepping to one side, he spun around, wielding his sword like a peasant wields a scythe. His victim squealed as it tried to jump backwards, then squealed even louder as the blade bit home.

Sergei felt the impact of steel passing through vertebrae and the rat-thing fell dead, the two halves of it scrabbling on the ground.

Before the strigany could rejoice at this terrible sight, the next two were upon him. They took up a position on each side, both feinting and dodging as the rest of the pack caught up. From the rabble behind them two more throwing stars span forward, and as Sergei ducked the whirling steel fragments his two tormentors closed in.

He lunged towards the first and then, as it ducked back, he changed direction and punched his blade into its belly. It collapsed, screaming as it clutched at its spilt intestines. Sergei snarled in triumph as he twisted his sword free and turned to face the next enemy.

But the next one had already ducked beneath his guard. The first Sergei knew of it was when, with a meaty chunk, Katerina sent the deformed triangle of its head tumbling back towards the river.

'Thanks,' Sergei gasped as more throwing stars sparkled through the shadows. The rest of their attackers were reluctant to follow their comrades into these swordsmen's blades. Although they outnumbered their prey six to one, their charge had faltered. Instead, they skulked back just out of striking distance and pelted their enemy with missiles.

Moving in perfect harmony, Sergei and Katerina closed in on them. Where they could, they dodged the flurry of thrown steel. Where they couldn't, they cut it out of the air. It was all too much for the assassins. Their fear was obvious even in the inhuman deformity of their whiskered faces, and they seemed about to break and run.

Before they could though, the second wave attacked. There were perhaps a dozen of them, and they charged the humans from behind. Their ragged forms were dripping with water from where they'd crossed the river. Although smaller than the humans, they were bigger than their comrades. Bigger and more aggressive.

Sergei, alerted by the horses, fought back a sudden feeling of despair.

To the hells with that, he told himself. However hopeless the situation, now was not the time for self-pity.

So, leaving Katerina to defend their backs from the throwing stars, he stepped into the new onslaught.

Monsieur Dodieu himself would have been impressed. His student moved with an instinctive, natural grace. The flicker of his blade brought down first one, then three, then more of the swarming attackers. He stabbed. He slashed. He parried. And even while he carved a path through their bodies, he managed to slip past their own lightning-fast blows. He dodged and swerved around a whole thicket of poisoned steel; his quicksilver moves relaxed and effortless. When one of his assailants was blinded by a stray throwing star, he even found the time to laugh.

Which was when a dagger buried itself in his thigh.

'Watch out!' He screamed the warning as he fell, the pain as nothing compared to his fear for Katerina.

The assassins, seeing him down, closed in around the two humans like the fingers of a strangler's glove. Katerina, her beautiful features twisted into a snarl of animal rage, prepared to meet them. But suddenly, with a blur of ivory fangs and golden fur, the skirmish was over.

All it took was the sight of Tabby. As soon as they saw her, the rabble of assassins turned and fled, squealing in terror as they raced away. The sabretusk sprinted after them, her tail switching back and forth with pleasure. As Katerina watched, one of the rat-things tripped a fellow straggler as it escaped. Tabby, barely breaking her stride, closed her jaws around its head and, with a quick shake, snapped the life out of it. Then she pounced upon the one that had tripped it. The creature shrieked. Writhing in panic it lashed out with a steel-barbed tail. Tabby pinned it down beneath one razor-taloned claw before tearing out its throat.

'Good girl!' Katerina laughed. Tears of relief ran down her cheeks as the cat bounded away in search of more victims.

For a moment, Katerina thought of following her, but a groan from Sergei reminded her of the blow he had taken. Squatting down beside him she examined the wound.

'You'll be all right,' she said as she leant over him. Ignoring his grunt of pain she lifted his leg and peered at the stab wound. It was narrow and deep, a triangular puncture from which blood flowed freely. It was bad, Katerina decided, but not really a problem. The blood which pulsed onto her fingers was too dark to be arterial, a good sign. It looked like the knife hadn't cut through anything but the meat of his leg. She'd tended a dozen beasts with similar wounds in the past and they'd all recovered.

'Does it hurt much?' she asked as she probed the wound.

'Not really,' Sergei lied through gritted teeth. He was pale and sweating, which was normal enough, Katerina supposed. The only thing that surprised her was the sound of his teeth chattering. Then she remembered that they were as unclothed now as they had been when the assassins had caught them bathing.

'Well, the main thing is that we're both fine,' she said with a wink and pinched him. Then, before he could retaliate, she went to grab their clothes. She put on her own shirt and flung Sergei his. Pausing only to listen to the shrieks that occasionally rent the stillness, she started to cut a spare piece of clothing into bandages.

Although it only took her a moment, Sergei was unconscious by the time she got back to him.

'Must be shock,' she muttered as she considered. After all, he hadn't really lost that much blood.

Well, no matter, she thought. She'd clean the wound and bandage it while he was out. Kneeling over him, she held his leg and, as gently as a cat with her kitten, started to lick the wound clean.

That was when she realised that something was wrong. It was the taste of the blood. It tasted horrible. Not that the blood of her wounded gnoblars had tasted particularly sweet, but this wound tasted as though it had been left to rot for a week. Alarm widening her eyes, she looked at the pale sheen of Sergei's unconscious face. Then she reached up and felt the pulse in his throat. It was so weak that it was barely there.

'Poison,' she muttered and spat the pinkness out of her mouth. For a moment she sat lost in indecision. Then, with a burst of violent activity she bandaged the infected wound, pulled his clothes onto him, and dragged him over to his horse. It was still dancing with terror and Katerina forced herself into calmness as she soothed it. As soon as it was still, she hoisted Sergei onto its back, leapt onto her own mount and turned back towards the city. Tabby, she decided as she broke into a gallop, would just have to find her own way home.

She was already praying that she wouldn't be too late.

'SO YOU FULLY intended to pay duty on the wine,' the clerk sneered from behind the safety of his desk. The huge lump of mahogany filled almost a quarter of his tiny office. Its surface was buried beneath papers, scrolls, books of regulations, a cudgel that served as a paperweight and an abacus. Opposite this mess was the door which led out to the harbour, and flanking this was a cloak stand and a small unlit brazier.

'Yes, we fully intended to pay duty on the wine,' Florin told him for the dozenth time, and wondered what would happen if he broke the clerk's nose. As if reading his mind the man pushed his chair back.

'And you just went to buy from the smugglers for the exercise, I suppose? The fresh air?' This time the official forced a laugh to show that he wasn't intimidated by the two men standing in front of him.

'I thought that only women suffered from hysteria,' Lorenzo muttered. The customs clerk stopped laughing. Instead he scowled.

'There were no smugglers,' Florin told him.

'That's not what Captain Culver says in his report,' the clerk snapped. He produced a document from the shoals of papers in front of him and waved it towards them. 'He says here that he was in the process of apprehending a smuggling vessel when the incident happened.'

'Who's that?' Florin asked, nodding curiously towards the narrow window that lit the office. When the clerk turned to look, Florin lunged across the table and snatched the report out of his hand. The man squeaked in outrage and leapt to his feet.

'That's an official document,' he complained. 'Give it back!'

'Shh,' said Florin. 'I'm trying to read.'

'Give it back or I'll call the guard!'

'No need for that.' Florin tossed the paper back down onto the desk. 'The good captain says here that we are in no way suspected of smuggling or any other activity deemed detrimental to the commonwealth or security of Bordeleaux, or Bretonnia, or any of the subjects and rulers thereof.'

'Culver would say that,' the customs clerk replied bitterly. 'You rescued him and his crew.'

'I'm sure you'd have done the same in our position,' Florin said, and for a moment the clerk fell silent. He was paid compliments so seldom that he found this one downright confusing.

But then Lorenzo spoilt the moment by sniggering, and the clerk bridled once more.

'Anyway, if you'll tell us what the duty is for three casks of Tilean wine,' Florin said, frowning at Lorenzo, 'we'll pay and be on our way.'

'I'm not convinced of your honesty,' the clerk flashed and thrust out his narrow chin in an almost comical look of defiance.

'I wonder what Captain Culver would say if he knew that you called him a liar?'

For a moment, rage and fear warred in the smaller man's eyes. It was a short-lived battle. With a heavy sigh, he slumped back down into his chair.

'Three casks is thirty-six crowns and thirty-three coppers,' he said, too defeated to notice Florin's wince.

'Don't you want to come and check our hold?'

But the customs official just shook his head in disgust. All he wanted was to get these horrible men out of his world. Apart from everything else, he could feel a headache coming on.

It would have been of some comfort to the harbourmaster, perhaps, to know how much the two failed smugglers had lost.

They tried not to think about it as they went about the business of finding a carter, manhandling the remaining wine casks up onto his wagon, and then escorting it back to their inn, the Ogre's Fist.

It was a small place, certainly no match for the one they had lost to the flames the year before. It consisted of no more than a dozen rooms, so small that they were little more than cupboards, and a bottom floor which consisted of a taproom and a kitchen. But although the Fist was small it was close enough to the port to be profitable. The rooms were ideal for the traders that clustered around the harbour like flies around a dungheap. The food and drink were also popular, especially amongst the longshoremen, tars and mercenaries that were the lifeblood of Bordeleaux's businesses.

And that was just as well. After this awful day, the inn once more comprised the whole of Florin and Lorenzo's fortune. But it was only after they'd slumped exhaustedly down into the taproom's best chairs that the full cost of the debacle hit them.

'A hundred crowns,' Lorenzo muttered into his flagon of ale.

'A hundred and three,' Florin corrected him. He took a sip of port and watched a trio of sailors roll into the bar. He could tell by their walk that they'd just returned from a long voyage, and he could tell from their exuberance that it had been a successful one. He tried to cheer himself up with the thought of how much money they were likely to spend, but it didn't work. After all, compared to today's losses what were a few coins one way or another?

'A hundred and three crowns,' Lorenzo repeated and took a swig of ale. Neither he nor Florin had fancied drinking any of the wine. The memory of all the casks they'd lost made its finely-balanced flavours taste as sour as vinegar.

'Let's look on the bright side,' Florin suggested as the sailors ordered their first round of drinks. Lorenzo looked at him as if he'd just gone insane.

'No need to look like that,' Florin told him with a wink. 'We're alive. We still have this place, and the boat. And it isn't even as if we lost all of the barrels.'

A horribly vivid memory of dripping sailors tossing wine overboard made Lorenzo groan as if in pain.

'No,' Florin continued obliviously. 'Today was a setback, but we won't starve. Why, last month alone we made almost a hundred.'

'We lost a hundred and three,' Lorenzo reminded him.

Florin regarded his comrade with a mixture of sympathy and irritation.

'Tell you what,' he decided with a conspiratorial nudge. 'What say we go to Madame Gourmelon's and make it a hundred and ten? I hear she's got some new girls in from the country. Apparently they're almost virgins.'

'Skinny then,' Lorenzo moped.

Florin shook his head. 'Not at all. Apparently they're as plump as grapes on an autumn vine.'

'Let's go then,' Lorenzo decided, swigging back the last of his ale and getting to his feet.

'You cheered up quickly.'

'Well,' Lorenzo grinned wide enough to show both of his teeth. 'There's more to life than money.'

'That's the spirit,' Florin nodded. 'And anyway... Hey, wait for me.'

He hurried after the older man, wrapping his cloak around him as he went. But no sooner had he stepped out of the tavern than he ran straight into his friend's back. He opened his mouth to complain then snapped it shut when he saw what had frozen Lorenzo in his tracks.

It was Katerina.

But what surprised him, and what had surprised Lorenzo, was that her face was wet and puffy from crying. Somehow, Florin had always thought that she was immune to such frailties.

'What's wrong?' he asked. The desperation on her face, as well as the sorrow, made him immediately suspect the worst. He wasn't disappointed.

'It's Sergei,' she told him, her eyes shining with moisture. 'You have to help me. He's been poisoned. I think... I think that he's dying.'

And with that Katerina Hansebourg, as diamond hard as anybody Florin had ever met, started sobbing like a child.

'There, there,' he said, wrapping a cautious arm around her shoulder. 'It can't be that bad.'

After a moment's resistance she melted into his arms and started howling with grief. Although the street was crowded, few of the passers-by paid much heed to the little tableau. After all, shattered hearts were no great novelty in Bordeleaux.

'There, there,' Florin repeated and wondered if he should say something else. When it came to grappling with treachery or sudden violence he thought of himself as being more than capable. When it came to comforting sobbing women, though... Well, what could he do?

A treacherous feeling of pleasure stole through him as she squeezed against his chest. The twinge of self-disgust that followed it served to snap him out of this quandary.

'Lorenzo, go get a carriage. Katerina, we'll go and see the crone. She saved me once.'

'Yes, boss,' Lorenzo said and plunged into the crowd of bodies like a swimmer into the sea. A moment later he was gone, just one more stooped and begrimed figure amongst the rest.

'But he's so sick,' Katerina snuffled and a shudder ran through her body. Florin swallowed and made himself push her away.

'I was almost dead when the crone saved me,' he told her. A sudden flash of memory, of burnt lungs and melted skin, made him clench his teeth.

Katerina sniffed and wiped her nose. 'Well that's good,' she said. 'My mother wanted to send him to the temple, but I knew that wasn't right.'

'How did you know?' Florin asked, as much to keep her mind occupied than because he really wanted to know. It was common knowledge that, despite the alms they took from the desperate, the temples were little better than taverns as far as the sick were concerned.

'I know,' Katerina said, a spark of hatred glinting within her bloodshot eyes, 'because she wants Sergei dead.'

'Ah,' said Florin. He almost asked if the old bitch had had Sergei poisoned but stopped himself in time. If that thought wasn't already in Katerina's mind, now was not the time to put it there. He thought about putting his arm around her whilst Lorenzo brought a cart but after a quick glance, decided not to. Her moment of weakness had passed. Now she was once more the Katerina he'd found ruling in the wilderness, a natural daughter for the ogre who had adopted her.

Florin smiled grimly. Blood or no blood, if the comtesse had spiked Sergei he didn't give much for her chances.

'Look, there's Lorenzo,' he said, relieved. 'Let's go and get hold of the crone. And don't worry, she won't let us down!'

CHAPTER FIVE

AND THE CRONE *didn't let them down. She dragged Sergei back from the very edge of death, working day and night to purge the poison from his blood.*

It wasn't easy, but he was strong. After two days he regained consciousness. After a week he was well enough to swing himself out of bed. And in a month he was almost back to his own boisterous self.

The crone was paid more than she asked for, and she'd asked for a lot. But, as far as Katerina was concerned, there wasn't enough gold in the city to pay for the miracle she had wrought.

Soon life was back to normal, and the tale of their battle in the forest had done wonders for business at Dodieu's fencing school, much to the old man's delight. And then, one day, Katerina realised that she had missed her monthly course. She waited until she was sure before telling Sergei that she was with child, and when she did he wept with joy.

Eight months later and Katerina Chervez was born. She had eyes as green as her mother's, as green as the depths of a summer's ocean.

They were magical too, those eyes. Or perhaps it was the baby that was magical. Or perhaps when the Hansebourgs finally welcomed Sergei into the family it wasn't magic at all. It was a gesture of gratitude for such a beautiful gift.

She grew well, and strong, and everybody spoiled her. And when she asked for a baby brother, well, what could they do but give in?

One year followed another, each better than the last, and the laughter of their children eventually became the laughter of their grandchildren.

And every day, in some quiet corner or moment of snatched silence, Katerina would thank the sun and the stars and the deep stone bones of the earth for saving her husband.

And she was happy.

'Katerina?'

She blinked, startled from her daydream. Not that it had felt like a daydream on this warm sunny day, in this place of the dead.

The garden of Morr stretched away on all sides, an entire tiered hilltop of age-rounded tombs. Between the rows broad flights of steps cascaded down, the perfectly kept geometries of their masonry a sharp contrast to the messy world below. And between the tombs there was perfectly smooth, perfectly swept paving.

The priests of Morr did their job well. Almost too well. The order and cleanliness of this high acropolis often struck those raised in the teeming chaos below as being eerie in its abnormality.

'Katerina?'

The voice was gentle and concerned. Wary too. But to Katerina it was just annoying.

A spark of resentment at the man who had dragged her back to reality flickered for a moment and then died. She didn't have the energy to feel angry. She didn't have the energy to feel anything. She just wanted to close her eyes and sleep; to sleep forever.

'Katerina. Come on. They're taking the body to the tomb. Don't you want to bid it farewell?'

A deep, shuddering breath tore itself from her body and she looked at Florin. He hadn't been invited to the funeral. Neither had Lorenzo. But then, they hadn't been invited to the house either. They'd come anyway. Her mother's porters had stopped trying to dissuade them when Lorenzo had explained what would happen to them if they succeeded.

'Come and bid the body farewell,' Florin said, deciding for her. She let him take her by the arm and guide her towards the Hansebourg family tomb. It squatted before the gathered mourners like a bloated granite beast.

Bloated, but always hungry.

As she watched, Sergei's coffin was carried towards its final destination. It was borne aloft by four of the Hansebourgs' men. Nobody knew where his own brothers might be, nor had anybody tried to find them. For the first time Katerina wondered if they would ever learn how he had died, or where.

Florin caught her as she stumbled, and together they followed the pallbearers into the tomb's gaping maw.

The inside was a cool oasis of smoothly polished marble. A great stone slab rested in the centre of the floor, and as Sergei's coffin was lowered onto it Katerina looked away, her eyes sliding sightlessly over the score of stone alcoves that hollowed the walls.

'Well,' Florin said, at a loss, 'I'll leave you to say goodbye.'

Katerina shrugged as, with a final squeeze of her arm, he stepped back out of the crypt. When he had gone, she walked over to the coffin, her feet seeming to move of their own volition. One hand reached out to brush against the polished walnut of her husband's coffin. It was cold and it was sealed. The poison had done horrible things to him before... before it had finished.

For a moment something moved in the still depths of her eyes. A glimmer of the humanity that she was trying so hard to disown, maybe. It glistened in the single fat tear that welled up and dropped, unnoticed, onto Sergei's coffin.

'Katerina. Are you finished? Let's go.'

The comtesse's tones rang out like steel toecaps on the stone walls. The expression in Katerina's eyes died, and her face became as hard and as still as a frozen lake.

'Or perhaps you'd like us to leave you in peace?' Florin's voice was tinged with anger, and when Katerina turned she saw him and her mother glaring at each other with ill-concealed loathing.

'No,' she said, waving a hand helplessly in the air. 'No. We can go.'

The comtesse smirked at Florin and, with all the eagerness of a card shark who has found a new mark, she bustled forward to sweep her daughter away.

Katerina's uncles, Gilles and Bouillon, were waiting impatiently outside. Now that they had done their duty their eagerness to be away had grown to a fidgeting intensity. They barely glanced at the girl as her mother dragged her along the path, merely bowed to the tomb with an unconscious formality before striding away.

'I'll come and visit you,' Florin called after Katerina.

'You're not invited,' her mother snapped back over her shoulder.

'I know,' Florin told her. 'But I'll come anyway.'

The comtesse paused as if she were about to argue. But then Katerina seemed to stir from her shock and the older woman hurriedly hastened her away.

'What a bitch,' Lorenzo said, his face even uglier than usual beneath his expression of contempt.

'Yes,' Florin agreed. He sighed and turned back to the tomb. The pallbearers were fretting, eager to seal it up and be away.

'Here,' Florin said, tossing a coin to one so that the gold of it flashed in the sunlight. 'You can go now. We'll do that.'

'Right you are, boss,' the man said. When he'd led his men away to the nearest tavern, Florin and Lorenzo went to stand by Sergei's coffin. Florin thumped a bottle of brandy down onto the woodwork, and Lorenzo dug three glasses out of his pockets.

The gurgle of brandy being poured and the whiff of alcohol filled the crypt.

'A toast!' Florin proposed, raising his glass to Lorenzo. 'To Sergei Chervez, a man as brave as an ogre.'

'Sergei,' Lorenzo repeated and they drank.

'A toast!' Lorenzo said once their glasses were refilled. 'To Sergei Chervez, a man more cunning than a wolf.'

'Or a debt collector,' Florin added, and the two of them laughed before drinking again.

And again.

And then some more.

Outside, the sun slowly melted away into the western sea. The shadows grew as deep as open pits beneath the tombs that cast them, and bats replaced the sparrows that had flitted amongst their stone bodies.

When Florin and Lorenzo finally stumbled back out of the tomb, Mannslieb was riding high in the sky. Florin waved the empty bottle at the moon cheerily, and decided to take it as a good omen.

They'd need one. They were once more men with a mission.

As the brandy had gone so had their thirst for vengeance grown. The oaths the two of them had sworn to defend Sergei's widow had been as binding as they'd been vicious.

The ferocity of their words had even impressed the invisible things that haunted this place, and they were not easily impressed. As Florin and Lorenzo staggered towards the cemetery gates, the silent chorus of the phantoms' approving whispers followed them out into the world beyond.

CHAPTER SIX

'AH MY BOY, my boy!' Mordicio wheedled happily. His yellow teeth glistened as he smiled within the rat's nest of his beard, and he examined the figure that stood before him with every sign of approval. It was as tall and gangling as he himself, and it belonged to one of the few people the old moneylender allowed into his private counting chamber.

The young man stood in the centre of the windowless cell, his face pale even in the lantern light.

'You're as handsome as your father!' Mordicio babbled on. 'Turn around and let me see that gold frogging. No, don't touch it! It has to go back to the tailor afterwards.' Rabin Mordicio obediently dropped his sweaty fingers from the gold thread and turned around. Although no more than thirty, he moved with the painful clumsiness of an arthritic grandfather. His face, as if to make up for this, had all the chubby vacuity of an idiot child.

'Yes, yes!' Mordicio rubbed the bony claws of his hands together. 'You look like a real gentleman, my boy, and no mistake. Just see that you don't spill soup on that waistcoat. It's silk and I can get almost full price back for it.'

'It's unlucky to sell your wedding suit, Pa.' Rabin spoke for the first time. He spoke in a petulant whine that perfectly matched his flabby features, but Mordicio didn't care. Today his boy was the greatest of all of his treasures.

'And anyway,' the groom-to-be carried on, 'after I marry the Hansebourg girl I'll be able to afford whatever I want.'

The older man stepped backwards, mouth open in horror, and seized the edge of his counting table as though about to fall.

'Able to afford!' Mordicio wailed, shocked to hear such words from his own flesh and blood. 'Able to afford! Are you trying to ruin me, your poor old father, just like your Uncle Chaim?'

Rabin thought of his Uncle Chaim. Just last year he'd finally died in the debtor's prison to which his brother had consigned him. The cholera had been quite bad in there, apparently.

'No, father, of course not.' Now the whine in Rabin's voice was obsequious.

'See that you aren't, my boy. See that you aren't. When you get married I'll take the girl's dowry, as is right. And I'll look after her fortune. For your own good.' The old man's eyes misted over at the thought of all the wealth Katerina's father had left to her. A third of the Hansebourg fortune, no less: a treasure of shares and ships and gold. It would make Mordicio a very happy man.

Rabin watched his father, his hatred carefully concealed. He'd seen the documents that would move Katerina's fortune from her control to his and then, just as freedom was finally in his grasp, over to his father. It was so unfair. He was doing all the work and the timing was hardly convenient.

It hadn't occurred to his father that the ceremony would take place the day after the wench had buried her previous husband. He'd had his own plans for today. Outside, a dozen of his hangers-on were waiting, still looking forward to a day at the dog fights. There were even some goblins on the bill today, and their antics as the dogs tore them to pieces were always amusing.

By rights, the Hansebourg strumpet's money should have been his. The gods alone knew that his allowance was barely enough to live on. He only managed to get by because of the terror Mordicio's name inspired in the tailors and tavern keepers of Bordeleaux. And now, just as he should be coming into his own, the greedy old leech wanted to rob him. Well, Rabin thought, we'll see about that. He rubbed his clammy hands together in unconscious imitation of his father and went back to looking vacant. He was good at it. He'd been practising for more than two decades.

'Now then, my boy,' Mordicio carried on. 'Here's your cloak. Watch the hem on the way out. The stone might wear on it.'

'It's not noon yet,' Rabin frowned. 'Shouldn't we wait?'

'Why wait?' his father shrugged. 'I'm hungry. Why eat my own food when there are tables of the stuff at the Hansebourg's? Very foolish with their money, the Hansebourgs. Very foolish. Katerina should be grateful that a man like me is going to look after it for her.'

Rabin said nothing, doing his best to keep the rage off his face. After all, he thought bitterly, this was to be a joyful day.

Rabin's henchmen straightened their backs respectfully as his stooped father stalked past them, and then looked at their master questioningly.

'Dog fight's off,' Rabin muttered, 'but never mind. We've a wedding to go to instead.'

'A wedding?'

'Yes. Mine. Something funny?'

But if there was, none of them were laughing.

'You must be insane.'

The Comtesse Hansebourg flushed bright red. She was unused to being spoken to in such a way, and she obviously wasn't enjoying the novelty. The trio of maids that waited behind her flinched and tried to hide behind the piles of lacy finery they carried.

'How dare you speak to your mother like that!' the comtesse yelled at her daughter. Katerina just grunted and turned back to stare out of the window. Her chambers were on the third floor of the Hansebourg mansion and the view below was busy with crowded streets, ragged roofs and the forest of distant masts that plied the harbour beyond.

To Katerina, none of it seemed real any more. The mist that last night had sucked in off the warm sea didn't do much to dispel the illusion, although it did soften the neverending squalor of the city. The hunched and desperate denizens that swarmed like rats in the streets below were blurred enough to look healthy, and the rot of Bordeleaux's architecture had been erased so that only the shapes of the buildings remained, as pure now as they had been in their builders' imaginations.

The comtesse's fine features grew even more thunderous as she realised that her daughter wasn't going to reply.

The girl hadn't washed or changed since Sergei had died. And her hair was as unruly and tangled as the mane of some wild animal.

Not only that, but the maids that the comtesse had sent to groom the girl had come back in floods of tears. One of them had even come back bleeding.

'Katerina,' the comtesse said, softening her tone. 'My dear. Let's not quarrel. This is the day of your wedding. A happy day.'

The comtesse attempted a smile which froze when her daughter responded.

'Don't be a fool,' she murmured. 'I'm not marrying anybody. And without both Uncle Gilles's and Uncle Bouillon's permission you can't make me.'

'Your uncles aren't here,' the comtesse spat. 'They left on business last night and they aren't back yet.'

Katerina waved a hand dismissively.

'Very well,' her mother said, a certain malicious pleasure creeping into her voice. 'Have it your own way. Oh, and by the way, did I mention that that animal that keeps following you around has returned?'

'Tabby, you mean?' Katerina turned to face her mother for the first time. The comtesse felt her malicious pleasure die. Katerina suddenly looked so young... The comtesse cleared her throat and ploughed on.

'Yes, Tabby. Ridiculous name. She's wounded, I'm afraid. When she wouldn't go into the cage one of the guards on the gate had to shoot her.'

'What!' Katerina cried. She sprang to her feet with such violence that her mother's maids retreated in panic.

'Oh, don't be so sentimental,' the comtesse told her. 'The animal will live. Well, perhaps it will. Sir Gerhardt, the keeper of the postern gates, has her safely locked up for the moment. But I think that he wants to kill her.'

Katerina drifted towards the old woman, her left hand behind her back.

'Where is she?'

Although little more than a whisper, the question carried more threat than a warrior's roar. The comtesse felt a sudden sheen of sweat dampening her forehead. She ignored it and forced herself not to flinch as her daughter approached.

'She's safe. For now. If you marry Rabin, you can have her back.'

There. It was out.

The comtesse felt relief and something else. She didn't realise until later that it was self-disgust.

Katerina froze, and considered.

A heartbeat later, trusting an instinct that nineteen years of strife had honed to a razor's edge, she decided. After all, what was a marriage? Just a piece of paper, no more. Nothing worth a single whisker from Tabby's soft muzzle.

Something glinted in her hand as she turned away and paced back to the window. The comtesse tried to convince herself that it was a piece of jewellery.

'I submit to your blackmail,' Katerina said, her voice as dead as the grave. 'I will marry whatever creature you choose. Then, within the hour of my doing so, you will reunite me with Tabby. Is it a deal?'

'Blackmail? What do you mean?' her mother blustered. She was suddenly conscious of the three pairs of eyes that had witnessed this scene. A fleeting fantasy of having the maids silenced crossed her mind, but she pushed it away. Instead she approached her daughter, one hand outstretched in a gesture of awkward reconciliation.

'Such a thing to say!' she said, and laughed a laugh that was as real as her pearls.

'Do we have a deal?' Katerina asked.

'Yes,' the comtesse sighed. 'We have a deal.'

And with that she turned and retreated. The maids took one look at their mistress's face and scurried away, but the comtesse ordered them to get back in there and dress her daughter. The girls eyed each other warily and crept back into the room like trappers approaching a wild animal.

'Come on then, let's get it over with,' Katerina snapped at them, and her mother winced.

What a daughter I have, she thought. As she made her way back to the grand hall to see that everything was in order she sighed, cursing the gods for her bad luck.

What a daughter. No decency at all. There was no telling what she would do when she found out that the damned cat of hers hadn't returned. The thought sent a trickle of apprehension running down the comtesse's spine, but she shrugged it off. After Katerina was married she would be Mordicio's problem.

That feeling came again, that oily nausea.

She ignored it and concentrated on the... the *consideration* that Mordicio had promised for her hand in this matchmaking. It would be enough to free her from her brother-in-laws' intermittent charity for the rest of her life.

She stalked off to bully the servants who were preparing the wedding hall. Despite the short notice, the comtesse had been able to summon a couple of dozen guests, and she wanted to make sure that appearances were maintained, for their sakes.

As if some dirty pet mattered in comparison to that!

The ceremony itself was held in the great hall of the Hansebourg mansion. It was a vast, echoing chamber and despite the short notice, it had been filled with a good number of guests. From all over the city the Hansebourgs' allies, trading partners and hangers-on had been summoned to witness the ceremony.

Those that had come tended towards the old and retired, but that was all to the good. As far as the comtesse was concerned, the more respectable the eyes that witnessed the marriage, the more binding it would be.

The guests stood amongst the great tables of food, little realising that most of the dishes were left over from Sergei's funeral party the day before.

The stonework was swathed with tapestries, and even the great columns that supported the roof had been decorated, wrapped with yards of festive cloth that made them seem like spirals of sugar-coated confectionery.

'Won't be long now,' Molly told her, her voice taut with excitement.

Katerina studied the maid with a cool look. She was small and plump, and blessed with the pretty dark eyes of a healthy rhinox. Katerina hadn't really paid much attention to her family's underlings since she'd arrived. As far as she was concerned they were just like gnoblars, silly chittering things that were made for her to rule with occasional flashes of praise or censure.

'How do you know that it won't be long?' Katerina asked.

Molly hugged herself nervously. Rumour had it that the young mistress's attention was the last thing you wanted to attract. Still, today was her wedding day. Maybe that would sweeten her mood.

'Because all the fine ladies and gentlemen are almost here, mademoiselle,' she replied. 'All but for Monsieur Rabin and his father. And don't you let anybody tell you anything about Monsieur Mordicio neither, mademoiselle. After all, what do they know?'

Katerina shrugged at the rhetorical question, but another voice piped up in answer.

'Everyone says that he had his own brother bankrupted,' the second maid volunteered with an obvious relish, 'and that he died in prison.'

'Hush now!' Molly scolded her. 'Miss Hansebourg doesn't want to hear such nonsense on her wedding day. Do you, mademoiselle?'

'Let the girl speak,' Katerina decided.

'And they say,' the other girl went on, emboldened, 'that he tried to ruin Florin d'Artaud once. It was all over a damsel's honour, I think. But anyway, Florin was too clever for him, and fought his way out of it!'

'And wouldn't you just like Florin d'Artaud to be too clever for you?' another girl said.

'Not that he'd have to be that clever,' someone else added.

'Or do much fighting!'

The maids burst into raucous laughter.

'Forgive me, Mademoiselle Katerina.' Molly was the first to recover. 'I don't suppose you know what we're talking about, being a lady and all.'

'Of course I do,' the bride-to-be said distractedly and looked through a gap in the curtains. There was a flurry of activity at the far end of the hall as a scruffy old man, who Katerina recognised as Mordicio himself, stalked through the doors. 'You're talking about mating.'

'Well, erm... yes,' Molly admitted, trying to hide her shock at this bluntness.

'I've done it often enough. After all, I *was* marr... married.'

For a moment Katerina's face crumpled like a fistful of parchment, and her green eyes shone as damply as dew on the grass. But then she was back in control. There was no time for this nonsense now, she scolded herself. She had to marry the moonfaced creature that had just followed Mordicio into the hall so that she could rescue Tabby.

After that she'd think about how to escape from this horrible city and make her way home.

And after that she'd think about Sergei. If she could bear to.

'Ooh look, mademoiselle. There he is. Isn't he, erm, handsome?' Molly said. Katerina followed the maid's gaze and watched Rabin lurching forward, moving with all the grace of a tailor's dummy. His face was as blank as a bowl full of dough; his idiot eyes small black dots within the pale folds of his flesh.

Katerina turned to look into Molly's kindly face. 'Tell me the truth. Do you really think that he's handsome?'

The maid averted her eyes and coughed into a handkerchief.

'Well, do you?'

'They say that real beauty is a thing of the soul, mademoiselle,' she evaded, and Katerina smiled. It was a brief, bitter thing, but the first for days.

'Molly,' she said as two of the Hansebourgs' porters strode over to escort her to the altar that waited at the end of the hall, 'you're a good and honest girl. I'm sorry I didn't spend more time with you.'

'Thank you, mademoiselle. But we'll still see each other after the wedding.'

'No.' Katerina shook her head. 'We won't.'

And with that, she stepped forward into the main hall and marched towards the altar. She ignored her escorts' pleasantries as they fell into step beside her and, moving forward with the grim determination of an execution squad, they soon reached the altar.

Ignoring the priest's murmured greetings, Katerina turned to watch Mordicio and his son approach. Their own wedding guests had followed them into the hall in a block, and now they veered off to one side. As they did so they revealed the daggers and swords that they wore about their belts. Not one of them seemed anything other than the hired thug that he was, which was perhaps why the Hansebourgs' dozen or so guests shied away from them.

As Katerina watched, Mordicio stopped and whispered something to his son. The man's face remained expressionless as he paused to lift the hem of his cape clear of the floor.

'Come on, come on,' Katerina snapped. The sooner everything was signed, the sooner she could get away to Tabby.

To her surprise, and to her relatives' consternation, her impatience was greeted with a bawdy roar from Mordicio's men. Katerina scowled at them and turned back to Rabin. Mordicio pushed him forward as they reached the altar.

'Make sure she signs in three places,' he hissed into his son's ear.

'Yes, father,' Rabin said, and stepped up to take his place before the priest. Katerina drew away from him, a look of disgust on her face.

'Don't be like that, dear,' Mordicio wheedled in a voice he thought was avuncular. 'He'll be your husband soon.'

Katerina just snorted as, his eyes darting nervously between the mismatched bride and groom, the priest started to read out the ceremonial words.

'We are gathered together in happy celebration on this day, to witness the joining of two young lives...' he began, apparently unaware of how uninterested the two young lives were.

'What are you looking at?' Katerina hissed at Rabin as he ogled her. Slowly, reluctantly, he dragged his piggy little eyes away from the smooth slopes of her cleavage and looked into the heat of her eyes.

Incredibly, he winked.

Katerina's nose wrinkled in distaste and she turned back to the priest. He droned on and, unbidden, a memory of her marriage ceremony to Sergei came to mind. It had been on a ship. The smell of tar and brine had been thick in the air, and the deck had been rolling beneath their feet as if in silent applause. Grief shifted lazily within Katerina's stomach and she clenched her jaw against it.

Now wasn't the time.

'...and even as the Lady herself looks down upon us here today, so we ask Shallya to also look down, and to gift these two young people with the life and fecundity with which she...'

Katerina wondered if she should tell the priest to get a move on. Probably not. He looked like the sort of dry old stick who'd just start again at the beginning, and there was no telling how long she had to rescue Tabby. Her mother had promised that the big cat was safe, but Katerina was worried about the wound she'd taken. After watching Sergei's festering death, she... she...

Something caught in her throat and she had to clench her fists to keep the tears locked inside of her.

'...for who can fail to be moved by the abundance of joy which is so apparent in these two?' the priest asked nobody in particular, his eyes lowered to the book from which he read. 'And who can doubt that their marriage is indeed a blessed thing, a glorious submission to the will of the Lady...'

Katerina turned to study her mother but if she had hoped to read anything on the comtesse's face she was disappointed. Her expression was hidden behind the traditional white veil she wore.

'...and in the days to come they will look back on today as one of the happiest days of their lives. Now, in the sight of your family, your gods and the Lady herself I ask you, Rabin Mordicio, burgher of Bordeleaux, do you take this woman as your wife?'

For a moment Rabin looked confused. Then he leered towards Katerina and said, 'I do.'

'And will you keep her and feed her, and get her with child?'

'I will.'

'And will you treat her with kindness and generosity for so long as you both shall live?'

Once more Rabin looked confused, but this time the priest came to his aid.

'At least,' the holy man said, eager to get things over with and start eating, 'in such a way as seems reasonable to you.'

'Certainly,' Rabin nodded.

'And you, Katerina–?'

'I do,' she said. 'Now, what do I have to sign?'

'You have to hear what the vows are first,' the priest told her.

'Very well, very well. Get on with it then.'

'Wait a moment,' he muttered. 'I've lost my place.'

'For Shallya's sake!'

'Ah, here it is. So, ahem, do you take this man to be your lord and master?'

'Yes, yes, yes.'

'And promise to obey him in all things?'

'Yes.'

'And to bear him strong sons, so that they may serve you both in your dotage?'

Katerina snorted. Then, seeing that that wasn't answer enough, she said, 'I do.'

'Very well,' the priest said, relief evident in his voice. He felt like a captain who had just shepherded his ship through stormy seas and into the safety of a port. 'Now then, if you'll just sign here... Yes, and here... Yes, I'm aware of that Monsieur Mordicio... and finally, here. Now you sir... Yes, Monsieur Mordicio, I'm aware of that too... Yes, that's it. Well then, it only remains for me to offer you my congratulations and...'

But Katerina had already left the little tableau gathered around the altar and paced over to her mother.

'Right then,' she said, standing in front of the comtesse with her hands on her hips. 'Where's Tabby?'

'What do you mean?' the comtesse asked, suddenly glad to be hidden behind her veil.

'Tabby. My cat. Where's she being kept? I want to go and tend to her wound.'

The comtesse shifted uncomfortably in her seat and looked towards the Mordicios for help. But father and son were still huddled over the altar, checking the signatures on the marriage document.

'Mother,' Katerina said, her voice becoming dangerously calm. 'Where's Tabby?'

The comtesse licked her lips, nervous for the second time in a decade.

'It was for your own good,' she said, and was immediately horrified at the whine in her voice.

'What was?' Katerina asked, although judging by the fury that was blossoming across her face she had already guessed. The comtesse got to her feet and, with an attempt at haughtiness, turned to leave.

Katerina caught her by the shoulder and spun her around like a top. By now a small crowd of guests had gathered around them. They had come to pay their compliments to the new bride, but now it seemed that something infinitely more interesting was unfolding. They held back and pretended not to be paying attention.

'Tell me, mother,' Katerina hissed as the guests pretended not to hear. 'Did Tabby return or were you lying?'

'Lying!' the comtesse bridled. 'What a thing to say! I wasn't lying. I was just encouraging you. For your own good. But no, now that you ask. I don't know where that damn beast is.'

Katerina's face drained of blood, leaving her features as white as porcelain except for the two red spots that burned on her cheeks. But before she could vent her rage on the comtesse, Mordicio interrupted them.

'Congratulations, my dear. Congratulations!' he said. And then, oblivious to any tension, he wrapped his skeletal arms around his daughter-in-law. Katerina didn't pay him much heed. She just pushed him off with a flat-palmed blow to the chest that sent the old man reeling back into Rabin's arms.

The guests drew back, trying to hide their delight at the way things were going. They'd be telling the story of the Hansebourg wedding for months.

But the Mordicios' entourage wasn't so sanguine. Even as the old moneylender was scrabbling back to his feet his men rushed forward, the clatter of their boots momentarily lost beneath the crash of an overturned table.

'The wedding's off,' Katerina snapped as her new husband let his father fall back to the floor.

'Too late,' her groom said, rubbing his podgy hands together and stepping forward.

Katerina raised her hand and he stepped back again, almost tripping over Mordicio in his haste to be away from his bride.

'Get her!' he squeaked to the first of his henchmen, his voice tight with alarm.

'I don't think there's any need for that...' the comtesse began, but nobody was listening to her any more. Rabin's men had grabbed all the guests' attention as they elbowed their way through them to get to Katerina. The guests got out of their way, their resentment not strong enough to overcome their fear of Mordicio's thugs. A moment later, the first of the thugs reached Katerina.

He was a big lad who didn't bother to hide the leer on his face as he reached confidently for the slip of the girl. His hands were the size of hams, and his outstretched fingers clawed into meat hooks as he grabbed at her.

Katerina, barely deigning to look at her assailant, seized both of his little fingers and snapped them backwards. The man shrieked with surprise as he buckled and fell to his knees. Ignoring his cry of protest, she jabbed her knee upwards beneath his chin. There was a crack of splintering teeth, a splash of blood onto the white of her wedding dress, and her assailant's cry was cut off.

The victim's companions hesitated as he slumped down to the floor.

'Well, go on then. Get her!' Rabin heckled them as he edged even further back. 'She's only a woman.'

Emboldened by this thought, or perhaps by the thought of what would happen to their reputations should they fail, the rest of the men charged forward. They knocked several of the guests to the floor as they did so.

'Stop. Stop!' the comtesse demanded, her voice shrill but ineffective. Even as she complained, a pair of men, their faces flushed with wine and anger, lunged past her and grabbed at Katerina.

But Katerina was no longer there. As they had closed in on her, so she had rushed past them, breaking through their line and racing around the scrum of guests in which they had become entangled.

'Don't let her get away!' Rabin cried as he scuttled back to hide behind the altar.

But if Katerina had had any thoughts of escape they were gone now. All of the miseries of the past few hellish days boiled up within her and found expression in the dangerous joys of rage and violence. Before Mordicio's men realised who was predator and who was prey, she had singled out one of the stragglers. Before he even realised that she was upon him she'd sprung forward, her gown billowing as she stamped down on his knee.

The crunch of gristle was inaudible among the shouts and cries of outrage that now echoed around the hall, but his scream as his kneecap was torn off wasn't. The man fell and Katerina jabbed forward, punching a single raised knuckle into his forehead. He collapsed into a boneless heap and Katerina leapt over his body. Her eyes blazed with a terrible green light as she closed in on her next target.

Had Mordicio's men been alone they would surely have captured her there and then. No matter how nimble she was, she wouldn't have stood a chance against their crushing weight of numbers.

But Mordicio's men weren't alone. Far from it. They were surrounded by wedding guests, and Hansebourg wedding guests at that. Although long in the tooth, their teeth were still strong and yellowed. They were people who were more used to pushing than being pushed. Especially not by hired louts like Mordicio's men. And especially not at a wedding.

The first to rebel, or so most people later agreed, was Monsieur Germian Berre. Although approaching eighty years of age, Monsieur Berre still possessed all the native viciousness that had seen him rise to control the whole of Bordeleaux's cinnamon trade. He also possessed a bone-handled walking stick which he'd thoughtfully had weighted with lead. So it was that, as one of Mordicio's larger thugs pushed rudely past him, the old man raised the stick and whacked it down on the back of his head. His victim's scalp split open as easily as the shell of a boiled egg and he fell forwards.

Unfortunately it wasn't the floor that broke his fall, it was the copious bosom of Herr Borscht's wife.

Herr Borscht, a grizzled old cutthroat who'd made his fortune by sailing tar down from the north, was most unimpressed by this breach of etiquette. Not being a man to let a grievance fester into ill-feeling, he finished the malefactor off with a kick to the groin before arming himself with a cudgel he snatched from the man's belt.

'Stop this!' the comtesse howled as the two old men turned gleefully onto another of Mordicio's number. This unfortunate had gotten himself tangled up amongst the train of somebody's hysterically screaming mistress. The last thing he heard before his two fellow celebrants fell upon him was the comtesse's wail of protest.

From behind the safety of the altar, Rabin added his own voice to hers. 'For Ranald's sake,' he scolded his followers, 'she's only a girl. Grab her.'

Even as he spoke, the party was turning into a riot, and the riot was spreading to engulf the rest of his men. Burghers, merchants and traders who hadn't raised a sweat for decades were flinging off their years as easily as if they were over-warm cloaks. In the first rush of delighted outrage they'd beaten perhaps half a dozen of their younger foes to the ground. Now that the element of surprise had worn off, things began to even up.

Not too much, though. Even the wildest of Mordicio's thugs knew what would happen to anybody who seriously injured these burghers. The burghers themselves, however, had no such qualms and hurled themselves into this wonderful blood sport with a wild abandon.

An entire row of tables collapsed as a struggling knot of figures blundered into them, their overburdened timbers falling like a row of dominoes.

Katerina, beside herself with the joy of combat, laughed out loud. For a moment, she thought of using this confusion to escape, but rejected the thought almost as soon as it occurred. Apart from anything else she couldn't leave her new allies to finish the fight alone.

No sooner had she reached this decision than a gaggle of screaming matrons scattered like hens before a fox, and a trio of Mordicio's men rushed towards her. Katerina turned as if to flee and leapt up onto a table. Pushing herself up off the corner, she turned again and jumped high. Before her pursuers could react she'd fallen back down amongst them, the speed of her fall increasing the impact of her elbow so that it struck like a thunderbolt. Bouncing off the body of her victim, Katerina lashed out with one daintily shod foot, kicking out at a man's leg then rolling beneath his falling body to drive her thumbs into his kidneys. He screamed in agony and Katerina backflipped away from him to face his remaining companion.

She chuckled as she saw the expression on his face. As he stood there, frozen between the desire to run and the shame of it, she fell upon him. Feinting to the right, she dodged and punched him in the throat.

Katerina laughed again, the sound as carefree as a child's gurgle. For the first time since Sergei had died she felt back in control of her life, exulting in the riot that surged before her. The hall had been transformed into a sea of struggling or inert figures, their finery torn and bloodstained.

Strangely enough, she didn't seem to be the only one enjoying the mayhem. Even as she watched, the oldest man in the room tripped one of Mordicio's thugs as he staggered past, and then fell upon him with a joyous roar.

Katerina was about to go and help him when, suddenly, the world exploded into a supernova of blinding white light.

And then there was only darkness.

'No, I don't think it's fun, my dear,' Mordicio muttered as he checked to see that she was still breathing. 'No, not fun at all. Only necessary.'

He slipped the golden candlestick he'd hit her with into an inside pocket, and checked that the marriage contract was still safely tucked there too. Satisfied, he huddled solicitously over Katerina and tried to catch the eye of one of his son's idiot followers.

Eventually, a pair of them emerged from the scrum beyond and Mordicio beckoned them over. Together, they dragged the bride out of the hall, elbowing their way past the knot of servants who stood uncertainly in the doorway.

'Get out of the way,' Mordicio snapped at one of them as he opened his mouth to protest. 'Can't you see that my daughter-in-law has been overcome by excitement? We need to get her home.'

Mordicio's carriage waited outside. The old moneylender and his henchmen threw Katerina's unconscious form into it as easily as if she were a sack of potatoes, slammed the doors after them, and made off.

Behind them cries of 'fire' had started to ring out from amongst the confusion. Seconds later and the first tendrils of smoke began to rise up from the windows of the Hansebourgs' great hall.

Mordicio glanced down at the inert form of the girl as a bend in the road rolled it to one side. Then he checked that the marriage documents were still safely inside his pocket. He smiled.

What a wonderful wedding it was, he thought, and cackled happily to himself as the first fire bells started to ring out behind him.

CHAPTER SEVEN

Bordeleaux's walls were massive. They had evolved over the centuries with the same relentless determination of all living things. The first primitive fishing village had grown into a town, which had grown into a trading port, which had, in turn, grown into the vast sprawl of streets and harbours and districts of which it was composed today.

Some scholars claimed that their city was even older than that first village; that it was older even than humanity itself. They claimed that the first human settlers had built their dwellings amongst the ruined remains of some other, more ancient race. For proof, they quoted ancient texts, although the texts were muddled after so many generations of copying errors. At other times they pointed to the delicately carved fragments of masonry which studded the patched daub and crumbling brick of the city, the beautifully worked stone as out of place as gemstones in a dung heap.

These scholars were usually ignored, a fact for which the saner ones were grateful. After all, if they had voiced their theories in the terrible lands of the north, who knows what might have been done to them? Burning at the stake was said to be the kindest of the witch finders' methods.

But in Bordeleaux there was little of this madness. The nobles who ruled this city cared as little about the dealings of their people as a farmer cares about the mooing of his herd. They didn't care what the populace did… so long as they did what they were told, of course.

Especially when they had other, more important concerns.

One of which was loping towards the eastern gate right now.

From the ramparts that loomed over the gate, Sir Guilbert watched the monster as it approached. He'd taken his helmet off so that he could feel the cooling breeze on his forehead, and also so that the long golden locks of his hair might flow with the wind, framing his handsome face.

The knight's eyes, normally perfect hazel ovals, were creased into slits as he peered into the rays of the setting sun.

The eyes of his sergeant-at-arms were narrowed too, although in his case the squint was a response to the blazing light that reflected from his master's armour. At this time of day the steel in which the knight was clad shone as brightly as a beetle's shell, the sweeps and curves of it flowing with reflected fire.

'My liege,' he said, bowing his head and punching a fist against the dully greased mail that armoured his own chest. 'There are reports that a fabulous beast approaches. The archers are standing ready and await your order to fire.'

Sir Guilbert frowned at his underling's show of initiative.

'Let them await,' he said. 'Let us see what kind of beast it is that approaches.'

'Some of the peasants say that it resembles an enormous cat, my liege,' the sergeant offered. 'One that has grown beyond all measure. Perhaps it is some creature from the forests of the elves?'

'No, no...' The knight waved the sergeant's suggestion aside dismissively. Thoughts of glory swirled in his mind as he considered the possibilities. Perhaps it was a fantastic beast from Estalia or beyond. Maybe a sorcerous creature that had flown here from the far shores of Lustria. Any knight who could best such a beast and take its head for a trophy would be the envy of his peers.

'Has it killed any of the peasants yet?' he asked, hopefully.

'None that I know of, my liege. Not that the good folk are taking any chances. See how they flee at its approach.'

The knight saw. The grubby peasants that toiled in the fields around the city parted before the tawny shape of the great beast like herring before a shark. Some of them had strayed into the cabbage fields that lined the road, and several arguments had broken out as a consequence.

The beast paid none of them any heed. Looking neither left nor right, it padded forward, content to pace slowly along as the crowd parted before it.

'I'm sure it must have,' decided the knight. 'It is our duty – my duty – to hunt down the beast and slay it. Summon my squire. Gather the knights. Have them meet me at the gates with all due haste. Oh, and sergeant?'

'My liege?'

'Bring my roan stallion, with the red caparison.'

'As you command, my liege,' the sergeant said, saluting, and hurried off to gather his lord's retainers.

The knight threw one last glance over the battlements before clanking off after him.

WHEN KATERINA WOKE up it was with a sense of relief. Her dreams had been a horrible fog of dread and confusion. She opened her eyes and breathed deeply, just taking a moment to enjoy the peace of lying on her bed.

A second later, the realisation hitting her as hard and fast as a boxer's fist, she remembered that Sergei was dead.

Her breath caught in her throat and she closed her eyes against a black tide of misery.

Then she tried to get up.

Tried and failed.

It took her a few confused moments to realise that the reason she couldn't move was because she was tied to her bed. But no, that wasn't right. This wasn't her bed or her bedchamber.

Her bruised head began to throb painfully as she started to piece together the events that had brought her here. The bloodied remains of her torn wedding dress gave her her first clue, and after that the memories came thick and fast. She remembered her marriage ceremony, and her mother's betrayal, and the fight.

But after that, nothing.

Well, never mind. Although beaten and disorientated, Katerina began an automatic process of prioritisation. The first thing to do, in fact the only thing to do, was to free herself from these bonds. She twisted her arms and legs experimentally. To her disappointment the movement was met with the clink of chains. Testing the limits of her freedom, she raised herself up onto her elbows and looked down at the manacles which held her. They were heavy duty lumps of grey steel, the dull surface of the metal marked by bright scratches.

Katerina turned her wrists and studied the small keyholes in the shackles. No help there. Even if she could find something to try and pick the locks with she had no way of reaching one hand with the other.

She fell back down and sighed. Then she took a moment to study the room. It was big, perhaps twenty paces across, and it was stone built. That suggested wealth. But, apart from the four-poster bed onto which she was bound, there was little other sign of wealth. There was a trestle table that wouldn't have looked out of place in a tavern, two rickety chairs and a chest that looked as though it had been nailed together by an amateur. Even the window was mean. Its single pane of glass had been fixed into the ceiling, the joinery around it so crude that it might have been put up there to cover a hole.

'Mordicio,' Katerina told herself, remembering the frayed rags in which Bordeleaux's richest man clothed himself.

Then she remembered his son, who was now her husband.

She swore, loudly and viciously. Then she tested the chains again with a new urgency. They didn't give an inch. Scowling with concentration, she abandoned the effort and craned her neck to study the bed frame to which the chains were fastened.

Unfortunately, it seemed to be the only thing in this draughty box of a room that was well made. The beams of seasoned timber were wider than her leg, and fastened together so tightly that, despite her most vigorous efforts, the joints didn't even squeak.

Katerina's heart began to race as she realised how hopeless this was. She licked her dry lips and ignored the twinge of panic that flared in the pit of her stomach.

There must be some way out of this. There was always a way.

But before she could find it, the door squeaked open and Rabin lurched in. Katerina could see immediately that he was the worse for drink.

Or maybe not. As he stomped across the room she could see that black patches had been singed into his fine clothes. He'd lost an eyebrow, too, and the red flush that she'd at first taken to be from too much wine covered only one side of his face.

Rabin approached the bed and paced around it warily. Only when he was satisfied that all of her chains still held did he shrug off his smoke-ruined jacket and fold it, with exaggerated care, over the back of a chair.

'Hello darling,' Katerina purred, her voice as smooth as honey. 'Are you all right? You look a little unwell.'

Rabin stared at her. His mouth opened and closed as soundlessly as a goldfish's.

'Unchain me and I'll see to that burn,' Katerina said, dropping her eyes demurely.

But not before she'd seen the comprehension that dawned in Rabin's eyes.

Damn, she thought. I shouldn't have mentioned the chains so quickly.

Rabin didn't reply. Instead he just sat and stared at his bride. Katerina could feel his eyes sliding over her body and forced herself not to show her disgust.

'Rabin,' she said with a sigh. 'You can let me go, now. We're married. I'm sorry I was rude but I was upset. That's all over now.'

She looked at him, but for all the reaction she got he might have been made of stone. Apart from his eyes, which continued to move like two pale slugs, that lingered on the patches of bare skin her torn dress revealed. Katerina felt that hint of panic again. If she'd been taken captive by a normal man, well, that would have been bad enough. But Rabin... There was something wrong with him.

Good, she told herself fiercely. You can find out what it is and use it against him.

Slowly her husband got to his feet, then, with a horrible deliberation, edged towards the bed. Katerina forced herself to lie still as he loomed over her. And when he touched her she even managed to wriggle.

'So you do like me after all,' she said, her voice as soft as her self-control was sharp. 'Well, come on then. Kiss me.'

Rabin's face twitched at the suggestion. He drew back and Katerina worried that once more she'd pushed too hard. But then she saw that he was only checking that her bonds were still fast. Once satisfied that they were, he leant forward, drool glistening on his lips.

'Kiss me nicely,' Katerina whispered as he lowered his head.

Then he closed his eyes.

And Katerina struck.

Her lips, which had been opened in invitation, peeled back to reveal sharp, white teeth, and her head snapped forward. She struck with the speed of a cobra, and before

Rabin had even realised that he was under attack, Katerina bit down viciously. With a sickening crunch she sheared her teeth through the gristle of his nose.

Rabin screamed and jerked and an explosion of coppery blood filled Katerina's mouth. For one terrible second she feared that she had bitten down too hard, and that she'd completely severed her victim's horrible snout.

But no. There was still a crunch of bone left to keep his nose attached to his face.

He screamed again, and Katerina gurgled through a mouthful of blood as he struggled like a hooked fish.

"Kee' 'ill,' she told him. "Kee' 'ill or I'll 'ite it off.'

Despite his terror, or perhaps because of it, Rabin understood. He stopped struggling. He whimpered instead and his eyes rolled in terror. The couple's faces were so close that his tears fell onto Katerina's clenched jaw.

'Dow 'et 'e go.'

'I don't have the key,' he whined.

'Den I 'te it 'o,' Katerina informed him.

'No, no! I have it, I have it. I just remembered.'

Slowly, Rabin reached into his shirt and pulled out a chain. An unadorned steel key dangled from it and he fumbled it into the first of her manacles. There was a twist, a click, and Katerina's left hand was free. She flexed her fingers then reached around to close them around the back of Rabin's neck, making sure that he had no chance of escape. She was tempted to release her sickening mouthful of blood and gristle, but fighting against her gag reflex she kept her jaws locked. There was no point in taking chances.

Rabin unlocked the second of her manacles and she brought her second hand up to grip his head. He whimpered miserably as she pressed one thumb to the side of his eyeball, ready for a gouging.

'Dow 'y 'eet,' she told him. Rabin shook his head thoughtlessly, then cried out at the pain it caused in his nose.

'I can't reach,' he wailed, and Katerina saw that he had a point. She cautiously removed her hand from the side of his face and plucked the key from his trembling fingers. Then, with a sudden burst of movement, she unclenched her teeth and punched him away from her.

Quickly, and spitting her mouth clean all the while, Katerina reached down and unlocked the manacle that held her ankles. She looked up to see what Rabin was doing, but if she feared that he might try to stop her she was mistaken. He'd already bounced back to his feet and fled back to the door. He turned to give her a last, hate-filled look, then rushed through it, already screaming for help.

Katerina unlocked the last of her chains. With a quick prayer of thanks that the mechanism had been well oiled, she sprang off the bed. Pausing only to unlock one of the chains from the frame, she made swiftly for the door, weighing the improvised weapon in her hand as she did so.

But although she'd been quick, she wasn't quick enough. She hadn't taken more than a dozen paces towards freedom when the door burst open and the first of her husband's men bundled into the room.

They slowed as they caught sight of her, and began to edge around her. More men followed them into the room, and the stink of spilt wine came with them. They had been celebrating their master's marriage, no doubt.

Good. That would make them weaker.

Katerina edged back and looked forlornly up towards the window. If only it wasn't so high. Given time, she probably could have escaped through it by dragging the bed over, but as it was, the pane of glass might as well have been a mile above her head.

That left her only one option.

Swinging the chain around her head, Katerina flung herself towards her foe. The first of them ducked down beneath the blurred links of the chain. The next one caught it around his neck.

And then they were upon her.

* * *

TABBY HAD ALWAYS loved the city. The great, teeming mass of prey animals that scuttled through the streets always sharpened up her appetite before feeding time. And even when she had a full belly she could sit and watch them for hours, her green eyes alive with fascination.

The only disappointment had been that her pack leader, Katerina, had never let her hunt the scuttling denizens of this tangled realm. But now that she was gone, Tabby found herself with endless opportunities in the world to indulge herself. Unbeknownst to her it was market day, and every one of Bordeleaux's streets was packed with the plumpest and healthiest merchants and farmers a hungry sabretusk could wish for.

Frustrating, then, that she had other, more pressing concerns.

In a human, the instinct which had kept her on Katerina's track might have been called loyalty. But there was really no room for ethics within the muscle-bound slab of Tabby's cranium. There was just hunger and cunning.

And perhaps a glint of loneliness.

Tabby, alone for the first time since she had been a kitten, had no capacity for even this amount of introspection. After dodging past the guards at the city walls, she had bounded through one of the many cracks in the city's tumbled-down walls and navigated her way upwards. All she cared about were the angles and slopes of the rooftops that she was prowling along. The streets she had left far below her. They were too crowded for swift movement, and the strands of scent that had led her back along Katerina's trail were long gone. They had been dispersed by the mob as completely as a drop of blood into a rushing river.

Not that Tabby minded. When it came to her pack sister she had another, more subtle power of detection. It was this sixth sense that kept her drifting slowly towards her mistress. She slipped over the tangled rooftops of the humans' warren as easily as a cloud, her half-ton of furred muscle seemingly weightless as she sprang from gabled end to tiled facing.

The big cat was getting close to Katerina. She knew this in a way that would have been indescribable to anyone except, perhaps, the mutant hunters of the northern lands.

Tabby knew something else, too. And that was that, now more than ever, her pack sister needed her. This instinctive knowledge was as sharp as the taste of blood and so, despite the dizzying drops that fell away beneath the crumbling tiles, she began to run.

THE FIGHT HAD been short and one-sided. Katerina had had neither numbers or surprise on her side.

Within minutes, she had been suffocated beneath the evil-smelling mass of her assailants. Not that their victory had been easy. Several of them were bruised and bleeding and one of them still lay where he'd fallen.

This had done nothing to improve her captors' tempers. They held her spread-eagled on the floor, two men clasping each of her limbs. Katerina knew that she should lie still, perhaps even feign unconsciousness, but the rage that fizzed through her blood was too strong. Despite the futility of the action she writhed and struggled, her bloodied teeth bared in helpless defiance.

Rabin waited until he was absolutely sure that his bride had been secured before skulking back into the room, clutching a bloody handkerchief to his face.

'Are you sure you have her?' he asked the leader of his troop.

'Yes, boss,' the man said, fighting the urge to mock the thick nasal quality of his master's voice. Through the snuffle of blood he sounded as though he was suffering from the world's worst cold.

'Good,' Rabin said, and peered cautiously over the shoulders of his men. His bride was held between them, quite helpless.

Rabin smiled. 'Look what you did to me,' he said with the barest hint of reproach.

'Come here,' she hissed, a savage triumph in her eyes, 'and give me a kiss.'

One of the men holding her laughed.

'Something funny?' Rabin asked.

'No, boss. No, not at all. I was just clearing my throat.'

'Hmmph.' Rabin dabbed at his nose with the bloodied handkerchief. He felt it move in a horribly detached way, and a sudden lurch of nausea reminded him that he should see a healer.

'I'm going to get this seen to,' he told his men before staggering away.

'What shall we do with her?' their leader asked.

'Well, Jean,' Rabin decided as his nose started bleeding again. 'She's not a virgin so you can do what you like. Just make sure she's chained and gagged afterwards.'

'Thanks, boss.' Jean smiled, his eyes lighting up with a horrible glee.

He waited until his master had staggered out of the room before, with a single stroke of his knife, he cut down the front of Katerina's bodice. The lace and pearls parted easily and the men cheered in anticipation.

Katerina felt her rage turn to panic as the first touch of cool air brushed against her naked skin. It filled her with a desperate energy, but her captors just roared approvingly and held her even more tightly as she struggled.

Silk tore with a high-pitched whine and her chemise was thrown back over a dozen heaving shoulders.

Katerina screamed and snapped her teeth at the nearest of the men. He responded with his fist, clipping her across the jaw. Katerina's mouth filled with her own blood and her eyes rolled back in her head.

Which was when she saw Tabby.

The cat was silhouetted against the blue square of sky beyond the window. Her flat muzzle wrinkled as she gazed down and her ears twitched curiously. Then her head disappeared so quickly that it might never have been there.

Katerina suffered a single heartbeat of doubt. It was silenced by a crash loud enough to drown the cries of Rabin's dozen men. A thousand shards of broken glass rained down and amongst them, her form as sleek as lightning, came Tabby. Even before her razored talons touched the floor, she was killing. The leader of Katerina's captors was the first to die. He looked up just in time to see the twin sabres of the big cat's incisors scissoring down towards him. A split second later and her jaws had encompassed his entire head.

There was a twist and a snap and Rabin's men saw their leader's head rolling clear of the monster who had slain him.

Amongst the chorus of yells and screams, some of them prepared to fight. Most, though, fled from the beast that had descended upon them.

Katerina caught the heel of the last of these, tripping him and leaping upon his back. She snatched his dagger from his belt, buried it in his neck, then sprang away, leaving him to die in a fountain of his own blood.

Tabby was already on her third victim. With a happy roar she tore her teeth from his torso and prowled forward.

'Good girl,' Katerina exulted as she exchanged a glance with the big cat. It seemed to smile back, baring the bloodied curves of its teeth. Then, shoulder to shoulder, woman and beast turned to face the remainder of Rabin's men. But beyond the litter of blood and glass and corpses there were hardly any of them left. Only one man remained standing. He waited in the doorway, his left shoulder turned towards them. The oaken slab of the door hung from the frame beside him, dangling from where it had been torn off its hinges by the stampeding men.

'Go away,' Katerina told him as she paced forward. Something about the lone man's stubborn courage made her hesitate to add his body to those that now lay cooling beneath her feet.

'I said go away,' she repeated as, Tabby prowling along behind her, she drew nearer to the man. 'If you don't, we'll…'

But she got no further. As soon as she was close enough to see the terrified whites of the man's eyes he turned, raising the crossbow that had been hidden behind his back as he did so.

Katerina rolled to one side as he fired, her body reacting in a perfect, automatic response. The bolt zipped past her head, so close that she could almost feel the sting of it.

It buried itself into something behind her with a meaty thud, but Katerina paid that no mind. She was already upon the bowman. Her splayed fingers flashed towards his face, the distraction blinding him to the stab of her knife into his stomach.

She twisted the steel through a rope of intestines and into his heart, pausing only to listen to his last breath before letting him fall forward.

'Come on, Tabby,' she said and led the way out of the bedroom and into a long, unfurnished corridor.

It took her a moment to realise that the cat was no longer behind her.

'Silly beast,' she muttered and paced back into the room. Although she'd scolded her pet before for feeding upon human flesh, she barely had the heart for it now. How could she, after what the cat had just done for her?

But a single glance told her that Tabby wasn't feeding, would never be feeding again. The crossbow bolt that had buried itself in the velvet fur of her chest had made that a certainty.

Katerina fell to her knees, feeling something inside her tear. Somewhere someone started to wail, a grief-stricken sound that seemed to be coming from a great distance. As she grabbed great fistfuls of Tabby's fur, some tiny, still part of her realised that it was she herself who was making the noise.

Her cries bounced off the bare stone walls and rough timbered floors. They echoed and magnified until those who Rabin's fleeing men had met believed in every talon, tooth, claw and scale of the terrible beast that had made its lair within the heart of their master's mansion.

And so it was that Katerina was left alone with the cooling body of the friend she'd raised from a cub.

CHAPTER EIGHT

'So TELL us again,' Florin said, crossing his booted ankles in a deliberately relaxed gesture. 'When exactly was Katerina married?'

The scorched chair squeaked beneath his weight, and he prepared to spring off it should it collapse. He wouldn't be surprised if it did. Most of the furniture in the Hansebourgs' great hall was already in ruins. The charred remains lay amongst the sodden rags that were all that remained of the tapestries.

The Hansebourgs had been lucky to have quelled the fire before it had spread to the rest of their mansion. The comtesse, though, did not look like a woman who was counting her blessings.

Far from it.

'Monsieur d'Artaud.' She looked down at her uninvited guest with an expression of extreme disdain. 'Where my daughter goes and what she does is none of your concern.'

'Oh, but it is,' he told her, fighting to keep his temper under control. A dozen terrible rumours had brought him here, each worse than the last. Now that he sat surrounded by this devastation, it was beginning to dawn on him that some of these wild tales might even be true.

The comtesse even looked a little shifty beneath her carefully applied make-up.

'Well, if you must know,' she said, 'Katerina decided to get married. And this time it was to somebody suitable.'

'Suitable?'

'Monsieur Rabin Mordicio.'

Florin swallowed his horror. 'So, scarcely forty-eight hours after we buried Sergei, Katerina decided to get married – to somebody she despised and had seen no more than three times. She really decided to do this?'

'Her family decided it,' the comtesse snapped defensively. 'A family of which you, Monsieur d'Artaud, are not a part. Now if you'll excuse me, I have things to see to.'

'Yes,' Florin said, casting his eyes over the ruins of the banquetting hall, 'so it would appear. Tales of your wedding party are everywhere.'

'Not my wedding,' the comtesse said with a hard glint in her eye. 'Katerina's.'

'We'll see,' Florin said with just a hint of menace. 'We'll see.'

IT WAS GOING to be a perfect summer day. The cool of the night still radiated from the battered hides of Bordeleaux's sprawling buildings, and the smell of the sea was fresh enough to compete with the rich stench of sewage and decay.

As yet, the sun had barely risen above the eastern horizon, which left the streets still pooled with darkness and shadows. It was amongst these shadows that the denizens of Bordeleaux had already begun to move.

There were porters hurrying to start their work, and courtesans glad to have finished theirs. There were merchants, either plump and comfortable within their carriages or skinny and panting beneath the weight of their wares. There were others of a more uncertain profession, their eyes alert despite the early hour and, here and there, knots of soldiers and sailors blinked in surprise as they realised night had become day whilst they caroused.

And amongst them all, still clad in the blood-splattered ruins of her wedding dress, walked Katerina.

She walked with the blank-eyed indifference of a carved statue. Most of the hurrying people she passed spared her no more than a glance. Whatever catastrophe had left her so shocked, they reasoned, was nothing that they wanted any part of.

She was no more aware of where she was than she had been during the darkness of the night. The only things that she was aware of were the facts of her new life. The two facts that had, between them, destroyed it.

And those were that Sergei was dead, and Tabby was dead.

She felt nothing as these two thoughts throbbed within her numbed mind. They seemed as meaningless as the beat of her feet upon the broken cobbles. Not that her thoughts or her feet felt like hers any more. They didn't. Instead they seemed to belong to somebody else entirely, to the hollow-eyed stranger in whose head Katerina had somehow become trapped. And as to where this hollow-eyed stranger's body was taking her, she had no idea.

Until, that was, she climbed out of the last stinking alleyway of the tanners' quarter and saw the spire of the Lady's temple in the distance. It jutted up from the squalor and grandeur of Bordeleaux's rooftops like a lance from a dragon's heart. The white column of marble was dazzling in the rays of the rising sun, and the statue of the Lady which stood on top of the stone shone like a fallen star.

With no more than a dull inkling of recognition, Katerina turned and started off towards the temple, and then she realised that it was where she'd been heading all along. She remembered visiting it with Sergei once when they had first arrived in this cursed city. The damsels within had told her of the Lady, who they said was the Bretonnians' own deity. To Katerina, raised within the robust faith of the ogres, it had all sounded sensible enough. This Lady, the priestess had said, sent her champions out to slaughter on her behalf. If anything, she seemed even more bloodthirsty than the Great Maw.

Katerina vaguely remembered the damsel getting strangely upset at her interpretation. A shame, as she and Sergei had wanted to ask her if they could climb the spire. They had gone to the harbour instead, where Tabby had gotten tangled whilst trying to pluck a mackerel from a fisherman's net. She had been so funny, so sweet…

No.

Don't think about it.

The memory vanished beneath the grey anaesthesia of her misery. In its place came the knowledge that, whatever had happened in the past, Katerina would climb the lethal heights of that spire today. She didn't know why. Or at least, she wouldn't admit to herself yet that she knew why, but she knew that she was going to do it.

The ground rose as she drew nearer. Now the shops which jostled each other along the filthy street were those of healers and fortune tellers. The herbs that went into their potions sweetened the air as the rising sun warmed it. Another time, Katerina might have enjoyed the scent. But today all she cared about was the temple whose shadow these charlatans used to cloak their deceptions.

Something flickered within the frozen confines of Katerina's chest as she remembered the healer who had failed to save Sergei. Then she reached the first high buttresses of the temple and the thought was banished from her mind.

It had grown with Bordeleaux itself, this temple. Deep within the cavernous halls of its interior there still remained the first four walls of the original shrine, and the even more ancient foundations upon which they had been built. Over the centuries the rest of this colossal edifice had grown around it like a pearl around a speck of sand, so that now it was the biggest building in Bordeleaux. Some even said that it was the biggest in Bretonnia.

It was as much a museum of architectural styles as a place of worship, and perhaps more treasury than either.

Its doorways were arched or squared or onion-shaped. Its colonnades were forested with a dozen different styles of pillar. And in every chamber the ceilings and walls were smothered in enough gilt and plaster to sink a ship.

But today Katerina saw none of these labyrinthine interiors. As soon as she reached the first of the temple's buttresses she began to climb.

It was hard work. Even though the masonry here wasn't as refined as that of the interior, the granite blocks fitted together with a workmanlike precision. There was barely a finger's width between any of them, and Katerina soon kicked off her shoes so as to be able to grasp the stone with her toes as well as her fingers.

She clambered up the buttress, and the going got easier as the angle began to curve inwards towards the temple wall. Once she'd reached that junction she paused, shrugged off the last ragged remains of her wedding dress, and used it to wipe the sweat from her hands. Then, clad only in her chemise and pantaloons, she began to climb again.

This time it was even harder work. There was no curve at all in the sheer face of the wall she was scaling, and the only traction she could get was from the tips of her fingers and toes. By the time she'd covered a few yards, her palms were once more soggy with sweat, and her fingers were starting to tremble.

When she finally reached the ledge she'd been aiming for she barely had the strength to haul herself onto it. Although it had looked as thin as a rope from the ground, it was just wide enough for her to sit on. She pressed her back against the chilly stone and closed her eyes against the blinding warmth of the sun.

The blinding part was good, she decided. Despite what she intended to do, she knew that to see the ground falling away below her would be a bad idea. She waited for her heart to slow and for the breeze to dry the runnels of sweat from her forehead. Only then did she start looking for her next perch, blinking the tears from her eyes as she scanned the masonry above.

It took her a moment to spot the first nest of gargoyles. They were up to her right, half a dozen weatherworn daemons. Half a century before there had been dozens of the things, a great flock of talons and tails and twisted, leering faces. But then the earthquake had come. In thirty-nine seconds it had felled the stone monstrosities with all the gleeful ease of a boy slingshotting seagulls. The temple's keepers had decided to take that as a sign and left the granite nests of the fallen beasts empty.

Katerina was bleeding when she rolled into the first of them. The stonework up here was cruder, the edges chipped and uneven. The masons had obviously not wanted to waste time chiselling away at surfaces nobody would ever see. Unfortunately, whilst that made the climb easier, it also meant that every yard smeared more of Katerina's skin off onto the stone.

So what, she thought vaguely.

As she settled herself into the guano-splattered perch she accidentally looked down. The drop was sheer, and the ground very, very far away. Deep within Katerina's numbed soul animal fear stirred.

But then it was gone, snuffed out by her despair as swiftly as a candle beneath a soaked blanket.

Empty-headed, Katerina inspected the glistening flesh of her knees and waited for the trembling to leave her exhausted hands. Not much further now, she thought, peering upward towards the wide gutter that marked the edge of the roof. Once there, she knew that the spire would be in reach, the final climb that she would have to make before she could take the last step of...

A sudden spell of dizziness broke her chain of thought and, with as little thought as a puppet on a string, she twisted around and started to climb.

Even as she did so, the feelings that she had been trying so hard to suppress started to well up inside her.

'I won't think about it,' she whispered, confiding in the blank stone face of the temple that which she could not quite confide in herself. 'I don't need to think about it. It will all soon be over.'

The breeze snatched the words from her as eagerly as a moneylender snatches a promissory note, and Katerina pulled herself eagerly up towards the final minutes of her shattered life.

'You HAVE THE nerve to show your face in my house,' Mordicio observed, surprise evident in every line of his wrinkled face. 'I always said that you were a very brave man.'

'Not at all,' Florin said. Lorenzo just watched the guards that stood behind Mordicio and admired the beating they'd so obviously received.

'I only came to see the new bride and groom,' Florin continued, 'to offer them my congratulations.'

Mordicio looked at him with undisguised scepticism.

'Then I'm afraid you're too late, my boy.'

'They've started their honeymoon already?'

'Not quite, not quite. At least, they haven't started it together.'

'Oh?' Florin raised his eyebrow.

Mordicio grunted with disgust. 'No, it seems that my son and Katerina have had a little tiff. You know how women are. She left to, ah, to clear her head.'

'That is a shame,' Florin said, and tried not to smirk. 'Where has she gone? Maybe I can talk some sense into her.'

Mordicio's beard twitched as he smiled. 'Talk some sense into her, yes. That's a very kind offer, my boy. A very kind offer. But I don't know where my daughter-in-law has gone. She is a free woman, after all. My only concern is that she's safe.'

'Or at least,' Lorenzo muttered to himself, 'that her purse is safe.'

'Oh, don't worry about that.' Mordicio, his ears as sharp as a wolf's, smiled as though he'd just received a compliment. 'I have all of that safely tucked away. For her benefit, of course. So if you had any ideas along those lines, my friend…' Mordicio let the sentence trail off, content that he had solved the mystery of Florin's concern.

The fact that the youngster looked so disgusted at the insinuation that his interest in Katerina was cash-based just made Mordicio like him more.

What an actor, the old villain thought approvingly.

'Well then, Monsieur Mordicio, we must be going.'

'Why rush? Stay a while. Have a drink. Now that I think about it, I have an idea you might be interested in. A business proposition. Shouldn't be difficult for a man of your abilities.'

'Perhaps another time,' Florin said, and got to his feet. He wanted to get out of here before either his temper snapped or Lorenzo's tongue bit. It wouldn't do to press the old gangster too far.

'Suit yourself, my boy, suit yourself. And if you do find my daughter-in-law, tell her not to come home if she doesn't want to'.

Florin, his hand already on the door, turned back.

'She's signed everything I needed her to.' Mordicio smiled and winked.

Bastard, Florin thought, and pushed Lorenzo out of the room before he could voice a similar setiment.

ONCE THEY WERE safely back on the street, the two men nudged their way through the stinking crowds, each lost in his own thoughts. As they trudged slowly back towards the Ogre's Fist, Florin was already wondering what their next move should be. He supposed that he should offer a reward to anybody who knew where Katerina was. The gold he'd got from the sale of the herring boat made that at least an option. But if he did offer a reward, that might encourage her finders to demand a ransom instead. Not that they'd find that easy; the casualties she was rumoured to have inflicted upon Mordicio's thugs was testament to that. Even so...

'Oh no.'

The shock in Lorenzo's voice stopped Florin in his tracks. He turned to his friend and frowned at the revulsion he saw on the older man's face. Lorenzo was not a man easily revolted by anything.

'What is it?'

But Lorenzo said nothing. He just stood and stared.

Florin, starting to feel the first rush of alarm, followed his gaze to a furrier's shop. It leaned out over the other side of the street, the ground floor open to the passing trade apart from a forest of pillars and screens. The owner and his apprentice sat outside, enjoying the sunshine.

'What's wrong?' Florin asked.

'Look,' the older man said, swallowing.

So Florin looked again.

Before he could see what had drained the blood from his friend's battered old face, the store's owner had crossed the street. He smiled widely and tugged respectfully at Florin's elbow.

'Good morning, sire,' the merchant said, and bowed.

'Not now.' Florin tried to wave the man away. Noticing that Lorenzo was already ambling his way towards the shop, Florin followed him.

And there, his own face suddenly as horror-stricken as Lorenzo's, he saw it too. In the very back of the room, stretched out on a skinning rack, was a huge spread of velvety fur. It was the burnished red of autumn leaves, and even though it was still stinkingly fresh it was a beautiful thing. The pelt's four corners ended in paws, and the head had been left on too. It was the head that drew Florin and Lorenzo forward, the two men open-mouthed with awful fascination.

From the twin sabres of the canines to the faded green of the glazed eyes, they knew every detail of this head.

It was Tabby's.

'Where did you get this?' Florin asked the merchant, who had remained attentively at his elbow.

'Ah, a rare specimen indeed. Of course it isn't cured yet but if your lordship wanted it... '

'Where,' Florin repeated with a dangerous patience, 'did you get it?'

'Ah, you know quality when you see it, sire! It's certainly a rare enough beast, and the costs involved in obtaining it were–'

Florin's patience snapped. The merchant's patter ended in a squawk as he was seized by the throat and dragged forward. His apprentice sprang to his feet, but he'd barely taken a step forward when Lorenzo unsheathed his cutlass and waved him back.

'Now,' Florin hissed, staring into the merchant's rolling eyes. 'Tell me where you got this skin or it'll be your own worthless hide that replaces it on the rack.'

'I got it from some men,' the merchant whispered hoarsely.

Florin drew his knife and the merchant's eyes rolled in terror.

'Mordicio's men, Mordicio's men!' he hurriedly added. 'They sold that skin to me. They must know that I am the only man capable of doing it justice.'

Florin released the merchant. The man's hand fluttered to his bruised throat and he fell back towards a workbench. With barely a pause he snatched up a curved skinning knife and shouted at his apprentice to go for help.

The youngster took to his heels with a will but Florin barely noticed. He had drifted forward to touch the smoothness of Tabby's fur. He remembered the first time he had tried to stroke her, and how Katerina had laughed at his fear.

'This was stolen,' he informed the furrier.

'So you say,' the man spat. Emboldened by the knife in his hand and the street to his rear, he had become a lot less reasonable. 'But how do I know that?'

Florin felt tears prickling behind his eyelids as he stroked Tabby's head.

'You don't,' he admitted, too busy worrying about Katerina to argue. Perhaps, he thought, she hadn't run away at all. The rumour mongers all said that she'd cuckolded Rabin and eloped. But then, the rumour mongers would say that. How was he to know that the Mordicios hadn't dealt with her in the same way they'd dealt with her sabretusk?

'I don't think it is stolen,' the merchant dared to say, and backed a little further out of his own shop. In his cloak he looked like a small, frightened bear.

'Think what you want,' Florin said, and came to a sudden decision. 'Here's half a dozen crowns. I'll buy it off you.'

So saying, he dropped a handful of coins onto the floor of the workshop and started to cut the sabretusk's hide down from the frame.

'Hey, wait a minute,' the merchant cried. 'Six crowns isn't enough.'

'Yes,' Lorenzo said, speaking for the first time. 'It is.'

The merchant looked at the scarred old bruiser and decided that, now that he thought about it, and in all fairness, six crowns would do nicely. He hurried to collect the coins from the dirt, keeping one wary eye on Florin as he took Tabby's hide. Without turning to look at the grovelling merchant, he threw the pelt over his shoulder and marched out of the shop.

The furrier counted the coins, weighed them in his hand, and smiled.

'Come again,' he called out after his retreating clients.

Business, after all, was business.

THE LAST TWENTY feet had been the hardest.

The base of the spire had been tough enough. It seemed that the long dead workmen had suddenly remembered what they were constructing as they'd reached the top of the building, and their workmanship had improved as a consequence. The blocks of polished stone they'd used had been fitted together with such razor-edged precision that they almost defeated Katerina. Luckily, the centuries-old lichen that furred the joints had offered some purchase.

The last twenty feet had been no more than a single, unbroken column of stone. The marble had been sheer and unforgiving. If it hadn't been for the carvings that surfaced the stone she would never have made it.

So it was that, as the sun rose to high noon over the stinking sprawl of Bordeleaux, Katerina rolled onto the top of the plinth. The gold-plated statue of the Lady towered above her, the goddess's form taller than any mortal woman's. She gazed down on the squalid glory of her followers' city with a hard expression, her gilded face as stern as any warrior's.

For a few uncounted moments the girl lay on her back, letting the sheen of sweat dry on her limbs and waiting for her muscles to stop trembling. Then, knowing that there was nothing to be gained by delay, she rose to her feet. Now that the hoarse sawing of her breath had quietened she could hear the voice of the wind that swept around her. It tugged at her hair, whipping it around her face in a merciful blindfold, and pushed helpfully between her shoulder blades.

Katerina was in no mood to be rushed. She used the statue to help her stand up straight, then turned to take a final look at the world below.

It would be a final look. The blinding madness of her grief had left her. In its place there had come a strange sensation of absolute clarity. The mood was as numbingly clear as spring meltwater and as it washed over her, Katerina knew that she hadn't come up here for solace. She had come up here to follow her man and her beast into the next life.

Ignoring the flutter of animal terror the thought conjured up, she stepped forward and hung her toes over the precipice below.

Beneath her, red tiled roofs jostled with thatched and slated ones, the architecture a vast quilt of poverty and affluence. Between the palaces and hovels the city crawled with the frenetic activity of an upturned anthill. Carts squeaked through the streets. Ships lolled in the harbour. People, looking smaller than ants from this height, scurried everywhere, each of them lost in their own personal maze of avarice and desire.

Katerina vaguely wondered how many of them there were down there. And among them, how many knew what it was like to have somebody like Sergei. Someone like Tabby. Then she stopped wondering, took a last breath, and stepped fearlessly into the abyss.

And yet, even as gravity claimed her, a hand seized her shoulder. The fingers held her with an effortless strength and, as easily as if she weighed no more than a dandelion seed, she was lifted up and set back down on the plinth.

The icy clarity with which Katerina had jumped was replaced by bewilderment as she saw who had caught her. At first she took the woman to be her mother, although there was a kindness about the face that had never appeared on the comtesse's. Then Katerina realised that she wasn't old enough to be anybody's mother. Beneath the flowing sweep of her mantle she was no more than a girl.

But a second later Katerina looked into the warm depths of her saviour's hazel eyes and knew them to be older than the oldest grandmother's. Even compared to the prehistoric plinth upon which they stood, they were ancient.

The statue had gone. She blinked with surprise and the woman threw back her head and laughed. The sound had all the gurgling joy of a cool brook on a hot summer's day. It washed around Katerina, and as it did so she was bathed with the scents of heather, lavender and the wild rosemary which had grown on the plains of the east.

Somehow, the scents brought an answering smile to her own face.

'That's better,' the lady said, the melody of her voice seeming to come from everywhere at once. She reached forward to brush a lock of sodden hair from Katerina's forehead, and her touch was as soft as dew. Katerina felt something stir within her; something she'd been trying to keep locked deep inside the confines of her soul. The woman smiled again, but this time it was sorrow, not joy, that smoothed the ever-changing lines of her face.

'Who are you?' Katerina managed to ask, her own voice tiny compared to her saviour's.

'That depends on who you are.' The lady shrugged. The tresses of her hair rippled with the movement, and for a moment they glowed like clouds in the moonlight. 'To the cold-blooded things that once ruled here I was one thing. To the fair folk that followed them, another. And now, to the knights who rule, I am something else entirely.'

'You're the Lady.'

The woman tossed her hair to one side, grinning with the mischievous delight of a little girl as the colour of it changed from oaken brown to spun gold. 'You could call me that. Yes.'

Katerina's mouth fell open and she stared, spellbound. As she watched, the smooth lines of the lady's face refined themselves, hardening into the angles and planes of a haughty empress.

'But I am also much more.'

'Yes.' Katerina nodded. 'I can see.'

The wind whispered between them, carrying with it the murmurs of the city below. It occurred to Katerina that she might be hallucinating, and she decided to ask the vision who stood before her if she was real.

But when she opened her mouth what she actually said was, 'Why did you catch me?'

Instead of answering, the lady turned to look out over Bordeleaux. As she did so, her face grew sad, as she studied the imperfections of the world below.

'The people down there,' she told Katerina, 'are weak. They are greedy and foolish. They steal from one another and lie even to themselves. Some are cruel, but not many. Not even as many as think it of themselves. Mostly, they are just foolish. And so, so human.'

As she spoke, her words rich with the sad harmonies of a funeral song, clouds blossomed in the blue sky above, appearing as mysteriously as mushrooms. A few of the busy men below looked up to see where the sudden shadow had come from, but not many.

'And yet,' the lady continued, her voice lilting into new, brighter harmonies, 'they are mine, these people. Just as are the fair folk, and just as the cold-blooded ones were that came before them.'

'I see,' Katerina said, her brows furrowed in thought.

'Though most of my people are never more than children, there are some amongst them who are more than that. Not many, but some.'

'You mean the knights,' Katerina said as the lady's face brightened and the clouds disappeared beneath a fresh tide of sunlight.

'The knights,' the lady said, 'and some others.'

Katerina met her eyes. She saw herself reflected there. For a heartbeat she saw herself exactly as she was being seen.

And she was terrified.

'Am I one of those others?' she asked, instinctively facing the fear, letting it wash over and through her.

Once more the lady shrugged.

'That depends,' she said, 'on how you return to the streets below. If you climb down, then yes. You will be blessed amongst those who toil down there, although they won't necessarily know it. If you jump, on the other hand... Well, if you jump then you'll be nothing.'

'But I miss my friends,' Katerina said. The thin whine of her voice sounded like somebody else's.

'Then,' the lady said, her eyes dark with a terrible compassion, 'miss them.'

And as Katerina's grief tore itself out of her like poison from a wound, the lady cradled her and rocked her and they looked for all the world like a mother with her child.

LATER, KATERINA DRIED the last of her tears and watched the sun falling down into the sea.

'What am I supposed to do, exactly?' she asked.

But she was all alone, with nothing but a statue for company.

Katerina searched the set lines of the thing's inanimate face, looking for any sign of life. When she realised that there was none, she turned and started the long, hard climb back to the world below.

CHAPTER NINE

'THAT'S THAT, THEN,' Florin said and stood back to examine his handiwork. He had placed Tabby's remains in a coffin, which had been placed besides Sergei's own.

It had been an expensive business; the cemetery's keeper had already been well paid by the Hansebourgs to guard the family crypt. But Florin had paid again, and paid with a will. Gold might be gold, but an oath was an oath.

And the oaths that he and Lorenzo had sworn upon this very tomb, it seemed, were about to be tested.

'The thing is,' Lorenzo said as the two of them left the crypt, 'Mordicio's house is a fortress. We can't be the first to have thought about breaking into it.'

Florin nodded his agreement and took a breath of fresh air. Bordeleaux's familiar smell of sewage and sea tasted wonderfully clean after the cloying stench of the tomb.

'It is a fortress. Maybe we should take them in the street, then.'

'Difficult.' Lorenzo frowned. 'They're usually mounted in carriages and surrounded by guards.'

Florin sat down, his back against the warm stone of the Hansebourg crypt, and looked down over the lower tiers of the acropolis.

'We could probably raise a fair bit from the Ogre's Fist,' he said as Lorenzo joined him. 'Enough to hire a score of mercenaries. Maybe even more.'

Lorenzo snorted. 'If you want to waste gold, why not just throw it into the sea?' he asked. 'The only thing mercenaries do better than run away is to jabber about their business to anybody who'll listen.'

Florin shrugged. 'Then we'll have to take them in the house.'

Lorenzo sucked his teeth thoughtfully and looked out towards the distant ocean. 'Let's not be too hasty,' he said. 'After all, we don't really know that the Mordicios have killed Katerina.'

'Of course they have,' Florin spat. 'You don't think she'd have let them get away with doing that to Tabby, do you? She wouldn't even leave the beast for Sergei.'

'But she did,' Lorenzo said. 'She left it to make its own way back when she brought him back from the... the poisoning.' Florin frowned and Lorenzo, seeing his advantage, pressed it. 'Maybe Tabby was killed at the gates. She wouldn't have stood a chance against the archers and the guards.'

But this time Florin just shrugged. 'Maybe, maybe not. Who knows? The thing is, Katerina was snatched by the Mordicios and now she's gone. That being the case, we have no alternative but to avenge her. Of course, it's possible that the Mordicios didn't kill her. But then, I'd rather do them an injustice than the shades we swore an oath to. Wouldn't you?'

Lorenzo glanced around at the listening tombs and swallowed nervously. 'There's always that,' he admitted.

'And anyway,' Florin winked. 'What are we so worried about? Breaking into a fortress, slipping past dozens of guards and killing the most paranoid man in Bordeleaux is nothing to us. We're the heroes of Lustria! The conquerors of the Ogre Kingdoms! The saviours of...'

Lorenzo grunted with disgust. 'Sometimes I think that you really believe all of that swill.'

'What should I not believe?'

'That we survived because of anything other than sheer luck.'

'We survived,' Florin proclaimed, 'because it is our destiny. Monsters, elements, treachery, steel – we survived them all. It can only be because of destiny.'

Lorenzo looked at his companion miserably. He should have realised from the start that Florin d'Artaud wasn't just keen to avenge Katerina because of the oaths they'd taken. Oh no. He wanted to avenge her because the alternative was running a peaceful business, and getting plump and rich. By Ranald's left ball, if he loved excitement so much why couldn't he have just stuck to gambling?

'Hey, cheer up,' Florin told his old friend, and punched him on the shoulder. 'We have to start thinking about how to get to the target.'

The target, Lorenzo thought. Lady help us, we've started referring to the most powerful merchant in Bordeleaux as the target.

They'd need a miracle, not a plan.

As Florin started talking about grappling hooks and black powder weapons, a miracle did happen. It came walking towards them through the city of tombs, its red hair tangled and its knees scraped. And when the miracle saw the two men it smiled, so that even beneath the coating of grime it was beautiful.

'Katerina!' Lorenzo yelled, springing to his feet. Florin followed him and together they rushed through the gravestones to embrace the girl.

'We thought you were dead,' Florin said, outpacing Lorenzo to seize her around the waist and hug her to him.

'Dead?' Katerina said, squeezing Florin back. 'Not me. I've got far too much to do.'

Then she smiled in a way that made Lorenzo realise that part of his relief had been premature.

* * *

Rabin had spent the day trying not to touch his throbbing nose, which itched abominably. Then, when his father had talked to him, he had forgotten all about not scratching it. He had been too angry.

The cheek of the old fool! The insolence! What business was it of his how Rabin treated his own wife? It wasn't as though she was worth any more happy than miserable. It wasn't as if she was worth anything at all – the documents she'd signed had seen to that. But apparently the elder Mordicio was worried about what her uncles might think. He was afraid of what the other merchants might think. He was even afraid of what Florin d'Artaud might think, although why, Rabin couldn't imagine.

Dabbing at his bandaged face, he paced up and down the bare boards of his study, swearing under his breath.

He had come close to telling his loathsome parent to mind his own business, damned close. But that wouldn't have done. Not just yet. Not when he could finally see a way out of the poverty in which the old goat kept him.

He'd stumbled upon his scheme whilst listening to the family's lawyer babbling on about the papers he'd have to sign. It seemed that Katerina couldn't sign her wealth over to her husband. No woman could. All she could do was to sign it over to his control.

Usually the distinction was meaningless, but Rabin had seen in the clause the key to escaping this penury. As Katerina's money wasn't officially his, he couldn't sign it over to his father, the bloodsucking leech. Of course, the old vulture's advisors were busily working out a way around the law, but by the time they succeeded, Rabin would have deposited the money, and himself, far outside of their reach. He just needed a few more days and everything would be set.

Somewhat mollified by the thought, he peered out of the small, leaded window. He could see a few masts in the distance, reminders of the vessel that was set to take him to his new life. For the first time since his marriage, Rabin allowed himself a smile, and he stomped over to the bell pull to summon a servant. After all, although he had to spend two more days in this miser's palace, there was no need to do it sober.

A few moments passed and he tugged at the bell pull again. It was almost a quarter of an hour before the door finally opened.

'What took you so long?' Rabin shouted as a serving wench bundled in. 'And why have you brought gin? You should know that I only drink wine!'

The woman mumbled something in reply, and Rabin saw for the first time quite how ugly she was. He frowned in disappointment. He preferred the pretty ones.

Well, never mind. A woman sobbing was a woman sobbing.

'I asked you a question,' he said, and stepped forward until he stood over the cowering wench. By the gods, she was ugly. A real crone. She seemed to be having some trouble speaking as well.

'What's that you're babbling about?' Rabin asked as she cowered even further down.

He raised his hand to slap her, but before he could, expert fingers grabbed his elbow and pinched the nerve. Rabin squeaked in surprise.

'I said,' Lorenzo said, standing up and letting his headscarf fall back, 'that Katerina wants a word with you.'

Rabin stumbled back towards the far wall. Instead of pursuing him, Lorenzo gave a shrill whistle. Katerina and Florin, who'd been waiting for the all clear, raced into the room. It took Rabin a moment to recognise them; both were swaddled in the voluminous skirts of washerwomen. But the disguise did nothing to slow their movements. In a heartbeat Florin had locked the door behind him and Katerina had cornered Rabin.

'Wait a minute,' Rabin pleaded, his eyes wide with terror above his bandaged face. 'You don't have to hurt me. I didn't do anything. It was you who hurt me.'

Katerina didn't deign to reply, apart from to produce a dagger from the folds of her skirts. Rabin's eyes opened ever wider when he saw that it was already bloodied.

'Don't,' he whispered, staring at the gory blade as though hypnotised. 'I didn't want to marry you. It was all my father's fault.'

Katerina pressed the edge of the dagger to the pale flesh beneath his jowl and he whimpered.

'You don't understand,' she told him, eyes glittering. 'This isn't for me. It's for Tabby.'

'No, not me. Don't blame me. It was all my father's fault. I swear it to you... Kill him instead!'

Something inside Katerina snapped. Before Florin realised what she was going to do, she slashed Rabin's throat.

Rabin felt no pain as he collapsed onto the barren floorboards. All he felt was regret for the freedom that had slipped through his fingertips.

Katerina watched him die, her face an unblinking mask. Florin looked shocked, but made no move to go to her side or inspect the body. Lorenzo's features revealed no emotion whatsoever.

Florin swallowed uneasily. As the last breath gurgled its way out of Rabin's ruined throat his face hardened. Justice, after all, was what they had come here for.

'What's in that purse?' Lorenzo asked as Rabin's body rolled onto its back.

'Let's see,' Katerina said and, unmoved by the slowing trickle of her husband's blood, she knelt on his chest and cut the purse from his belt. There was a clink of coins as she hefted the leather bag, and with a contented grunt she hid the purse inside her clothes.

'Right,' she decided, getting back to her feet and wiping her hand on her apron. 'Let's go.'

'Wait a minute,' Florin said, and shifted his boot so that the spreading pool of blood wouldn't stain the leather. 'Where are we going? You don't mean to kill Mordicio as well, do you?'

'No.' Katerina shook her head. 'He probably deserves it, but not from my hand. Let's go, before we get caught.'

'What a good idea,' Lorenzo said, and rearranged his headscarf.

At any other time, Florin might have sniggered at his friend's apparel. But not now.

Katerina slipped though the door of Rabin's study and led the way back into the maze of corridors beyond.

Most mansions this size would have been stuffed with carpets and paintings and finely crafted furniture. They would have been lit by crystal chandeliers and studded with mirrors. Not Mordicio's, though. His uninvited guests' footsteps echoed alarmingly against barren wood and undressed stone, and their way was lit by no more than tiny windows. Even now, with the sun riding high in the sky above, the interior was dark and gloomy, a place of shadows and cold, dank walls.

In a way, this was a good thing for the trio. There was none of the usual gaggle of servants that inhabited such great houses. The little that Mordicio had to dust he was content to leave dusty. He obviously wasn't the sort of man to waste money on cleaning. But the emptiness also had its disadvantages. Amongst these barren corridors and locked rooms, even their disguises left them looking out of place. From the mould that patterned the walls to the grime that hid the floorboards, it was obvious that no cleaning women had been here for a long time.

When they heard the thunder of boots ahead, they knew that they had nowhere to hide.

'Gods curse it!' Katerina swore as shouted orders mingled with the approaching clatter of boots on floorboards. 'I knew we should have killed those guards.'

'No. It was enough to tie them up,' Florin said.

'So it seems,' Katerina said, sarcastically.

'They'd have been found anyway,' he replied, raising his voice against the racket of the approaching guards.

Lorenzo watched the two of them squabbling with slack-jawed amazement. Then he snapped his mouth shut and turned.

'I can see that you're too busy to run,' he said over his shoulder. 'So I'll see you later.'

Florin and Katerina exchanged a single glance then bolted after him.

Despite the lack of any distinguishing features in the empty halls, Lorenzo led the way back to Rabin's study with the unerring accuracy of a rat in a sewer. Once there, he drew a dagger and threw himself at the window. Behind him, Katerina bolted the door whilst Florin, cursing at the unfamiliar fastenings, began to undress. Sweating like an escapologist, he struggled out of two shawls, one frock and a series of petticoats to reveal the rope he had coiled around his midriff.

'How do you women wear all of this stuff?' he gasped as he kicked the petticoats away and started uncoiling the rope.

'I don't,' Katerina said.

Florin paused. Then he pushed away the image that had sprung into his mind and got back to work. As if to remind him of the urgency of the situation, a hail of knocks bounced off the study door.

'What is it?' Florin mumbled in what he hoped sounded like Rabin's voice.

But any attempt at impersonation was dashed when, with the cheerful tinkle of smashing glass, Lorenzo popped the window from its frame. The guards outside howled in alarm and started kicking the door instead of knocking it.

'What's below?' Florin asked Lorenzo as he tossed him one end f the rope.

'A roof, and then the street,' the older man said, and threw his end of the rope out of the window.

The door boomed as something heavy was swung against it.

'We need to tie off on something heavy,' Florin told Katerina. The two of them looked frantically around the room but the furniture here seemed to have little weight. There were just a couple of chairs, a rickety table and a single candle stick.

There was also Rabin's body.

'Congratulations,' Florin told the dead face, now as white as chalk from all the blood loss. 'You finally get to be useful.' So saying, he threaded the rope around the scant furnishings of the room and finally tied it off around the corpse.

The blows against the door, meanwhile, had grown sharper. Florin gestured for Lorenzo to start climbing. The tangle of dead meat and furniture squeaked across the room then stuck against the wall beneath the window.

'You next,' Florin told Katerina. She seemed on the verge of arguing when the first plank of the door gave way, splitting asunder with a flash of white wood.

The cautious eye which peered through the hole appeared just in time to see Katerina rolling out of the window. The sight encouraged the guards to redouble their efforts, and even as Florin was following his friends down the rope the door burst open. He saw the first of the guards that charged into the room and, trapping the rope between the soles of his boots, he began to slide down it.

Florin glanced down as he did so and saw the warm red tiles of the roof below him. Katerina and Lorenzo were already clambering over the edge of it as he descended, and he supposed that they'd found some handy drainpipe.

But suddenly, he realised that he wasn't descending after all. Despite the rope that slipped through his reddening palms, he was going up, not down. Confusion writ large upon his features, he looked up and saw the florid faces that leaned out above him. Then he got it. The rope was being pulled back up even faster than he was sliding down it.

'Ranald's left ball,' he swore, and released the rope from between his feet.

The rope whiplashed through them as he began to descend again. It whined with a heat that Florin could feel even through the leather of his boots. His palms, meanwhile, screamed with a sudden burning pain.

Swallowing the agony, Florin looked down, judging the distance he still had to go. If he let go too early he'd be likely to snap his spine, or at least to crash through the tiles below. Palms searing, he gritted his teeth and held on. The agony lasted for perhaps three more seconds, but they were the longest seconds of Florin's life. When he finally did let go it felt like letting go of the blade of saw, and he stumbled across the tiles with his wounded hands clasped to his chest.

'Over here,' Katerina called, waving from the edge of the roof. Florin raced towards her, ducking instinctively as a crossbow bolt zipped past him. Then he was over the edge of the roof and descending once more. This time, all he had to grip was the rusty iron trunk of an ancient pipe, and each handful was an agony against his ruined skin. By the time he finally reached the street below, his face shone with tears of pain.

'Let's go,' Lorenzo snapped at him. He stumbled forward, dizzy with the exertion, and let his two friends guide him into the milling embrace of the crowded street.

CHAPTER TEN

Gilles and Bouillon Hansebourg were not sentimental men; far from it. Sentimental or not, Katerina was their niece. And apart from the fact that they wanted to honour their dear departed brother's memory (which they did mainly to annoy their bitch of a sister-in-law) the two men had their pride. Fortunately for the comtesse, this precluded any physical violence against her.

'I should have you chained to the gateposts and whipped,' Gilles told her, his pockmarked face a gargoyle's mask of hatred.

If the comtesse was afraid, she did a good job of hiding it.

'Don't threaten me, Gilles,' she told him. 'If anybody's blood is going to be spilled in front of the mob it won't be mine. After all, I've never dealt in your sort of contraband.'

Gilles exchanged a look with his brother. Bouillon twirled his carefully waxed moustache, and walked over to sit down beside the comtesse. Although the great hall was still in ruins, her own quarters were not. That was the second reason why they had decided to talk here.

The first was that two solid oak doors ensured their conversation could not be overheard.

Even so, Bouillon lowered his voice as he leant forward on his overstuffed armchair. 'If our business dealings should ever come out, I'm sure that our heads will be on the block, but I can assure you, sister-in-law, that so will yours.'

The comtesse regarded him with a level expression. The bone china perfection of her features remained completely still apart from the flickers of light and darkness that the fire cast. Bouillon had to admire her nerve.

'I know that it will, brother-in-law,' she told him, 'which is why you can tell Gilles to stop fiddling with that dagger he has hidden in his sleeve. You know that I'll never talk.'

Gilles turned and spat into the fire. The three of them listened to the hiss as his spittle fried, then returned to their deliberations.

'The thing is,' Bouillon told her, 'that we were a little surprised to hear that you'd married Katerina off to Mordicio's son.'

'Surprised!' Gilles repeated the word, his voice high-pitched with outrage.

'And we wondered if you realised quite what a stupid idea that was.'

The comtesse stiffened and her cheeks coloured.

'And then,' Bouillon continued, 'we find that, not only have you married her off to Rabin Mordicio, a drooling imbecile, but that he's lost her. You can imagine how upset we are.'

'Rabin Mordicio.' Gilles shook his head in disbelief. Then, suddenly unable to contain himself any longer, he left his post by the fireplace and started to pace around the room.

'Oh, calm down,' the comtesse told him. 'I don't know why you're so upset, anyway. You never wanted anything to do with the child and she's been nothing but trouble.'

'It's her dowry we're worried about, you stupid woman!' Giles yelled. His hands bunched into fists and he turned on her with barely restrained violence. Bouillon looked at him disapprovingly.

'Oh, well. If money is all you're interested in…' she said, as if disgusted by such base matters. The fact that Mordicio's bribe to her even now nestled beneath the cushions that supported her plump bottom did nothing to diminish her expression of disdain.

Giles and Bouillon exchanged another look. Bouillon raised one eyebrow in an unspoken question. His brother shrugged helplessly.

'Yes, well, what we're concerned about isn't money. It's the lack of it.'

'What do you mean?' the comtesse demanded, looking uneasy for the first time since her brothers-in-law had returned.

'I mean that we don't have Katerina's share any more.'

The comtesse, for once, was speechless.

'Those damned herrings,' Giles muttered, and for a moment the comtesse thought that he'd finally gone mad, but then she understood what he was talking about.

'But the herring shoals were very good this year,' she reminded him.

'Exactly. But we thought that they wouldn't be. Sooo…' Bouillon trailed off, too embarrassed to continue.

'So we sent our boats up to collect salted fish from Kislev,' Giles finished for him. 'Then the herring came in. They were so plentiful and cheap that we could barely give our salted stuff away.'

'But Franz's share of the business is supposed to be worth almost a hundred thousand crowns!'

'Yes,' Bouillon said, taking some small comfort from his sister-in-law's distress. 'It is. Imagine how surprised Mordicio will be.'

The three of them imagined it.

It wasn't much fun.

'So we'll have to try to annul the marriage,' Giles decided.

'Getting to be quite a habit of ours, isn't it?' Bouillon sniggered, quite inappropriately in the comtesse's opinion. 'I've got a feeling that she'll be happier separating from that pig's bladder Mordicio's son than from the strigany.'

'No, we can't do that,' the comtesse said. She'd just remembered how much of Mordicio's gold she'd spent on repairing the fire damage from the wedding. Even if she wanted to return his... gratuity, she wouldn't be able to.

'Why not?' Gilles asked testily.

It took the comtesse a moment, but then inspiration struck. 'Because it will look a little suspicious if, a day after Katerina disappears from his house, we annul the marriage. He'll think that we're hiding her.'

'So let him think that,' Gilles snapped and prowled back to look at the fire. 'The old goat can think what he wants to. We have the men and the steel to deal with him if he gets cocky.'

'But not,' the comtesse reminded him, 'the money.'

Bouillon rubbed his chin and stared into space.

'The first thing to do,' he decided, 'is to find our beloved niece. Once we've got her, there are a thousand things she can accuse Mordicio's son of. Some of them are probably true. And even if we don't get the marriage annulled straight away, we can keep it locked in the merchants' court, which will be just as good.'

Gilles frowned. 'How will we find her?'

'Considering that she only has one friend in the city, I'd suggest starting with Florin d'Artaud,' Bouillon said.

The comtesse's nose wrinkled with distaste.

'Ah yes. D'Artaud. Nice lad,' Gilles reflected. 'I don't see why you didn't marry her to him. His brother's quite well off by all accounts.'

'My daughter will never marry that vagabond,' the comtesse snarled.

'Fancy him yourself, do you?' Gilles leered.

'How dare you,' the comtesse barked. 'In fact, get out of my chambers!'

'Your chambers? I don't remember you paying–'

'Come on Gilles,' his brother cut in. Much as he enjoyed these family blood sports, now was hardly the time. 'Let's go and find our niece.'

Gilles grunted with disgust and, turning on his heel, stomped out of the room.

The comtesse didn't rise to see her brothers-in-law out. She was too busy thinking about how she might hold on to the coin that Mordicio had given her for arranging the marriage.

All in all, she decided, it would be best if her daughter disappeared for good.

The comtesse watched the fire die. Yet even when the flames had gone, her eyes still shone, glittering in the darkness like diamonds.

DESPITE THE BONE-ACHING chill of the place, the waiting man felt none of the cold. His gaunt frame shivered, but even as he rattled the lantern he clutched in one bony hand, he felt warm. Hot, even. The flames of hatred that burned inside his scrawny old chest were more than a match for the subterranean temperature.

He paced about in the clammy darkness, his boot heels clicking on stone. Usually it was anxiety that set him to scuttling back and forth. Tonight, though, it wasn't anxiety, it was impatience.

After an hour, the first faint breeze stirred the frozen air. The man turned to face it. It had come from the passageway that led up from the depths to this hidden meeting place, and brought with it the whiff of something bitter and poisonous.

'About time,' the man grumbled to himself and pulled at his beard disapprovingly. But he had to wait for another five minutes before the liquid blackness of the deep hole spewed out its occupant.

'Welcome,' the waiting man said, hiding his irritation. 'Welcome. It seems that I have another little piece of business for you.'

The thing that he had summoned chittered excitedly, its teeth as yellow as butter in the lamplight. 'Yes, yes,' the assassin squeaked, and its tail thrashed the ground with excitement. Ever since it had returned from its last mission, it had been hoping to work for the manthing again. Or for anybody else who'd pay in warpstone. The assassin wanted more, wanted it badly. More of the stuff which even now waited in the lead box the manthing carried.

'Do you remember the girl that you weren't to kill last time? Red hair, white skin. Killed lots of your friends.'

'It's a lie!' the assassin hissed, his thoughts still befuddled by what was in the lead box. 'I didn't kill her.'

'Yes, my fellow. Yes. I know. But now I want you to.'

The red beads of the assassin's eyes swivelled upwards to study the man-thing's face. Even beneath the agony of its need it was surprised by the cold hatred it saw there. It was quite impressive, for a human.

'So I kill the female. Yes. But you pay first.' The assassin edged forward, revoltingly human fingers stretching out as greed sharpened its rodent face.

'A little bit now,' the man said, ignoring the stink of the thing's breath as it drew near. 'Yes, I think a little bit is all that will be good for you right now.'

Skrit's tail flickered back and forth behind him and, as if by magic, a curved shard of steel appeared at the end of it. 'Pay now,' Skrit insisted, his nose wrinkling as he snuffled at the box that the man still clung to.

The man's face remained impassive as he watched his confederate twitch and shudder. 'No.' The man shook his head and, for once, decided on absolute honesty. 'I won't pay you now, because if I do, you will have more than enough to kill yourself. And looking at how far you're gone, I think that you will.'

The assassin took a step back, peeled its lips back from its fangs, and made a shrieking, gurgling sort of sound.

'Yes. I'll kill the female quick. Now you give me warpstone quick. Yes?'

'Yes,' the man said and tossed over the leaden box.

The assassin snatched it out of the air, pressed it into the broken stone of the floor, and prised the lid off with a twist of a knife. The cancerous green glow lit up the joyous snarl that creased the assassin's snout, and the air filled with the sour tang of ammonia as it urinated in sheer delight.

'Lots more where that came from,' the man told the thing, although it was barely listening any more. 'All you need to do is to bring me her head. And Skrit?'

The creature looked up.

'Kill anyone you find with her. Or see near her. Or who you think she might have looked at.'

'For more stone?'

'For more stone.'

'Yessssssssssssss,' the creature hissed. Then, suddenly paranoid, it closed the box and hid it within its ragged robe.

The man watched it go, scuttling off into the darkness like a giant cockroach.

He thought about how it would be to meet your death at the hands of such a living nightmare. It wouldn't be quick. Ah well, the man thought with a smile, at least he wasn't dying in vain. By the time he'd finished with Katerina even her mother wouldn't be able to recognise her.

'MONSIEUR D'ARTAUD, WHERE have you been?' Jeanette asked. 'Why do you look so worried? What are you doing?'

'Nothing,' Florin told her as he herded a dozen complaining patrons out of the Ogre's Fist. The last of them seemed strangely reluctant to leave his drink. Florin's boot changed his mind. Having thus cleared the taproom Florin slammed the bolts closed on the door, wincing with pain as the metal touched the raw flesh on his palms. Then he spun around, pressing his back against the wood and the grumbles of complaint from outside.

'Nothing's going on?' Jeanette asked him, openly sceptical from behind the safety of the bar.

'That's right,' Florin agreed, and with a last nervous look around the empty bar gestured for Katerina and Lorenzo to go upstairs. After a night spent holed up beneath the relatively safe house of Madame Gourmelon, the three had decided to risk returning to the Ogre's Fist.

'And who's she?' Jeanette asked, scowling at Katerina's back as she rattled up the staircase.

'Nobody,' Florin said, pushing past the serving wench to make sure that the back door was locked.

'Nothing and nobody,' Jeanette repeated, following him through.

'Is anybody in the cellar?' Florin asked.

'Who do you think might be down there?'

'No–'

'Nobody,' she finished for him, and clicked her tongue in disgust.

Florin slipped his arm around her waist and kissed her on the cheek. Jeanette tried to maintain her scowl as she wriggled against him, pressing her breasts against the hardness of his chest.

'You know how much I think of you, Jeanette,' he said, brushing a lock of hair back from her face.

'Oh yes,' she said with a pout. 'Every time you want something.'

'Yes,' Florin said, and smiled with such sudden brilliance that she quite forgot to be annoyed. 'That's why I'm going to make you a partner.'

'You mean…?'

'That's right.' Florin nodded. 'From now on you run the inn. You almost do anyway, but from now on you can keep a third of whatever you make.'

'Oh.'

'Thought you'd be pleased,' Florin said and, with a slap on her nicely rounded rump, he left her to decide if she was disappointed or not and rushed upstairs.

He found Katerina waiting for him.

'Are you sure you want to come with me?' she asked as he pushed past her. 'There's no reason why Mordicio's men would have recognised you.'

Florin stopped moving for long enough to roll his eyes at Lorenzo.

'What?' Katerina snapped. She was in no mood to be patronised.

She never was.

'The thing is,' Lorenzo told her as he copied Florin's example and started to stuff clothes into a trunk, 'we can't take the chance. If Mordicio has even the slightest suspicion that we were there, then...' He made a chopping gesture across his neck and did a passable impression of a man with a cut throat.

'I see. Well, you're welcome to come with me.'

'And you with us,' Florin said as he lifted a section of flooring. A tangled cache of weapons lay within the hiding place. They gleamed with the dark lustre of a thousand murderous possibilities. Most of them were cutlasses or cleavers, but amongst these was a leavening of other weapons. There was a crossbow, a heavily greased T of sprung steel. There were great blocks of spiked iron, which had obviously been forged to fit around fists bigger than any man's. There were also a few contraptions that were so strangely crafted that Katerina took them to be no more than ornaments.

'Help yourself,' Florin told her, picking out a stabbing sword for himself before rushing off to start rolling up his clothes.

'Where did you get all this stuff?' she asked as she picked up the crossbow and tested the mechanism.

'They're mostly from customers who couldn't pay their bill,' Florin shouted back from another room.

'And who were too drunk to fight back,' Lorenzo added, cackling happily as if at some fond memory.

Katerina selected a cutlass from amongst the confusion of weapons. It was a well-balanced object, and as sharply curved as one of Tabby's tusks. The comparison brought a sad smile to her face as she checked the scabbard before buckling it to her belt.

Florin came back into the room, cramming a velvet hat onto his head and swirling a silken cape around his shoulders. He winked at Katerina, swept his hat off, and bowed.

'Mademoiselle,' he said, 'what a lovely cleaver that is you have strapped to your waist. And those rags – designed by the great Paravaldi of Tilea, no?'

Katerina laughed, exposing most of her sharp, white teeth. 'And you, monsieur, must have stepped straight out of the duke's palace. And, to judge by the smell of you, into a pigsty.'

'This scent is the very latest fashion amongst the aristocracy,' he replied haughtily. 'Why, King Louis himself smells of nothing but griffon dung. As well as impressing the ladies, it gives the skin a certain lustre.'

Katerina laughed again. This time the sound of it was too much for Jeanette, who'd been eavesdropping below. With a jealous scowl on her face she pounded up the stairs to see what was going on.

'Are you all all right?'

Although she was speaking to Florin she didn't take her eyes off Katerina. They weren't approving.

'Yes, we're fine,' Florin said.

'Thought I heard an ox being strangled,' Jeanette said.

'Ahem,' said Florin, and wondered how to distract Katerina. By the flash of colour on her cheeks she seemed to have realised that she was being insulted.

'This is Jeanette,' he said. 'She's concerned about the livestock arrangements because she is my and Lorenzo's new partner.'

'What?' Lorenzo cried.

No sooner had he asked the question than something pounded against the front door of the inn; something a lot heavier than a drunkard's fist.

Florin was almost glad to hear it.

'Quick,' he said. 'The tunnel.'

'What do you mean about Jeanette being a partner?' Lorenzo demanded.

'Nothing.' Florin shrugged. Then, even as Jeanette began to shout her own complaints, he grabbed everything that he could carry and bolted down the stairs. He reached the bottom just in time to see the door bounce against its hinges and led the way through the back room and down into the cellar.

It was a dank place, although not an unpleasant one. The smells of wine and gin mingled with those of oaken barrels and beer casks. Florin dropped his gear onto the floor and attacked the stack of crates that leant against one wall. Katerina joined him, and the two of them started to sweat with the effort of clearing them away.

Lorenzo was too busy squabbling with Jeanette to help.

'By Manann's chamberpot, will you two be quiet?' Florin cursed.

'Then tell Lorenzo that I'm a partner,' Jeanette demanded. She put her fists on her hips and pouted in a way that Florin usually found quite sweet.

'She's a partner,' Florin told Lorenzo, who cursed long and loud. Jeanette smirked.

'And perhaps,' Florin grunted as he dragged the last of the crates away, 'Jeanette will be kind enough to put these back over the trap door when we've gone. That is, unless you'd rather stay here and try to argue her out of her share?'

Lorenzo stopped complaining.

'Don't know why you didn't cut her in sooner,' the older man told Florin as the two of them stooped to lift the trap door. 'After all, she does practically all of the work here.' Florin opened his mouth to reply and then shut it again as the sewer stink roiled up to greet them.

'Hurry up,' Jeanette told them. But she was too happy to sound really urgent. It wasn't just that she'd settled her claim to a partnership with Lorenzo that made her beam with happiness. It was also that she'd realised that Katerina's lithe body and beautiful hair were about to be dunked into a river of liquid excrement.

Florin swallowed as he peered down into the eye-watering stink of the blackness below him. Swirls caught the lamplight here and there, and shone queasily.

'Get a move on,' Jeanette urged him as the front door boomed again. 'I'll tell everyone that you went out the back entrance an hour ago.'

'Thanks, partner,' said Florin. He managed to conjure up a smile for her despite the fact that his stomach was already heaving. Then he took the lantern she passed to him and crawled down into the sewer.

Jeanette waited until she'd heard Katerina's silkily smooth legs splash into the churning filth below. Only then did she close the trap door and, with a big smile on her face, go to see who was making a mess of her door.

THE STINK WAS so thick that it was almost a vapour. The sludge of sewage from which it rose was curdled with horribly recognisable lumps; partially dissolved things that felt like the contents of an overcooked stew. The splosh of the three escapees' footsteps echoed along with sounds of dripping water and the distant squeaking of rats made bold by darkness and numbers.

In a way, Lorenzo told himself, these were all good things. Even if their escape route was discovered, who but the most desperate of pursuers would follow them down here? Yes, he told himself as something slithered past his leg, this was a wonderful place to escape through.

Wonderful.

Then he stopped trying to fool himself and concentrated on trying not to vomit instead.

Ahead of him, her narrow waist and flowing tresses no more than a silhouette in the scant lamplight, Katerina ploughed a path through the sewage. Lorenzo would have felt better had she shown some sign of sharing his revulsion. As it was, she remained untouched by the filth even as it slurped around her skin. She looked around as they trudged forward, her eyes wide with nothing but interest as she studied the thickly encrusted architecture of this place. They sloshed along, lowering their heads as the sewer narrowed. Katerina's head brushed against the ceiling, the brickwork smeared with shit from some high tide of sewage. She flicked the worst of it off her hair, so unconcerned that the filth might have been no more than soap suds.

There was, Lorenzo decided, something distinctly unusual about Katerina Hansebourg.

The sewer narrowed further, and as the roof closed in the tide of refuse grew higher. When it had risen high enough to spill over Lorenzo's belt and into his breeches, Florin stopped and led the way into a side tunnel.

Although so narrow that the trio's knuckles dragged along the walls as they scuttled forward, it was relatively clean with no more than a dribble of dirty liquid running down the middle of it. Lorenzo, realising where they were, felt a rush of relief. Up ahead was an entrance to one of the open sewers that served the city above.

Even as he started to wonder how far ahead it was Florin stopped, turning to hand the lantern back to Katerina. The flame within flared in the rush of air, and for a moment the begrimed wooden door in the ceiling stood out from the smeared brickwork.

'We'll climb out here,' he told her, his words tight lipped against the sewer air. Katerina nodded and held the lantern up as Florin reluctantly pressed his fingertips against the door and pushed upwards.

After a minute of trying he gave up, wiped his fingertips against his shirt, and looked miserably at his injured palms.

'Why didn't you just ask me to do it?' Katerina said and, before he could reply, she passed the lantern back to him and slapped the palms of her own hands against the filthy underside of the trap door. The thin cords of her muscles grew sharper as she strained upwards but despite her obvious effort the door didn't move an inch. She stood back and cursed. 'Are you sure that it opens upwards?' she asked Florin.

'Yes, of course it does. Otherwise people would fall through. It opens onto Brewers Street, opposite the–'

'Shhhhhh,' Lorenzo hissed.

'What is it?' Katerina asked, but he just waved her into silence.

A heartbeat later and they all heard it.

'Probably nothing,' Florin said reassuringly, and looked anxiously up towards the jammed door.

The sound grew louder. It was almost like footsteps. Almost. But there was a pattering quality about it that was more animal than human. It seemed to come from everywhere at once, due to the sewer's distorted echo.

'I think it is something,' Katerina said. 'I think that Florin's tavern wench betrayed us.'

'Why would she?' Florin asked, in half-hearted defence of Jeanette.

Katerina shrugged.

'Here, let me try the door,' Lorenzo said. Katerina and Florin shuffled along the passageway to give him room as he pressed upwards. For a moment he thought that he felt something give, but he was mistaken. The door remained firmly closed.

A sharper tone had emerged from the pattering rush of whatever it was that was approaching. A tapping counter-point of something like hobnailed boots. Or perhaps, Lorenzo thought as he tried again, claws.

'They can't have followed us from the tavern,' Florin decided as he watched Lorenzo sweat. 'If they had they'd be sploshing through the sewage, not pattering along on brick.'

Katerina grunted her agreement.

'Then they must be coming from ahead.'

The two of them peered into the darkness. For all they knew it went on forever, down into the very roots of the world or the hells that lay beyond them.

The pattering of feet grew louder.

Nearer.

'Let me get a hand on to that,' Katerina said, and squeezing up against Lorenzo, she pushed upwards. Unfortunately, he was in no mood to appreciate the soft curves of her body.

'If we run,' Florin said, talking to himself more than to his struggling comrades, 'whatever it is will catch us from behind.'

'Depends on how fast we run,' Lorenzo volunteered. But the only reply he got was the sibilant hiss of steel on leather as Florin drew his sword.

He was about to suggest running anyway when the trap door flew open. Lorenzo saw the end of the cart which had been parked on top of it disappear and, as welcome as a watery mirage in the deserts of Araby, the patch of blue sky beyond. Never one to stand on ceremony, he accepted Katerina's offer of a hand up and leapt out of the sewer and into the street.

It was the first time in his life a Bretonnian street had appeared clean to him, but he didn't let that distract him. He was too busy hauling up first Katerina and then Florin.

Florin kicked the door shut behind him and the three of them hastened away from it and into the next street.

'I wonder what that was?' Florin said as they headed down towards the docks.

'Probably just your imagination,' Lorenzo told him.

'What was my imagination?'

'The noise.'

'What noise?'

'The one that you imagined.'

'But I was talking about the one that you heard.'

'I didn't hear a noise.'

'Then how do you know what I was talking about?'

'I didn't.'

'Aha! So you admit it.'

Katerina listened to the exchange then rolled her eyes. 'I hate to interrupt,' she said, 'but I'm off to find a well.'

'Good idea,' Florin agreed.

'I wondered when you'd remember how dirty you were.'

'Oh, it's not that. I just want to help you undress.'

'That's what she meant,' Lorenzo told him. Katerina snorted with laughter and for the first time in years, Florin found himself blushing. He was almost glad of the smearing of filth which hid his embarrassment.

Usually, Skrit would have killed the underling who'd brought him the news. He would have gutted him, or flayed him, or had him nailed to a plank and fed into a fire, inch by screaming inch. Right now, though, he didn't feel the need. For once, the warpstone that coursed through his veins had made him passive. He lay slumped against a wall, drooling happily as his mood was borne upwards by delusions of invincibility.

Not that this happy state of affairs did much to diminish his underling's terror. It grovelled before him, its lifted tail glistening with the musk of fear. Skrit's mood, it knew, was as reliable as a roulette wheel after he'd taken the stone. For him, the line between glaze-eyed calm to frothing psychosis was a thin one, and getting thinner all the time.

'Sooooooo, tell me again,' Skrit said, his words slurring through a delightful sense of paralysis. 'Where did you see the man-things?'

'In the upper level, my lord. They were only there for a few moments. A few seconds. They were hardly trespassing at all.'

'You let them trespass in my territory?' Skrit asked. Although his head still lolled, a dangerous clarity was returning to the pink marbles of his eyes.

His scout felt its heart accelerate in an almost unbearable explosion of adrenaline. 'I went to kill them as soon as I found out,' it chittered, the words running into each other as it fought the urge to flee. 'But Rikit didn't tell me in time to catch them. He was too lazy. Too lazy. Should I punish him, master?'

Skrit gurgled with laughter at his underling's pathetic attempt to shift the blame.

'Yes. Punish him. But first,' he said, raising a single claw to prevent the runt from scurrying off, 'I heard something interesting about these trespassers.'

'My lord?' the underling squeaked, white spots of panic swimming through his vision. Damn and curse Rikit for his treachery! They had agreed not to mention any of the details.

'Yes-yes,' Skrit replied. The lash of his tail twitched into sudden life like a waiting viper. 'I heard that one of them was the ancient's female. The one we are looking for.'

'I... I... I mean Rikit... His fault... not mine... I wanted to tell you... not certain...'

Skrit let the underling chitter on, his hysteria growing. Under the influence of the warpstone he'd eaten, the assassin found the scent of his underling's terror an irresistible perfume. Even so, when it started to shiver with the beginnings of a complete nervous collapse, he silenced it. Although it would have been fun to watch, Skrit still had enough presence of mind to realise that losing the underling now would be a waste of resources.

'Be calm,' he hissed and forced his muzzle back down to hide his teeth. 'I won't punish you. You'll be too busy for punishment.'

'Thank you, my lord,' the scout whimpered, collapsing onto the floor as relief washed through it.

Then it realised what had just been said, and the relief vanished. 'Busy, my lord?' he asked, his whiskers twitching with trepidation.

'Yes,' Skrit giggled. 'You'll be busy tracking the man-thing's scent through the overworld.'

'Yes, master. Yes. I'll take Rikit with me.'

The scout rubbed its bony paws together, its terror lifting as it thought of what it would do to its treacherous comrade. There would be plenty of opportunity, of that he had no doubt. The only question was whether he would use steel or poison.

'Go then,' Skrit said, suddenly impatient. 'Go now. Find the female. Find out where her new burrow is.'

'Yes, my lord.'

'Then come back and tell me. I want... I want to finish off the job I started.' Skrit's tail writhed thoughtfully, and his teeth bared as he thought about killing the female. To kill her would be wonderful. It would be ecstasy. He could almost see how it would be, the warpstone lending a razored clarity to his imaginings. He could almost hear her scream, almost see her flesh ruined, almost watch the light going out of her eyes... These were thrills he could hardly wait for.

No. No, they were thrills he *wouldn't* wait for.

Shivering with a sudden, exhilarating rush of warpstone addiction, Skrit sprang to his feet. Steel flashed in his paws and tail and he blinked away the hallucinations to find a victim.

But there were none to be found. His entourage, veterans of their master's murderous mood swings, had already fled. Only the echoes of their footsteps remained as they followed the scout up into the relative safety of the world above.

IT TOOK FLORIN, Katerina and Lorenzo almost two hours to find a place to clean the sewer filth off them. When they did it was neither a well nor a bathhouse, but something even better. It was a laundrette.

At first sight (or rather, at first smell) of Florin and his companions, the owner armed himself with a pounding stick and prepared to shoo them out of his premises and back into the gutter. But a flash of gold was enough to change his mood. Minutes later, the three stinking fugitives were soaking in three neck-deep vats, wallowing in the soap suds as happily as pigs in swill.

Katerina couldn't remember the last time she'd been so completely, wonderfully relaxed. Pink-faced from the heat of her bath she lay back, letting the tresses of her hair fan out like the fronds of some fabulous sea plant. She sighed and lifted a foot clear of the soap suds. Wiggling her toes brought her a sense of childish delight and she smiled in a moment of perfect, blissful contentedness.

It took her a while to realise that Florin was outlining his plans for the future.

'The first thing to do,' he said, 'is to find a ship.'

'Like the last time we had to run from Mordicio,' Lorenzo sniffed.

'But this time we've got the gold to book a passage to somewhere civilised.'

'We had the gold last time, too,' Lorenzo reminded him. 'Before you lost it.'

Florin shrugged, unconcerned. 'That's true. But back then I was young and foolish,' he explained for Katerina's benefit. 'Some might even say rash.'

Lorenzo opened his mouth to reply. Then he changed his mind. Lounging neck-deep in the perfumed warmth of his vat he felt too good to argue. He couldn't imagine why he hadn't tried the novel experience of taking a bath sooner.

The three of them sunk into a companionable silence, content to do nothing but soak.

'Let's call in the owner,' Florin suggested at length, 'and see if he can get a tailor to come and bring us some new clothes.'

'Waste of money,' Lorenzo muttered, but not loud enough for anybody to hear.

'Then we can go and start looking for a ship.'

'So where are you going?' Katerina asked.

'South, I think. Maybe Tilea. In fact, yes, Tilea. We can go and find Castavelli. I'm sure that the hero of Lustria will be pleased to see us.'

Katerina sighed again and lent back to stare at the ceiling. 'Well, I wish you luck,' she said.

'Wish us...? Wait a minute. You have to come with us.'

Katerina just shook her head and Florin and Lorenzo exchanged a surprised glance.

'Oh, I see,' Florin said with what he thought was sudden understanding. 'You want to go somewhere else. You should have just said so. Where do you have in mind? Just don't say Kislev, for Manann's sake.'

'I'm not going anywhere,' Katerina explained. 'I'm staying here.'

Her decision was met with a moment of stunned silence, after which both of her companions started to talk at once.

'What? You're mad. You can't stay here. We're ahead of Mordicio for now, but that won't last. Half the town owes him money and the other half works for him. No, no. We have to leave Bordeleaux. And we have to leave quickly.'

'Don't worry,' Katerina told them. 'You two can leave. But I have to stay.'

'But why?' Florin asked helplessly.

'I don't know exactly,' she admitted. 'But there is something I have to do here. Some task.'

Florin bit his lip thoughtfully. 'You mean your destiny?' he suggested.

Katerina just shrugged. 'If you like.'

'But how do you know that you're destined to do something here? Maybe you're supposed to go to Tilea.'

'No,' Katerina told him, the green fire of her eyes stone cold with absolute certainty. 'I will stay here.'

The calming effects of the suds and hot water were completely ruined for Florin, and he pinched the bridge of his nose between thumb and forefinger. Lorenzo watched him miserably. Both men knew how stubborn Katerina was, and both men remembered their oath to protect her.

'In that case, then,' Florin decided, 'we'll have to stay here, too.'

Lorenzo looked as though he'd just heard a death sentence read out. For a moment, he seemed on the verge of tears, but instead he just nodded his agreement.

'That is good news,' Katerina said, and ducked her head beneath the suds to hide the smug smile that painted itself across her face. When she re-emerged, Florin and Lorenzo were still looking like condemned men.

'Cheer up,' she told them. 'This city is like a thousand rat-runs. There must be somewhere we can go where Mordicio won't find us.'

'Oh, he'll find us,' Florin frowned.

'Unless,' Lorenzo suggested, 'we go to the Sump.'

Florin's frown deepened.

'What's the Sump?' Katerina asked.

'It's between the harbour and the labourers' quarter,' Florin told her.

'So it's where the poor people live.'

'No. The people who live in the Sump are way beyond poor. They're the dying and the diseased. Or freaks, hiding from mobs and witch hunters.'

'Or,' Lorenzo added, 'from other things.'

'Sounds perfect.' Katerina smiled and happily blew a blob of foam across her tub. Lorenzo and Florin exchanged another horrified glance. And then, because there was nothing else to do, they burst out laughing.

* * *

LATER, WHEN THEIR skin glowed pink and their fingertips had become as wrinkled as dried grapes, the three friends climbed out of their baths and into swaddlings of borrowed sheets. A tailor waited in the next room, his measuring tape draped around his scrawny neck like a badge of office. A pince-nez glittered on his hawkish nose, the spectacles low enough down to reveal eyes as sharp as the pins which bristled from his sleeves.

Katerina was the first to submit herself to his ministrations. To her relief, he showed no sign of embarrassment when it came to stretching and measuring her limbs. Neither did he show any sign of lechery. As far as the tailor was concerned she might just as well have been a straw-stuffed dummy.

'Thirty-four,' he muttered to himself, scratching the number down onto a wax tablet.

'Thirty.' He'd wrapped the tape around her hips as carelessly as if they'd been no more than cold hams.

'Thirty-four.' He nodded at her chest, as coldly approving as a tutor checking a mathematical calculation.

'Five feet and... don't stand on your toes... five feet and seven inches. Hmm. Not bad.'

'Thank you,' Katerina said, an edge of sarcasm in her voice. The tailor, seeming to realise that she was a human being for the first time, cleared his throat.

'Colour?' he asked, and gave her a critical look.

Katerina shrugged.

'Hmm,' the tailor said, slipping back into the safety of dispassionate appraisal. 'I'd say green. As it happens I have a frock with me in exactly that colour.'

'No, I want breeches and a tunic,' Katerina told him. 'And a woollen cloak.'

For a moment he looked as if he was about to argue. Then he shrugged and looked back down at her measurements.

'It will cost more,' he told her. 'I'll have to restitch some of the clothes I have with me. Especially the tunic. Side panelling, perhaps.'

'You better get started, then,' Katerina told him and draped the sheet back over her shoulders.

It was dusk by the time the tailor had finished reclothing Katerina and her two companions. Even Lorenzo, who hated to see money spent almost as much as Mordicio did, had to agree it had been worth the time and the expense. For the first time since they'd killed Rabin they looked respectable; more burghers than burglars.

CHAPTER ELEVEN

A SCREAM ECHOED out of a narrow alleyway. There was no mistaking the pain in the voice. In the weak light of their single oil lamp, the travellers couldn't see any sign of the victim, and Florin was glad of it. He had no desire to witness the sort of atrocities that were committed in the Sump's moonless depths. Even so, he peered into every shadow and flicker of darkness as he led his companions past the dark maw of the alleyway. This was no place to be taken unawares.

Behind him, the cry of agony was drowned by a chorus of high, inhuman giggling. He glanced back over his shoulder and was relieved to see that Lorenzo was nervously keeping a watch to their rear. The older man's cutlass was bared, its razored edge perhaps the only clean thing in this squalid place. In any other of Bordeleaux's quarters, walking around with a drawn blade would have been an invitation for trouble. Not in the Sump, though. Here, a drawn blade was merely a sensible precaution. Florin had taken to carrying his own unsheathed sword as easily as citizens of other quarters carried walking sticks or their trays of goods. There was, he'd already learnt, no telling where the next attack would come from.

With a last glance behind him he squelched forward along the unpaved street. As he did so, the giggles turned into grunts of exertion, and the splatter of torn meat could be heard.

Manann's chamberpot and all its contents, Florin thought as the slobbering echoes of some terrible feast caught up with him. I can't believe we got talked into this.

At first he had thought that it wouldn't be so bad. They had money, after all. Not a fortune, but more than most of the denizens of these squalid streets would see in a lifetime. Unfortunately, far from smoothing their way, their wealth had just made things harder. Their fresh clothes and well-nourished frames had attracted the starving inhabitants of this quarter like piranhas to the scent of blood. This was all new to Florin. Usually he and Lorenzo, being both healthy and well-armed, had little trouble with footpads. But within these starving rat-runs their obvious strength made little difference. To the hollow-eyed desperadoes who'd sunk to these depths, the possibility of a violent death held no terrors.

Faced with the certainty of slow starvation, they had nothing to lose.

So far, Florin and his little gang had been driven out of two flophouses, their weapons wet with the blood of their hosts. They'd fought off half a dozen gangs of footpads, their victories robbed of any glory by the malnourished state of their attackers. And they'd taken one casualty. Thankfully, the sliced meat of Lorenzo's shoulder still showed no sign of festering. Even so, all three of them desperately needed a safe place to rest and get some sleep.

Florin noticed that the first grey light of dawn had crept up on them, and he greeted it with a curse. He blinked the gravelly feeling from his bloodshot eyes, stifled a rib-cracking yawn, and came to a sudden decision.

'I've had enough of this,' he said, turning to face his companions. 'We need to find somewhere to hole up, and we obviously aren't going to be able to do that here. I think we should go to the labourers' district. Try to hide in one of the barracks.'

Lorenzo rumbled his exhausted agreement but Katerina shook her head. 'No,' she decided, sounding as fresh as if she'd just awoken from a night in a feather bed. 'This place is better. I've been thinking about it, and I'm sure we should stay here. They say Mordicio has offered a reward for us. Even if he has, he'd never believe people from here. They're starving, so they'd say anything.'

Florin shrugged. 'So what? If we stay here it's only a matter of time before we're overwhelmed. Haven't you noticed how the gangs that attack us keep getting bigger? My guess is that the survivors are joining up with others, then coming back for another try.'

'He's right,' Lorenzo chipped in, for once too tired to squabble. 'And even if he wasn't, another day without sleep and we'll be finished anyway. After we collapse they can take our purses and slit our throats at their leisure.'

'Don't worry about that,' Katerina told him. 'I've decided what we have to do.'

'Oh have you now?' Florin asked irritably.

'Yes,' Katerina told him. 'It's quite simple, really. We have to found a tribe.'

'Found a tribe?' Florin snapped, his exasperation finally getting the better of him. 'What in the name of Ranald's balls are you talking about? Let's just get out of this pit and back to civilization.'

'Wait a minute,' Lorenzo said. 'Let's hear what she has to say.'

'What I mean,' Katerina said, 'is that we have to find a place here that's easy to defend. Then we have to round up the inhabitants and bend them to our will. It's just the same as what I did with the gnoblars back home... I mean, back in the east.'

'Good idea,' Lorenzo said.

'What?' Florin could hardly believe what he was hearing. Apart from anything else, the Lorenzo he knew was no more likely to take advice from a woman than he was from a dog. Maybe he was becoming delirious.

'Well, what else are we going to do?' the injured man insisted. 'This is the only place in the city where we might be able to hide. She's right, we need to join forces with some of the natives.'

Florin looked from Lorenzo to Katerina, then back again. 'Fine,' he said. 'Have it your own way. But if you think that–'

'Good. Well, that's settled then,' Katerina interrupted. Then, before Florin could take offence, she squeezed his arm and pressed up against him seductively.

The complaint died on his lips.

'And I think I know exactly where we should go. Remember that dead end we came to yesterday? The one at the end of that little path? We'll go there.'

'Why?' Florin asked, the swell of Katerina's body combining with two sleepless nights to dull his wits. But Katerina had already turned on her heel and started leading them back the way they had come. Florin realised that he had been left with no choice but to follow. He cursed under his breath and trudged off after Lorenzo and the girl. He just hoped that nobody ever found out who had ended up following who.

EVERYBODY IN THE Sump recognised the distinctive squeak of Monsieur Tulvi's cart and they knew it for what it was, the sound of death. Most welcomed it, some even drew reassurance from it, taking some comfort in the knowledge that their bodies would be carted up to the garden of Morr and not left for the rats. And for this, they had Monsieur Tulvi and his squeaking cart to thank. He alone was willing to handle the bloated remains that appeared every morning in the mud of these streets. Whether the bodies had been rotting for a day or a month, Monsieur Tulvi undertook the back-breaking task of carting them away.

All he got for his morbid labour were the few pennies that were sometimes scattered around the corpses, a paltry communal offering from a community that could scarcely afford even that.

He was not a man given to morbid introspection, which was fortunate considering his job. Nor was he a man given to much curiosity. So it was that when he noticed the first of the ragged creatures that scuttered past him in the grey light of dawn, shapes that moved as lightly as windblown leaves, he paid them no heed. His profession had always proved armour enough in the past, protection against the footpads and outcasts that haunted these quagmired streets.

The corpse collector couldn't help but watch them, these dark shapes. Even from the corner of his eye he could see enough of them to know that they were... they were...

What was the word?

Ah yes.

That was it.

They were *different*.

Although roughly human-shaped, they ran with the low, skittering energy of cockroaches. They ran as silently, too. Neither a splash or a tap marked their passing, and for a moment, Monsieur Tulvi wondered if they were no more than phantoms. Quickly, knowing that he'd been mad to look too closely at the things that even now turned back to look at him, Monsieur Tulvi drooped his head over his cart. Its occupant, a woman who'd been patiently waiting for his services all week, winked up at him with the dead orb of her remaining eye. The undertaker didn't mind. The sight was infinitely preferable to the lash of a scaly tail that he'd seen slip from beneath one of the shadowy runners' cloaks.

He couldn't help but look up to see if they'd noticed his unconscious appraisal. To his relief, the street seemed empty. The tailed things had gone as silently as they had come. Monsieur Tulvi lifted his hat back and ran his fingers through his thinning hair. Silly to worry, he scolded himself. Even the twisted need burying. Why, there had been that man with the extra arms. He'd treated him as well as anyone. And the one with the tentacles he'd had to lop off in order to smuggle the body into the communal grave. Yes, in the next life there'd be a few who owed him favours.

And on that happy thought, Monsieur Tulvi's life ended. There was an eyeblink of biting steel, a heartbeat of blinding pain, and then nothing.

Conscientious even in death, the corpse collector's body fell forward and landed neatly in his own barrow.

Its assassins detached themselves from the shadows into which they'd melted and scuttled forward to inspect their handiwork. It was Rikit who had thrown the weapon, and his whiskers bristled with pleasure as he inspected his handiwork. The man-thing's sallow skin was already blossoming with the dark bruises of internal haemorrhaging, and Rikit chittered happily. The poison he'd used had been perfect.

Chiselled teeth bared in triumph, Rikit twisted his throwing stars free of his victim's back. It had buried itself deeply between his ribs, and by the time he'd worked it free the rest of the pack had gathered around.

'You kill without orders,' one of them said. 'You show yourself to the man-things.'

Neap was indistinguishable from the rest of the pack beneath his hood, but there was no mistaking his voice.

'It saw what we were,' Rikit whined, the joy of the kill quite spoilt by his leader's interference.

Neap chittered with unpleasant laughter. 'Don't tell me,' he sneered, 'tell our master. I'm sure he'll be interested to learn why you broke his order and interfered with the man-things.'

Rikit's tail twitched nervously.

'Our master likes listening to you, yes?'

Understanding dawned in the pink marbles of Rikit's eyes. 'What?' he squeaked. 'What? I don't understand.'

But Neap had already faded away back into the shadows. He didn't want to waste any more time. They'd already lost the scent of their prey once, after it had disappeared into the launderer's house. It had taken them a dozen false starts until they'd found it again, and now it was so clear and fresh that it might have been a gift from the Horned Rat himself. The might have located their prey by sunset, Neap thought, and after that he'd tell his master of his success.

And after that, he'd turn to the more important matter of having Rikit dealt with, once and for all.

AT FIRST, FLORIN had thought Katerina's comparison of humans and gnoblars had been ridiculous. He'd seen gnoblars first-hand; they were runty little greenskins that the ogres used as a combination of pet and self-propelled snack. Even compared to the goblins of the west, they had been stooped and puny things. They had always seemed to be naturally malnourished, too. The only lively thing about their crooked little bodies had been their eyes, the yellow slits moving with the constant fear of attack. But now, as he followed Katerina into the hovel she'd just kicked her way into, he realised how horribly similar some of his fellow humans were to these creatures.

There were perhaps ten of them gathered in this single-roomed hovel. Most of them, grubby little children, were even the same size as gnoblars. They huddled behind their mother's skirts, the tears of their frightened sobs drawing clean white runnels down their unwashed faces. In front of this pathetic tableau, the men of the house had gathered in desperate defence. They were scrawny, malnourished, and hollow-eyed. Even so, they were obviously prepared to fight off the warriors who had barged into their home.

Or, judging by the stones and bits of wood with which they were armed, to die in the attempt.

Katerina was pleased to see it.

'Good morning,' she greeted them, strolling through the splintered remains of their doorway. 'Why didn't you answer when I knocked?'

'Get out,' the oldest of the men told her. Despite the fact that his home had just been invaded, there was no anger in his voice. Just a low, weary despair.

'Are you the leader here?' Katerina demanded to know.

'This is our home,' he told her, 'and my family. It is all I have. Do you think we haven't already been robbed of everything else? Do you think we haven't been beaten and terrified and driven from one place to another by scum like you?'

Suddenly, the despair was gone. In its place was a rage that had had long to mature.

'Hush, father,' one of the man's sons said, edging closer to his parent. 'There's no point provoking them.'

'And why not?' the outraged elder cried, flecks of spittle glistening on his beard. 'What do we have to lose? We have nothing to call our own, not even the rubbish they throw away, not even the food that falls on the floor. The rats live better than us.'

Despite the fact that Florin and Lorenzo had followed Katerina into the shack with swords drawn, the man fearlessly waved a sharpened chairleg at her. 'I don't care any more what they do. We're better off dead than living in this cursed place.'

Katerina waited until his rant ended before replying. 'So are you their leader or not?'

'No,' the man said and, with a ragged cry, he threw his piece of wood into the wattle wall of the hovel. 'No, I'm only their father. And I've failed them.' So saying he dropped to his knees and began to sob. His sons looked mortified as their mother, the crying children still clinging to her ragged skirts, bent down to comfort him.

His sons looked away. So did Florin and Lorenzo. Embarrassment filled the room like the Lustrian heat, so intense that the four of them started to sweat. The only person unmoved was Katerina. She waited with disinterested patience until the man had brought himself under control.

'You needn't look so miserable,' she told him. 'The reason I've come to you is because I am now your leader.'

'Don't mock me, woman,' the man said, knuckling his eyes furiously.

'I'm not mocking you. I will arm your sons and feed your children. And I will help you to protect them all. Them and everybody else in this street.'

It was all too much for the eldest son. Still burning with embarrassment on his father's behalf, he couldn't keep quiet any longer.

'Big words for a wench,' he sneered. 'Why should we–'

With barely a flicker of movement Katerina jabbed a thumb into the soft spot behind the youngster's ear. He collapsed with a surprised squawk, his makeshift weapon dropping from his nerveless fingers. His brother raised his arm in retaliation, but before he could strike, Katerina turned and revealed what she held in her other hand.

The glitter of silver stopped her assailant as surely as a crossbow bolt.

'Take it,' she told him as he goggled uncertainly at the wealth. 'Pick up your brother and go buy some food.'

The lad looked at his parents. Eventually the father managed a nod and the coin was snatched from Katerina's hand.

'Who in Shallya's name are you?' The old man asked as his lad bit experimentally into the silver.

'I am Katerina Hansebourg,' she told him, and her emerald eyes flashed proudly in the gloom. 'And the Lady has sent me to save you.'

There was a single, silent heartbeat; a knife-edged moment that was balanced perfectly between suspicion and belief.

It was ended by the mother. She bowed her head to the hard-packed earth, as if this grubby hovel had been transformed into a shrine. After some hesitation, her husband followed her lead and, with a final look at the coin she'd given him, so did the son.

'The Lady,' the mother whispered. 'I knew she'd answer my prayers.'

Katerina waited until they had all knelt before telling them to stand up again.

'I said that the Lady sent me,' she smiled as she helped the woman back to her feet. 'Go with your sons to the market while I introduce myself to the rest of the tribe.'

'The tribe?' the father asked.

'That's right.' Katerina spoke with an air of perfect assurance. 'You and everybody else who lives around this courtyard. You are now all under my protection.'

'Do you want me to introduce you?' the man asked. Suddenly self-conscious, he started to wipe the tears from his face, although the more he smeared the dirt away from his eyes the more obvious it became that he had been bawling.

'No need for that,' Katerina decided. 'I think that I can introduce myself.'

'Yes,' he replied, blinking his eyes in relief. 'I suppose that you can.'

Florin and Lorenzo exchanged a worried glance before following Katerina back into the mud of the little square. It wasn't much of a kingdom she'd chosen to conquer. Barely a dozen hovels clustered around the little cul-de-sac, the rotting buildings as dirty and dilapidated as the people who huddled within them. And yet for all that Florin could see the sense in recruiting the denizens of this place. It was small enough to hold, and it was controlled by a single, easily defended entrance. In fact, the charred remains of a gate still lay in the entranceway, proof that someone had once succeeded in securing the little community, if only for a short while. Still, he remained troubled, and it wasn't Katerina's strategic sense that worried him.

'Katerina,' he murmured, keeping his voice low as he hurried to overtake her.

'What is it?' She stopped and turned to face him.

'What you said back in there. All that stuff about being sent from the Lady. Maybe you shouldn't say it quite so often.'

'Or,' Lorenzo mumbled his agreement, 'maybe you shouldn't say it at all.'

Katerina scowled in confusion. 'But why not?'

'Well... it's not that either myself or Lorenzo are superstitious. Far from it.'

Lorenzo grunted, and looked shifty.

'But the thing is, it's better not to take the Lady's name in vain. Even if these peasants believe you, it's still unlucky.'

Florin flashed her his warmest smile, and wondered if he dared to give her a friendly kiss.

He soon realised that he didn't. After a moment even his smile wilted beneath her cool appraisal, dying like a sunflower in the snow.

For Shallya's sake, he told himself. She's only a woman.

'It isn't unlucky to use the Lady's name,' Katerina told him, her face unreadable. 'She has sent me to save these people. You didn't think that I was lying, did you?'

Florin opened his mouth. Then he closed it. Katerina's face was a blank slate of perfect honesty. Could she really believe what she was saying? By the gods, he hoped not.

'All right then,' he finally said, although it was only because he couldn't think of anything more appropriate. 'Whatever you say.'

Katerina smiled, and the flash of happiness softened her features. She planted a quick kiss on his cheek before heading off to the next hovel.

'Well,' Lorenzo said sourly as she marched out of earshot. 'That certainly told her.'

Florin shrugged a little guiltily. 'Just be glad I never faced her across the poker table,' he said. 'We'd have lost our shirts.'

Lorenzo sniggered in spite of himself, then prepared himself for action as Katerina started banging on the next door. This time the occupant wasn't quite so shy. Barely five minutes after she'd started knocking, the door was flung open and a man as short as a dwarf stomped out, a rusty meat cleaver held in one fist.

'Touch that door again and I'll kill you,' he growled, waving the weapon threateningly in front of him.

Katerina watched it, unmoved. 'Why are you here?' she asked.

'What business is it of yours?'

'The Lady sent me to lead you to a better place.'

'How dare you come to my door with such blasphemy? I've been robbed of everything else, but I–'

The short man didn't finish his sentence. With a blur of movement, Katerina grabbed his elbow and dug her thumb into the nerves in the crook of his arm. The man's weapon thunked into the earth at his feet. Pressing up against him as tightly as a courtesan, she reached up and pinched one of the arteries in his neck.

'Don't ever accuse me of blasphemy again,' she whispered, her voice as soft as a razor on a whetstone. 'I told you that the Lady sent me. Are you calling me a liar?'

Through the first black spots of unconsciousness that had started to whirl through his vision, her victim saw the two warriors who stood behind his tormentor.

'Say no,' Florin advised him.

'No,' he choked out, and Katerina released him.

'Good,' she said, letting him fall back against the door. 'Now, why are you here?'

'I was a butcher,' the man gasped, rubbing at his bruised throat. 'Lost my business to the moneylenders.'

'I see,' Katerina nodded. She picked up his cleaver from where it had fallen, examined the edge, and handed it back to him.

'I could use a butcher,' she told him as he cautiously received the weapon. 'In fact, I've just had an idea. Come with me and we'll round up a few more people. Then you can take them to buy a pig. You can prepare the carcass, and tonight we'll all feast.'

'Buy it with what?' the butcher asked, his eyes wary. He had come to the conclusion that this girl was insane. She certainly wasn't the only one down here. The Sump was full of those who'd succumbed to madness, poor souls whose wits had been shattered by the gods alone knew what unspeakable events.

'We'll buy it with silver,' Katerina told him, and showed him a coin.

The man's eyes swivelled downwards, drawn by the silver like iron filings to a magnet. 'Is that real?' he asked, speaking more to himself than to this incredible slip of a girl.

'It's real,' Katerina assured him. 'Now, if you don't have any more questions, we should go and round up some men to help you. You can tell them what to buy and what to do with it. If you want to, that is.'

The butcher licked his lips, and swallowed. 'Yes,' he said at length. 'I want to, your ladyship. Indeed I do.'

'Don't call me that,' Katerina told him. 'Call me Katerina. And what shall I call you?'

'Butcher will do,' the man decided, a wistful look in his eye. 'Butcher will do nicely. Just wait for a second, would you?' He disappeared back through the doorway into his hovel and silenced his waiting family's questions with a rough bark. When he re-emerged, he was strapping an apron around his waist. It was striped with the butcher's traditional blue and white, the simple pattern occasionally broken by brown blossoms of ancient bloodstains. Somehow the cloth made the butcher seem bigger. His back was straighter than it had been, and his head was held higher. Even his skin seemed less sallow.

As they set off to drag the next household into Katerina's tiny fiefdom, Florin realised what she'd given the bankrupt tradesman. It had been a lot more than the promise of a full belly. Perhaps, he decided as she started hammering on the next door, this might work after all.

CHAPTER TWELVE

IT HAD BEEN born a thousand miles away, fathered in the deep ocean by irresistible winds and immovable depths.

To every race it was known by a different name. To the cold-blooded rulers of the southern jungles it was known as Tel-Iqsa, and avoided for the chill it brought. To the dying races of Ulthuan and Naggaroth it was known as Dromarie. To them it was a thing to be greeted as a welcome ally, for such was their art that they could spin and weave it into cloaks large enough to swathe entire fleets.

To the cruder folk of the Empire it was known as Nachtnabel, but to the inhabitants of Bordeleaux it was simply the fog.

They had no word to distinguish it from the lesser mists and drizzles that dampened their city. They needed no separate word. Everything that they knew about the fog, and everything that they dreaded, was carried in the way the word was pronounced.

The fog.

A soft, dull, suffocating word for a soft, dull, suffocating thing.

And yet, for all that softness, it was a thing with countless teeth. They took many forms, these teeth. Sometimes they were vast granite canines, biting into ships whose pilots had been befuddled. Sometimes they were tiny, microscopic things that feasted on lungs weakened by icy moisture.

The sharpest of all the fog's teeth came in human, or in almost human, form. They chewed their way through the blinding confusion with a hungry glee. Murderers, kidnappers, rapists – these and dozens more waited for the fog to drench their city, hibernating in between times like daemonic seedlings, lying dormant before some nightmare spring.

Not that all of Bordeleaux's denizens possessed such patience. As the fog poured through the grimy arteries of that sprawling city, it touched the remains of crimes committed in other, fairer weather.

In the pauper's grave that his father had purchased for him, it found the body of Rabin, even more pale and bloated in death than it had been in life. In the looted interior of the Ogre's Fist it found the body of Jeanette, the girl lying in the position in which her murderers had left her. And in the filthy thatched rooftops of the Sump it found other, worse things. Things that were a horrible combination of man and rat. Things that were perhaps the sharpest teeth of all.

Skrit led his minions over the rooftops. It wouldn't be long now until he had the female's head, the grisly trophy that he needed to unlock the man-thing's claws from his next portion of warpstone.

Sometimes, when he let his thoughts stray, he was seized with a terrible fear. A paranoia that the man-thing had been lying to him, and that he would try to disappear without giving him the stone. Skrit tried not to dwell on such thoughts. The anger they created in him was almost more than he could bear, a terrible blinding thing that threatened to cripple him with fresh madness.

And that he could not afford. So, keeping himself even more tightly disciplined than his nervous followers, he rushed forward, barely noticing the fog as it rolled over him to mask his scuttling advance.

When he did notice it, he welcomed it as a gift from his abominable god. Even one as stealthy as he found the muffling blanket of the fog a help, especially as it did nothing to dampen his scout's sense of direction. After all, what skaven was ever fool enough to rely entirely on his weak little eyes? Neap obviously wasn't. Skrit knew this because of the jest he'd played on his underling. He had offered him a reward for finding the female manthing so quickly. Then, when the scout had finished snivelling his gratitude, Skrit had told him that, whatever reward he chose, it would be doubled and also given to his rival, Rikit. The entire clan had been impressed when, after some thought, Neap had decided that he wanted to be blinded in one eye.

Skrit was still snickering at the memory of Rikit's expression when a whispered squeak cut through the fog. He froze, whiskers twitching, and listened as the call was repeated. Excellent, he thought, rubbing his claws together in a grotesquely human gesture. That was Neap's call. They must have already reached their target. This was going to be easy.

Even so he waited, staying as still as a tumour in the darkness, until the scout came and made his report.

'It's sleeping,' the miserable creature told its master. Its words were muffled by the dirty thatch of the roof that it grovelled down into.

'Be still,' Skrit told it, afraid that it would alert whoever lived below.

'Yes, master,' Neap squeaked, a little too loudly.

Irritation flashed red in the marbles of Skrit's eyes, and his underling cowered even lower.

The pain from Neap's empty eye socket was terrible, but even as he wept blood onto the straw, he knew that it had been worth it. Even now, the traitor Rikit was wandering the sewers, blind prey to whatever came upon him first. It was a pleasant thought, and it gave him the courage to address his master.

'The girl is with other man-things now,' he dared to say. 'All sleep together in one of the tall burrows. There are others around, too. Other man-things. Many.'

'All sleeping?' Skrit asked.

'Apart from two.'

'Armed?'

'Yes. Very armed.'

Skrit gnawed at one of his whiskers. If he sent in his followers first then it would be safer for him. And safer was the same as good. On the other claw, they were worthless things, his underlings. Any one of them might wake up the female's companions and that would mean a fight. Ordinarily, Skrit wouldn't have minded, but tonight he needed to take the female's head. Skrit bared his teeth and thrashed his head from side to side.

'I will go first,' he decided. 'I will kill the female. You will follow me. When I have killed her, you will kill the others. All of the others.'

'Yes-yes master. Yes-yes-yes.'

'But if you – if *any* of you – wake her up before I am finished, I will make an example that they will hear of even in Skavenblight. Understand?'

Neap chittered his acquiescence before slipping away into the safety of the fog. He was eager to terrify his comrades with these orders, just as he himself had been terrified.

When he returned, Skrit let him lead the way. The rest of the pack followed him over the rooftops, moving with the effortless coordination of a shoal of fish. Soon they surrounded the little courtyard that Katerina had spent the day conquering. Even through the fog, Skrit could see the glowing remains of a big cooking fire, and his snout wrinkled at the smell of charred meat and rotten grape juice. Man-thing food was revolting, but at least it had knocked most of them out. The only ones left awake were the yawning sentries, the pair of them keeping a useless guard on the newly mended gate.

Skrit waited for almost half an hour more, lurking in the fog until he was sure that there were no surprises in store for him below. Only then did he begin to slither towards the hut where Katerina was sleeping.

KATERINA WAS SLEEPING soundly. The meat and wine had combined with a week of sleepless nights to drop her into a slumber that was almost catatonic. She barely had time to organise a rota for guard duty before collapsing into the hut that she had commandeered.

Barely six hours ago it had belonged to a trio of cutpurses. They were long gone now. Of all the courtyard's inhabitants they had had the temerity to refuse the offer of Katerina's rule, and for that they had paid. If it hadn't been for Florin's restraining influence they would have paid even more dearly. As it was they had merely been driven away.

Katerina twitched in her sleep and rolled onto her back. Her arm fell to one side and landed on Florin's chest. He grunted something in his sleep and rolled towards the warmth of her body.

After burning the lice-ridden rags that the hut's previous occupants had left behind, the fugitives had decided to spend the night on the freshly swept floor. The hard-packed dirt felt remarkably comfortable and the three of them were tangled into a single, snoring heap.

LURKING ON THE roof above them, Skrit could hear the sounds of their slumber. They sounded as mindlessly content as a herd of pigs. The assassin had to bite his tongue to contain the chitter of excitement that welled up inside him. This was going to be so easy.

BARELY NINE FEET below the skaven, Katerina shifted then wriggled comfortably against Florin's chest. His snores turned to snuffles as the silk of her hair brushed against his cheek.

* * *

SKRIT, ICILY PATIENT despite the cravings which gnawed at his thoughts, waited until this slight disturbance in their sleep had smoothed itself out. Then he started to pick gently away at the thatch of the roof on which he crouched. Slowly, one piece of straw at a time, the assassin burrowed a peephole through the roof. When it was finished he pressed himself into the straw and blinked into the darkness below.

KATERINA TURNED TOWARDS Florin and buried her face in the hollow beneath his chin. He shifted back and, his dreams still unbroken, slipped an arm around her waist.

A SINGLE RED eye blinked in the darkness above them. Then it was gone. Skrit had sensed enough. The time to strike, he knew, was now. He'd kill them as easily as kittens.

Quickly, working with a barely contained excitement, the assassin started to test the thatched roof, clawing through the mat of straw and parasites until he'd uncovered all the beams that supported it.

Only when he knew the strength of every inch of the roof did he signal for his underlings to start moving.

They swarmed down into the courtyard, moving through the fog with the silent speed of a cloud's shadow. Half a dozen slipped towards the dozing sentries, the men as unaware as any of their sleeping comrades, while the rest gathered outside of the door to Katerina's hut.

INSIDE, KATERINA MOANED and dragged Florin's arm tighter around her. Florin, his own dreams kindling with images of Jeanette, stroked her. Katerina moaned again and turned towards him.

SKRIT, HIS OWN heart pattering with darker passions, ignored the movements from below. A couple of slashed throats were all that stood between him and more of the stone. He started to dig faster.

* * *

KATERINA, HER EYES still half-closed, took a handful of Florin's hair and turned his head towards her. For a moment they breathed in each other's breath. Then, almost as though it was an accident, their lips brushed against each other.

Skrit watched them through the hole he'd made. The assassin enjoyed this moment even more than they did. He felt his muzzle pull back from the chisels of his teeth, and curved knives appeared in his paws, two silver smiles in the midst of the fog's grey misery.

FLORIN'S EYES opened half way as, beneath the smooth warmth of Katerina's touch, he realised that his dreams had seamlessly merged into a reality that was even better. He inhaled the warm smell of the girl and, wondering if she was awake or not, nuzzled her ear.

Which was when Lorenzo turned, lifted one leg, and broke wind loudly and long.

Katerina's eyes flashed open. Florin recoiled from the confusion he saw in her gaze.

'I was just going to wake you up,' he lied.

Before she could ask why, Skrit struck. He fell upon them with a wild shriek, his dark shape as purposeful as an arrow amongst a confusion of falling thatch and splintered timber. Behind him, his ragged vestments flapped upwards like a meteor's tail, and in his paws steel flashed like lightning. A split second after his claws touched the ground he stabbed downwards, three blades slicing through the darkness in a single, lethal blow.

But tonight, for the first time in a long and bloodthirsty life, he missed.

Perhaps it was because of the effects of the warpstone he'd taken, perhaps it was just his desire for more. Whatever the reason his poisoned blades struck the space between Katerina and Florin and buried themselves hilt deep into the hard-packed earth of the floor.

The darkness and the swirling fog was suddenly filled with cries of warning and alarm as the humans rushed for grab weapons and lanterns. Skrit cursed and plucked two of his knives free. Only the curved blade of his tail-knife remained stuck, and he shrieked with frustration as he tugged at it. It was his last mistake. Although still blinking in the darkness, the assassin's cry was all Florin needed. He dragged his sword from its scabbard and, as inelegantly as a butcher chopping bacon, slashed blindly towards the inhuman noise.

The weapon jarred in its hand as it connected and Florin felt a flash of panic. He had just realised that, in this confined darkness, he was more likely to have hit one of his comrades than anything else. But Skrit's sudden squeal of pain ended his doubts. It became almost too shrill to hear as Florin's sword bit deeper, and although terrible, it certainly wasn't human.

Florin, the force of his blow spent, twisted his blade free. There was a horribly satisfying crunch of tearing sinews, and a warm splatter of blood painted itself across his face. The assassin's shriek became a death rattle and the body collapsed amongst the last falling pieces of straw.

Lorenzo managed to spark a lantern into life just as the fire was fading from the assassin's eyes. They went from red to pink then rolled upwards as it exhaled its last, foul-smelling breath.

The three humans watched the scaled serpent of its tail twitch and stiffen. Its almost-human claws relaxed around the hilts of its poisoned weapons and its snout peeled back to reveal jagged teeth, razored incisors as long as daggers. Florin and Lorenzo's faces twisted with disgust at the horror which lay bleeding at their feet. Katerina, though, didn't feel even a tinge of disgust.

All she felt was hatred.

'That thing,' she said, and kicked the verminous cadaver with her bare foot. 'It's like the things that killed Sergei. The rat-things.'

'I see,' Florin said. The first fleas were already leaving their host, hopping away in little flashes of movement that disappeared into the darkness. He grimaced as he watched them.

'So do I,' Katerina said. 'I see now what my task is.'

'What task?' Florin asked, stooping to clean his blade on the thing's cloak. It was so thick with filth that he gave up after a moment.

'Extermination.'

Florin and Lorenzo glanced at each other. Lorenzo shrugged as his friend stood back up.

'I see,' Florin said, although only because he wanted to say something. He didn't know how Katerina intended to eradicate this thing any more than he already had. Maybe she was talking about burning it.

'Yes,' Katerina said. 'Yes, we will track these things down. We will find them in their lairs and in their sanctuaries and we will cleanse them from the face of Bordeleaux. Maybe the world.'

A smile played across her fair features as she outlined the lunatic scheme. She might have been discussing a night at the opera or an evening's dancing. But however easy her smile, the expression didn't reach her eyes. They were as bright and unforgiving as the light of a funeral pyre.

Florin swallowed uneasily. Somehow, the look on her face was more terrifying than the living nightmare which lay cooling at their feet. After all, he'd faced and defeated other monstrosities, many of them more lethal than this one. Or if not defeated them, at least survived.

He'd never had to deal with anything quite like Katerina Hansebourg though. There was something about her that was as impersonally lethal as a precipice or an avalanche. What made it even worse was that, deep down in his bones, Florin knew that he could no more escape from the destiny that she was carving out for them than he could sprout wings and fly.

And, Sigmar help him, he liked it. Ever since he could remember he'd always felt the pull of the abyss. From gambling tables to duelling squares to uncharted wildernesses he'd sought destruction with the unconscious enthusiasm of a hound following the scent of its prey. And in Katerina he'd met somebody whose will to destruction seemed greater even than his own.

For the first time, he began to wonder if he was in love.

He sighed and looked up. Amidst the confusion of his thoughts, it took him a moment to realise that the lights which glittered and blinked around the edges of the ruined roof were more than stars.

'Ah, shit,' he said, and at that, Skrit's followers rained down to avenge their master.

FOR ONCE IT was the comtesse doing the pacing. Her two brothers-in-law were hunched over the new table that had been set up in the great hall, their lips moving as they read the documents that the family's lawyer had brought.

'Are you sure Rabin's dead?' the comtesse asked for the dozenth time.

The lawyer, without a single trace of irritation, told her the same thing that he'd told her twelve times before.

'Madam, I have been assured that Monsieur Rabin is not just dead but in his grave.'

'And he died... what was it you called it?'

'As far as we know, he died intestate.'

'So Katerina inherits her dowry back?'

'That's right. As well as any other monies that her husband might have had.'

'And how much was that?'

Before the lawyer could reply, Gilles turned on her. 'Stop jabbering, woman,' he snapped. 'Can't you see that we're trying to concentrate?'

'You must forgive me, Gilles,' the comtesse snapped back. 'I forgot how difficult it must be for you to read. Shall I call one of my maids to help you?'

'Yes. Tell her to tie your jaw closed.'

The comtesse flushed.

'As always, your manners are the equal of your intelligence, Gilles,' she told him as the redness in her cheeks narrowed to two little dots.

The comtesse returned to her inquisition of the lawyer.

'And if it's true that Katerina's lover killed him... not that it necessarily is... that wouldn't alter that fact?'

'I don't think so,' the lawyer told her. 'In fact, I'm almost sure it wouldn't. Women are weak, foolish creatures, easily led by men. Even if Katerina was at the scene of Rabin's murder, then she was undoubtedly under the influence of Florin d'Artaud. And in any case, no young lady could possibly have had a hand in such brutality.'

Bouillon glanced up at the comtesse and snorted.

'Did you want to add something, Bouillon?' she asked him, but her brother-in-law just shook his head.

'Not really. It just seems that all of these recorded cases back up our friend the lawyer's statement. In fact, even if she did kill him–'

'Which she undoubtedly didn't,' the lawyer cut in.

'Then we'd still get her dowry back *and* Rabin's estate.'

The lawyer pursed his lips. It seemed a shame to disturb the moment of peace which had fallen over the three Hansebourgs, but he hadn't reached his present position without possessing a keen sense of duty.

'In point of fact,' he mumbled, 'Katerina inherits the estate, not her family.'

'But she's only nineteen,' the comtesse frowned.

'That doesn't matter. As a widow, she is no longer legally bound to her guardian's will. In fact, she no longer has any legal guardians.'

'The selfish little thing!' the comtesse exclaimed, as though the law had been created by Katerina with the sole purpose of thwarting her. The lawyer just shrugged noncommittally.

'Well, I've had enough of all this.' Gilles shoved the papers to one side. 'The main thing is that Mordicio's no longer entitled to Katerina's share of the business. And as long as she doesn't come back, we're keeping it.'

'Nicely put, brother,' Bouillon told him, and winked.

'What about Rabin's estate?' the comtesse asked. 'That should be ours... hers too.'

Gilles and Bouillon broke into a peel of mocking laughter.

'Let's see if I understand you,' Bouillon said. 'You want to go and tell Mordicio... Mordicio, mind... that because our niece's lover has murdered his son, then, not only does he not get her dowry, but he also has to give us his son's possessions as well?'

Gilles's face twitched and hardened into what was supposed to be a mask of well-meaning support.

'Actually, sister, I think that you're right. We seem to be finished here. Perhaps you could go and tell Mordicio yourself. It will come easier if he hears it from a pretty woman rather than two scarred old villains like us.'

The comtesse glared at him.

'Not at all,' she told him. 'I'm only a woman. What do I know of these matters? It would be much better if you went to speak to Monsieur Mordicio in person.'

Gilles looked like a man who has just remembered why it's a mistake to spit into the wind. He was still spluttering around for an excuse when Bouillon stepped in and saved him.

'No,' he decided. 'We'll leave Mordicio well alone. It's enough that he doesn't have Katerina's share of the business any more, and Katerina isn't likely to reappear. The girl we found at d'Artaud's tavern told us that they've escaped the city. As long as Katerina remains a fugitive she's unlikely to present us with any more problems.'

'Not that she would have presented us with any at all if some damn fool hadn't dragged her back here in the first place,' Gilles added, but the comtesse ignored him.

'Well, if you aren't men enough to protect your niece's inheritance then I want nothing further to do with you,' she told her two relatives. So saying, she stuck her nose in the air, swivelled on her heel, and flounced out of the room.

Only when she was back in her own chambers did the comtesse let her excitement show. For the first time since her daughter had been brought back to the city, she was actually worth something in and of herself. There was no need for any further manoeuvrings and alliances on the comtesse's part – all she had to do was find the wretched child and get her to sign her share of the Hansebourg fortune over.

The beauty of it was, the comtesse thought with a happy smile, Katerina couldn't even read. Still smiling, the comtesse scribbled a note, sealed it with wax, and summoned one of her maids.

'Give this to the lawyer when he leaves, and only when he leaves. In fact, have his carriage stopped at the gate and give it to him there,' the comtesse told the girl. 'Also, tell him that I'll meet him in his offices at ten o'clock tomorrow morning.'

'Yes ma'am,' the girl said and hurried away. It was unnerving to be around the comtesse when she was so cheerful. It usually meant that somebody was about to get hurt.

IN YEARS TO come the short, desperate struggle between Katerina's first followers and the skaven was to be known as the Founding Battle. Ballads were written about it. Heroics were created, and then embellished, and then inflated up into feats of god-like magnificence. Even Lorenzo gained an air of martial nobility. But the reality, as always, was very different. There were no grand strategies or spectacular displays of the warrior's craft; no daring assaults or clear-eyed heroics.

No. All there was was fog and darkness, and breeches soiled by terror, and a panicked hacking at an enemy barely seen. Had it not been for the fog then things might have gone differently because, for once, it worked against the skaven. The billowing stink of it blinded their human opponents to the true horror of the things they were facing. Filled with the courage of the ignorant, they fought instead of running. At the same time, the confusion the fog brought fuelled the vermin's instinctive paranoia. It stoked their cowardly imaginations and peopled the night with phantom armies of vengeful humanity. The ringing tones of Katerina's curses made things even worse for them. Even to the skaven's inhuman ears the joy in her voice was obvious and, punctuated as it was with the backbeat of steel hacking into verminous flesh, quite terrifying.

It took only seconds for the assassins into the hut to realise what a mistake they had made, and a few seconds more for the last of their torn corpses to end up on the floor. Most of them lived only long enough to shrill their terror into the night, filling their brethren outside with panic, even before Katerina burst out of her quarters. She left half a dozen of her foes in there, a slaughterhouse debris of smashed bone and severed muscle, and led Florin and Lorenzo into the melee that raged in the yard outside.

And that was when the battle ended.

With their leader dead, the assassins' morale deserted them. Those that could, fled, scampering up walls and drainpipes to the sanctuary of the rooftops, skittering away from the victorious humans like rats from a burning barn.

It took Katerina a moment to realise that the battle was over. When she did, she sounded alarmed for the first time since the violence had begun. 'Don't let them get away!' she called, squinting through the suffocating greyness. 'We need to capture one!'

But although her followers had been willing to fight, they weren't willing to pursue. Even Florin had other ideas – he'd already stumbled towards the embers of the cooking fire and was busily trying to coax them back into life.

'Bring some more wood,' he called out, coughing in the smoke.

This order proved a lot more popular. Within minutes, fresh flames were licking upwards. As even more fuel was piled onto the fire, the heat of it started to lift the fog. Gradually, inch by sodden inch, it retreated to hover above the blood-soaked square like a wet rag over a butcher's block.

It left behind it the smell of rotten seaweed, the smell of spilt blood and the bodies of a dozen casualties. The balance of these casualties was scarcely believable. Of the untrained rabble who had fought, not a single one had been killed. Two were bleeding from wounds barely deep enough to need stitching, and one had lost an eye, but that was all.

Without exception, the bodies that littered the blood-soaked ground belonged to the enemy. Most of them had been hacked to pieces by the workman's tools with which Katerina's tribe had fought. There were a few, though, that seemed to have died of no more than flesh wounds.

Katerina studied them and licked her lips. Perhaps, she considered, they were merely feigning death. Cautiously, she prowled over to one and turned it over with her foot.

There was no movement from the flea-ridden body, nor any sign of breath. Squinting in the darkness Katerina saw why. She stooped to study the dagger that had been buried, hilt deep, in the thing's back. The handle seemed almost a part of its twisted form, growing out of the crooked spine as naturally as a stalk from an apple. On close inspection, its design was such that no human hand could have created it. Whatever these things were, they had obviously had no intention of leaving their wounded behind.

Katerina frowned, then stood and went back to stand by the fire. Her people were huddled around it. Despite their victory, most of them looked terrified, as wide-eyed and slope-shouldered as a herd of sheep.

Well, that wouldn't do.

'Butcher,' she called out, selecting the first man whose name she could remember. 'Get somebody to help you make sure those things are all absolutely dead.'

Which, Katerina thought, they certainly were, but that wasn't the point of the exercise.

'Right you are,' the butcher said. His shoulders squared with new purpose and he turned to start giving directions of his own.

'Now you two,' Katerina selected the brothers from the first family she had recruited. 'When they've checked them, you drag them over here. Start stacking them up for burning.'

The lads hastened to obey as, in pairs or small groups, Katerina set the rest of her people to work. Some tended to the children, others the wounded. The sentries were doubled, and scouts were sent reluctantly up onto the thatched roofs to keep an eye out for further attacks. Only when everybody was busy did Katerina allow herself the luxury of washing the blood off her face and hands and then went to dry off by the fire. Florin and Lorenzo, who had already busied themselves with a wineskin, welcomed her with a cupful.

'Thanks,' she said and knocked the drink back. As she did, the first of the corpses was hoisted onto the fire. At first, the weight of it dimmed the flames, the fur and cloth doing little more than singe and smoulder. But then the thing's melting fat leaked onto its rags and the corpse started to burn like a candle.

As it flared, the smell of it grew strong enough to drive everybody back from the fire.

'Sergei's killers. I wonder what they are?' Katerina asked, and absentmindedly watched one of the thing's eyeballs pop. As if in response, the flames devouring it started to turn green.

'I don't know,' Florin admitted.

'I think that I do,' Lorenzo muttered. Katerina turned to him, the sizzling remains forgotten in the face of her quickening interest. Lorenzo seemed not to notice. He just took another cupful of wine and lapsed back into silence.

'Well, what are they then?' Katerina finally asked.

'What? Oh, them. Well, there are always a lot of people who go missing when the fog comes.'

Florin grunted dismissively.

'That's because of murderers, not necessarily these things.'

'Some of them are slain by murderers,' Lorenzo nodded. 'Some by kidnappers. But some… Well, some are just taken. You must have heard about them. The vanished, they're called. Or the disappeared.'

He took another drink, the plight of his fellow man seeming to add relish to the wine.

'Never heard of 'em.' Florin shook his head.

'I have.'

The interjection came from one of the lads who Katerina had sent to gather the bodies. She turned to him now and he blushed so deeply that it was visible even in the firelight.

'Have you really?' she asked.

The lad swallowed nervously and looked as though he regretted ever having spoken. He looked to his brother for help but got no more than a shrug.

'Don't look so nervous,' Katerina told him, and prowled over to place a reassuring hand on his arm. 'You fought well tonight. Very well. That's why I asked you to take charge of burning the bodies. I knew you'd be capable.'

She smiled at him and his back straightened. His chin lifted, too, and for a moment he actually did look as capable as Katerina had told him he was.

'I've heard of the disappeared, is what I meant to say,' he told her. 'And I think that the grandfather is right.'

'Grandfather,' Florin smirked and elbowed Lorenzo in the ribs. To his delight the older man scowled. The lad looked at them before realising that he should be looking at Katerina instead.

'Yes, they're usually taken from around here. Sometimes from around the docks. Usually they're people who are on their own. Foreign sailors who get lost in the town. Girls who... who, you know.' All of a sudden the blush was back but he ploughed on anyway. 'Sometimes they take families, but not often. They only want healthy people, see. Healthy and strong.'

The group of men who'd gathered around the fire to listen to the conversation muttered their agreement.

'They want to sacrifice only the healthy to their gods,' one said.

'Or to eat. I always heard they were cannibals.'

'How can they be cannibals if they aren't human?'

'Easily.'

'No. I heard they use their victims as slaves.'

The lad listened to the dispute until he saw that he had lost Katerina's attention.

'Anyway,' he said, gesturing towards the misshapen skull that was blackening in the fire. 'It's these things that take them, for whatever reason.'

'Are you sure about that?' Katerina asked, and the lad, seeing the enthusiasm in her eyes, nodded vigorously.

'Oh yes. Look at this one.' He gestured to one of the bodies that lay waiting for incineration. 'See, it's got a web wrapped around it to catch people with. And some of those others have got vials of potion. Sleeping potion, I'll warrant.'

'I think he might be right.' Florin, wineskin in hand, had gone over to examine the cull more closely. 'Look, they've all got coils of rope wrapped around them. Must be for tying up their captives.'

The lad nodded vigorously.

'That's what I said,' he said proudly, and turned back to Katerina.

She nodded approvingly. 'Well done,' she said. 'What's your name?'

For a moment it seemed that the lad had forgotten. It took his brother's sniggering to refresh his memory.

'Jacques,' he told her, and shuffled his feet with embarrassment.

'Jacques,' Katerina replied. 'I'll remember it.'

He beamed beneath the dirt and splattered blood which begrimed his gaunt face, and swelled with pride. Then he turned back to his task with a will, driving his brother before him.

'I don't understand why I never heard of these things before,' Florin said, and used his dagger to lift the hem of one of the robes. Sure enough, a length of webbing was wrapped around its midriff. 'You'd think that somebody would have killed some of them from time to time.'

'Maybe they're just very careful.' Lorenzo shrugged. 'Maybe that's why they only take lone victims.'

'No,' said one of the gathered men. 'It's because they've got magic. Sorcery. Makes them invisible.'

Florin winked up at Lorenzo. 'If their magic makes them invisible, then how can we see them?' he asked.

For a moment the expert seemed nonplussed. Then, with the same single will that will turn the heads of every cow in a field, the assembled people turned to gaze at Katerina.

A miracle, they thought, although none of them quite dared to say it. And because none of them quite dared to say it, nobody quite had the nerve to disagree. And because nobody had the nerve to disagree, it became the truth.

Katerina remained unaware of the awe in the faces of those who watched her. She was too intent on the burning bodies of her enemies. There was a hunger on her face as she watched them dissolve beneath the flames. A hunger and a look of hard appraisal.

With a surreptitious glance at his beloved leader, Jacques hurled another craeture onto the charred remains of the first. The quickening heat was enough to incinerate it as easily as if it had been a torch. Katerina's eyes narrowed as it flared into life, squinting with feline concentration as she watched it burn.

She seemed not to feel the heat that was driving everybody else back, pace by pace. However fiercely it burned, the pyre was no more than a dying spark compared to the holocaust that she was planning.

The rest of these filthy things would live to regret the day they'd taken Sergei.

Although not, she thought, for very long.

IT TOOK THE comtesse barely a week to succeed where her brothers-in-law had failed. What's more, she had succeeded with none of the blood and expense that had accompanied their ham-fisted efforts. All it had taken had been the ounce of common sense that the two buffoons so obviously lacked.

Where Gilles and Bouillon had blundered around the city like drunken bears, the comtesse had merely gone from one dress-maker to the next. The fog scarcely hindered her driver as he piloted her carriage through the mean streets of Bordeleaux and in the competitive game upon which these petty merchants depended, the superbly dressed comtesse's custom was a prize worth winning.

The comtesse, knowing this, was surprised that her search took as long as it did. Despite her ploy of asking after a brown-haired girl, the tailor's description of Katerina was perfect. He remained miserably certain that the woman he had clothed had been a redhead. Not only that, but the wardrobe she had insisted upon had been both expensive and inappropriate. Which, thought the comtesse as she followed him to the laundrette where he had found her, was a damn fine description of her daughter all by itself.

Barely an hour later, she was sitting in the steaming shop where the three fugitives had washed away the sewer filth. A contract for the Hansebourg family's linen cleaning requirements lay on the table in front of her. Wax stamped and triple signed, it looked just as grand as the passport to prosperity that it surely was.

The launderer, his eyes flitting between the numbers in the contract and the comtesse's jewels, had told her everything that he could. Then his wife, who was obviously an expert at listening from the next room, introduced herself and told the comtesse a lot more.

The older woman blanched when the Sump was mentioned. As always, it seemed, Katerina was determined to be selfish. She had probably gotten herself killed already.

Scolding herself for such defeatism, the comtesse put the final stamp on the contract and strode back out to her carriage. Although her first instinct was to go to the Sump immediately, common sense dictated otherwise. It was already too dark. Not only that, but it would be wiser to take more men than just her footman and driver.

Wiser to hire them privately, too. It wouldn't do for her brothers-in-law to get wind of what was going on. When Katerina had signed her share of the Hansebourg fortune over, then she would tell the two fools what she had done. In fact, she was looking forward to it.

Until then, everything must be done secretly, even though that meant delay. Not even her driver suspected what lay behind his mistress's sudden interest in housekeeping.

'No! No! WHEN I say stab forward, you stab forward *whilst* throwing your other shoulder back! Don't throw it back *before* you stab forward. Lorenzo, why is he throwing his shoulder back before he stabs forward?'

'You can't be explaining it to him clearly enough,' Lorenzo told his friend, and winked at the bemused-looking trainee. He was one of the score that Florin had ranked up on the freshly swept earth of courtyard, there to learn the nastier points of street fighting. The weapons the men carried were no less murderous for being scavenged and makeshift.

'I'm not explaining it clearly enough?' Florin wailed. With a deep breath, he started to explain this most basic of manoeuvres all over again.

'Look, it all starts with the feet. Let's go back and do the footwork again. Remember how it goes? Feet apart... that's it... Then it's right foot to the right... Good... Left foot to the back... That's right... Then... Wait for it... Bend your knees, stab forward and throw your shoulder back. All at the same time. Now, do it really slow. Yes! Yes! That's it.'

Florin beamed at the trainee who smiled cautiously back.

'Now, back to the starting stance. We'll speed it up this time. Ready? So it's one... two, three. Yes, you've got it! He's got it. Lorenzo, he's got it.'

The older man rolled his eyes theatrically at Florin's enthusiasm, and laughter rippled through the ranks as Florin rushed over to embrace the man who'd finally completed the manoeuvre.

'Right then, lads. I think that this is a good time to eat. Don't drink too much wine. We're sparring this afternoon.'

Florin watched them hasten to the trestle table where their womenfolk were ladling out the first bowl of stew. He smiled as he listened to their cheerful banter.

Compared to the huddled vagabonds they had been when Katerina had found them, they were men reborn. Their new equipment and the first signs of new meat on their gaunt bones was only a part of it.

The greatest gift that Katerina had given to these people had had nothing to do with the gold from Rabin's stolen purse.

'How are they doing?'

Florin turned to find Katerina standing behind him. He forced himself to frown and Lorenzo followed his lead.

'As well as we might have expected.' He shrugged.

'Unfortunately,' Lorenzo added.

'I thought that they were coming on quite well. You're a fantastic trainer.'

She flicked back her hair and stepped so close to him that Florin could feel the warmth of her body. For a minute he forgot to look depressed so Lorenzo scowled deeply enough for both of them.

'All that means is that Florin's a bit less useless than they are,' Lorenzo told her.

Florin sighed and nodded his agreement. 'I hate to admit it, but I think he's right. They'll need months of training before we can even think about this plan of yours.'

'Maybe half a year,' Lorenzo added.

'Although probably no more than twelve months,' Florin said, looking thoughtfully at their little army.

Katerina shook her head. 'We'll implement my plan the next time the fog rolls in.'

'But they won't be ready.' Florin was the first to get his protest in. 'Look at what you've given them. How happy they are. Why waste all that by murdering them all on some whim?'

Expecting an angry response, both he and Lorenzo were surprised by her bark of laughter.

'So let me see if I understand you,' she said, and squeezed both of their arms. 'It's our people you're worried about. Not me. The fact that I'll be using myself as bait when the rat-things come slaving isn't what's bothering you.'

Florin opened his mouth to reply. Then he closed it again.

'Well.' Katerina gave a little pantomime sob and pushed them both away. 'I thought that I meant more to you than that.'

She raised a hand to hide her face from Florin and winked at Lorenzo. Despite himself, the older man sniggered.

'It's not funny,' Florin told him. 'Remember what we swore over Sergei's grave? How we're bound to protect her?'

'And you will,' Katerina cut in.

'What, by letting you get captured and dragged off to Sigmar knows where? No. No, you can't do it. It's madness.'

'I know what I'm doing,' she told him. 'I'm doing exactly what I am supposed to. Those rat-things murdered Sergei. They tried to murder my herd... I mean, my people. So I will track them and destroy them. Next time the fog comes they will hunt, they will find me, and they will take me back to their lair. You will follow them, and when we know where it is, we will destroy it.'

She looked at her friends' horrified expressions and shrugged impatiently.

'It's really not that complicated. We used to wipe out packs of sabretusks with the same trick back home. The only difference is, this time we'll use me as bait and not a rhinox.'

Not for the first time, Florin wondered if events had driven her crazy. She didn't look mad, he had to admit. He'd seen plenty of lunatics in his time; he'd often taken girls to watch the hilarious antics of the inmates of Bordeleaux's asylum. But although Katerina showed none of their symptoms, to suggest that she would allow herself to be taken by the horrors that hunted through the fog...

'Wait a minute,' he exclaimed, a sudden hope dawning. 'You're joking, aren't you?'

'No.'

Florin rubbed his eyes and Lorenzo shrugged hopelessly.

'Well, the lads honestly aren't ready. Give us another month at least.'

'I'm sorry. I know you mean well. But I must follow the will of the goddess. And you have to have faith in me.'

Florin waited for Lorenzo to curse at the word. But all he did was to shrug and say, 'I suppose that we do.'

'Thank you,' Katerina beamed, and kissed his cheek.

Florin realised that he was defeated. All that was left to him was to be a good loser.

'All right, I'm convinced. Anybody who can kiss Lorenzo without throwing up is probably tough enough to handle a few vermin. They weren't really that big, after all.'

This time he did take the opportunity to wrap an arm around her.

I'll just have to hope the fog holds off for a while longer, he thought, then looked up as the lookout shouted something from the gate. The man didn't sound particularly worried, but that didn't matter. There was no point in wasting an opportunity to practise a drill.

'To arms!' Florin cried, brushing Katerina to one side. 'To arms!'

And the men, as if determined to make a liar out of him, bolted to their posts as professionally as any militia company.

CHAPTER THIRTEEN

THE FATIMA LOOKED exactly like what she was. Her hull was tar painted, the darkness of it a fine uniform for the task for which she had been built. Her sails were also drab, stained with tanner's juice. The usual Arabyan pride in the spotless whites of their ship's canvasses had given way to another, more practical consideration.

The *Fatima's* low silhouette also helped. Even unladen, she was lower in the water than most other merchant ships her size, a fact designed to make her as inconspicuous as possible. Even another five minutes of invisibility could be worth the loss of seaworthiness.

At least, it was to men engaged in the *Fatima's* trade.

The only part of the slavers' ship that hadn't been sacrificed to the demands of stealth were her masts. They were as high and as thick as she could bear. All three of them were built to support great stormclouds of canvas, and the rigging that wove between them meant that the sails could be tacked as swiftly as silk beneath a seamstress's touch.

Yet for all these advantages the ship's master, the self-styled Emir of Jubail, kept her lurking far out to sea. The horizon was a single line that stretched all around her, unbroken apart from the occasional white-capped wave. The Bretonnian coastline lay to the east, still hidden by the curve of the globe, and the great port of Bordeleaux lay sprawled along it.

Occasionally, in the distance, specks of movement would set the lookout to shouting warnings down to his increasingly nervous master. So far, none of the traders or fishermen who hugged the distant coastline seemed to have seen her. But now, as he waited for the fog to return, the emir fretted over the fact that *seemed not to* have seen her wasn't necessarily the same as *hadn't* seen her. For all he knew, there could be a naval sloop heading out to question him even now, perhaps a squadron of sloops. Some of them could even be working their way around him, skulking below the horizon as they circled like hyenas around a wounded antelope.

The Arabyan glanced unhappily towards the smooth line of the southern horizon, his chins wobbling with concern. If these meetings with his Bordeleauxan partners weren't so lucrative he would have abandoned this one days ago. In fact, he would have abandoned it anyway if the truant fog hadn't remained to blur the western horizon.

He had no idea why it had evaporated so quickly. Once it rolled into Bordeleaux it usually maintained its stranglehold on the city for weeks on end. This time, though, it had barely reached the coastline before recoiling, blowing back out to the open ocean like a wounded beast returning to its lair.

Well, to the hells with it, the emir told himself. He would wait. He couldn't afford not to. With a last resentful look at the fog that lay cowering to the west, he waddled back to his cabin.

'Damn this stinking northern weather,' he muttered as he squeezed past the massive lump of his bodyguard and locked the door behind him. If only he'd brought a woman, too. He had expected to have some fresh ones by now, captives willing to do just about anything to escape the dank hell of the slave hold. With another curse, the emir collapsed onto a sofa and started to eat.

Barely an hour passed before the fog started to roll back towards land. It moved with the deceptive speed of all great predators, the silent mass of it swallowing up rank after rank of choppy waves as it raced back towards Bordeleaux. The emir had barely finished his third course when the grey wall of it rolled over his ship. When it dulled the light that came from the porthole he looked up, a hopeful smile lighting his greasy face. Then he returned to his feasting. He'd need to keep his strength up for the exertions of the days ahead.

THE COMTESSE STEPPED down from her carriage, a scented kerchief held beneath her wrinkled nose. Almost everything around her, from the crumbling buildings to their wretched inhabitants, seemed to be rotting.

In fact, the only wholesome thing in the entire awful place was the palisade and wooden gate her driver had brought her to. It stood perhaps a dozen feet tall, a freshly built wall that stretched between one crumbling building and the next.

It had taken the comtesse's driver a long morning, spent sprinkling coppers amongst the mongrel breed who lived here to find this place. And now they were here even the guards she had hired from the docks looked a little uneasy. They spread out around the carriage, hands on sword hilts, and eyed the street warily.

To think a young lady of the Hansebourg household was living here!

'Hello down there,' somebody called down from the palisade. It was the first cheerful voice that the comtesse had heard since entering the Sump, and she squinted upwards to see who was addressing her in such an inappropriate way.

The man was leaning over the top of the palisade, his elbows rested on the crude woodwork as he grinned down at the comtesse and her entourage. When she recognised who it was, her estimation of her daughter did the impossible and dropped even farther.

'D'Artaud,' she said, pronouncing the name as though it were a curse.

Florin's smile grew even wider and he swept the hat off his head. 'Comtesse Hansebourg,' he crowed, loud enough for Katerina to hear him. 'What an honour to find you at our humble abode.'

'Our humble abode?' the comtesse snapped. 'Who else is in there with you?'

'Oh, you know,' Florin said, and waved his hat around vaguely. 'Just a few friends.'

'And what about my daughter?'

'Lovely girl,' Florin said, avoiding the question as neatly as an opponent's blade, but the comtesse wasn't to be put off so easily.

'I mean is she in there with you?' she demanded.

Florin started to blather, when Katerina appeared at his side.

'Hello, comtesse,' she nodded.

'Hello, my dear,' the comtesse replied, sounding for all the world as if she was pleased to see her child. 'It's certainly a relief to find you well. I've heard all sorts of terrible rumours. That's why I decided to come and find you.'

Florin and Katerina exchanged a wary glance.

'Well, as you can see, I am well,' Katerina told her.

'Good, good,' the comtesse beamed happily. 'Good.'

For a moment the conversation stalled. It was Florin who finally broke the silence.

'Would you like to come inside and take a glass of wine with us?' he asked.

The comtesse, ignoring the glare which Katerina shot towards her companion, snatched at the offer.

'Maybe a small one,' she agreed, and Florin disappeared from the palisade to open the gates.

'Come in,' he said, with a small bow. 'And welcome.'

The comtesse bit back the tart reply that sprang to mind and tipped her head graciously. Her guards followed her through into the courtyard, keeping a respectful pace behind their employer as she appraised the situation. The buildings around the hard-packed earth of the little courtyard were scarcely any improvement over the usual hovels which littered this quarter, although at least they looked tidier. The denizens looked cleaner, too, and better fed. In fact, were they carrying weapons?

'Stand easy,' Florin told them, proud of the men's bearing. For a moment, a flash of regret that Katerina was so keen on leading them to their destruction turned his smile into a frown.

'Are these your servants?' the comtesse asked as Katerina climbed reluctantly down from the palisades and prowled over.

'Hardly,' Florin told her, aware of how far the comtesse's voice carried. 'They're our comrades. We've teamed up to... to... Oh look. Here's Katerina.'

'Hello my darling,' the comtesse gushed, and embraced her daughter.

'So,' Katerina said as she untangled herself from her mother. 'What do you want?'

'To see that you're all right, of course.'

'And what else?'

A flash of irritation darkened the comtesse's features. She hid it behind her kerchief.

'Nothing really,' the comtesse said, glancing back to the footman who had the papers. It seemed that her daughter was keen to be rid of her, which meant that she'd probably be willing to sign just about anything just to accomplish that. Unfortunately, d'Artaud was likely to start asking all kinds of awkward questions. He might be many things, the comtesse decided, but he was no fool.

'I wonder if you'd like to come for a drive with me?' the comtesse suggested, happily. 'I'd like to talk to you. We didn't really get off to a good start, I suppose. And although I only wanted what was best for you... Well, things didn't quite work out as I expected.'

'Unfortunately, I don't have time right now,' Katerina told her. 'Maybe you can come back tomorrow?'

'Yes,' the comtesse nodded after a second of rapid calculation. She had waited for almost two decades to inherit her late husband's share of the Hansebourg fortune. She could wait for one more day. 'Yes, I'll come tomorrow. Maybe we can go to a dressmakers.'

'Good idea,' Katerina smiled. 'Well then. Until tomorrow.'

The comtesse, realising that she was being dismissed, accepted the indignity and kissed her daughter again. This time Katerina kissed her back.

'Oh, by the way, comtesse,' she called out as the older woman walked back to her carriage.

'Call me mother, my dear,' the comtesse cooed.

'Very well, mother. I just wanted to ask you to bring a lawyer with you. I want to go over my inheritance.'

'Your inheritance?' the comtesse asked lightly.

'As a widow, I am entitled to whatever is left of my dowry. And as Rabin didn't have a chance to spend any of it, I expect to recover it all.'

The comtesse gave no sign of the chill that ran down her spine.

'I'm afraid you're mistaken, my dear,' she said, kindly. 'But don't worry. I won't let you go without.'

It was Florin's peal of laughter that finally cracked the veneer of the comtesse's composure.

'Please accept my compliments,' he told her good-naturedly. 'I used to make a living at cards… '

'Some living,' Lorenzo muttered.

'Yes, a good living.' Florin pretended to have misheard his friend. 'But you, Comtesse Hansebourg, have got the best gambler's face I've ever seen.'

He swept off his hat and made a low bow. The comtesse, her face suddenly as pale as a corpse's, apart from two flares of red which burned on the elegant angles of her cheekbones, froze. She looked at her head guard, a murderous light in her eyes. The guard, a heavy-set thug whose face was marked with the scars of a dozen successful retreats, gestured towards the men that waited, swords drawn, along one side of the yard. He shook his head, and the comtesse, thwarted, started to grind her teeth.

'Well,' she said, finally containing her temper with an act of almost superhuman will. 'You must have your little joke, I suppose, but I will bring the lawyer tomorrow. Who knows, a man who has spent a lifetime studying the law might even know a little more about it than Monsieur d'Artaud.'

With that, the comtesse turned and, resisting the temptation to storm out, paced carefully back to the carriage.

She would bring a lawyer tomorrow. She had no doubt that she could bully or bribe the old fool into lying for her. She'd also bring a lot more guards. Let Florin d'Artaud try to interfere then.

Please gods, the comtesse thought with a small, vicious smile. Let him try.

BUT THAT NIGHT, even as the comtesse was cajoling the family lawyer into breaking just about every one of the rules which supposedly bound his profession, the fog returned to Bordeleaux. It swallowed up the ships that lay in the harbour, and slipped up the streets that radiated away from the docks. It drifted over the labourers' quarter and then prowled into the Sump. Eventually, the mass of it grew heavy enough to creep up the slopes to encompass even the wealthier quarters.

As the temple bells began to ring midnight, the fog had even reached the foot of the Lady's temple. It swirled around the smoothly chiselled marble and ancient granite foundations, the stinking billows of it making the stone slick with beads of dirty moisture, and crept guiltily into the portals and arches of the lower tiers. Soon, the whole great sprawling mess of Bordeleaux was hidden beneath the sodden mass of the fog.

Only the pillar upon which the form of the Lady stood rose above it. Her golden eyes gazed down sightlessly, doubly blinded by night and fog. Yet, however heavy the fog, and however dark the night, she watched her people as they slept or crept or coupled in the endless maze of the city beneath her.

And, far below, knowing that she watched, Katerina prepared to act.

CHAPTER FOURTEEN

RAFAEL WASN'T A bad man. Not at all. He was kind enough, in his way, and he was never unnecessarily cruel. Which meant, he considered, that he was never really cruel at all.

No, Rafael thought as he padded through the fog. Considering who I am, I'm actually a pretty decent sort of man. I don't even grope the women, although all the rest do.

A low whistle from ahead distracted him from this happy line of thought. He froze, waiting. Coils of mist wrapped themselves around him, the cold grey tongues muffling the few distant sounds of Bordeleaux's deserted streets.

Despite this, Rafael could sense the rest of his comrades as they too waited in the darkness. They'd hunted through the foggy streets dozens of times in the past, and each time they'd become more proficient, more aware. Silent and unseen, they slipped through the darkness with the instinctive coordination of a shoal of piranhas.

Like piranhas, their leaders had developed a finely tuned appreciation of what was prey and what was not. That was why, as the cobbled boots of two longshoremen echoed drunkenly through the murk, Rafael and the rest of the slavers remained still.

Only when the dock hands had turned a corner did the little party scurry back into motion, the felt slippers they wore over their boots masking any sound. They turned one corner, then the next. Then they froze again.

Rafael waited and this time his patience was rewarded. The murk in front of him darkened into a shadow that resolved itself into the shape of a hooded man. His leader wrapped his arm around Rafael's shoulder. Leaning close against him, he made a funnel of his hand and pressed it against the slaver's ear. Only then did the leader whisper his instructions, speaking in the smoothed-down language of those used to dealing in silence.

'One man. Paffed out. We'll gif him a niff of the fleeping humour anyway. You and Wallaf can take him back to the wagon. Underftand?'

'Aye,' Rafael whispered back, taking care to avoid breaking discipline with the sibilant hiss of a 'sir'.

He followed his leader towards their prospective victim, and realised that he could smell the man before he saw him. The whiff of stale sweat and cheap brandy was strong enough to cut through even the seaweed stench of the fog.

Their victim gave a sudden snort and the five men froze, waiting until he had slipped back down into the carefree depths of his drunken stupor.

Only then did Rafael's leader move in. Even to his comrades, the slaver's silent movements could scarcely be seen. Only the sudden acid whiff of the sleeping humours signalled his advance and, to ears trained by a thousand such painless assaults, the sound of the victim's changed breathing pattern told the rest of the story.

'Rafael and Wallaf.' Their leader's disembodied voice drifted back from the body. 'He's under. Take him away, but be careful to carry him face down. Don't want another one to drown in his own vomit.'

Wonderful, Rafael thought sourly. Why do good men like me always get such rotten luck? Why doesn't anyone else ever get the pukers?

Rafael had more sense than to voice these thoughts. Instead, he grabbed the inert form of his captive, waited for Wallaf to lift the arm and leg on the other side, and set off back to the wagon.

A few moments later, their unconscious captive, his body rebelling against the noxious stew of the rotgut he'd drunk and the narcotics he'd inhaled, did indeed begin to throw up. Rafael winced with disgust as the bile splattered off the cobblestones and onto the felt of his boots.

'Come on,' Wallaf chided him as he came to a stop. 'Don't hang about. Let's get rid of this one and get back. It's our turn to take one of the women.'

Rafael rolled his eyes at the leer in his comrade's voice. Our turn to take one of the women indeed.

He'd never be so damned lucky.

Good men never were.

'This is madness,' Florin muttered as he peered into the fog. He, Lorenzo, and two other men were sitting in the darkness of one of the houses that faced the street. The wattle had been scraped away and a pair of holes had been cut through it. Florin was peering through one now, a thin viewing slit that gave a waist-high view of the street outside.

At least it was supposed to give a waist-high view of the street outside. In fact, all he could see at the moment was a blank wall of sodden darkness.

Sitting beside him, Lorenzo was using the other hole. The strand of thread that he held disappeared out through it at ankle height. He kept a firm grip on the piece of cotton, the other end of which was firmly nailed to the other side of the street. If anybody walked through the invisible line then he would be able to feel them, but they shouldn't notice a thing as the cotton was plucked through his fingers.

That, at least, was the theory.

'This,' Florin muttered, with an increasing amount of mutinous unhappiness, 'really is madness.'

'Congratulations,' Lorenzo told him.

'What do you mean?'

'That's the hundredth time you've said that in the last hour and each time has been more irritating than the last.'

Florin's scowl was hidden by the darkness. 'I suppose you think that this is a good idea then?'

'No, I think it's madness.'

'Then what are you complaining about?'

'Just because I think something, doesn't mean I have to keep saying it over and over again.'

'Oh no. Not you. You've got more important things to do. You've got to sit on your arse and twiddle your thumbs. You've got to start arguments about nothing. You've—'

'Sssshhhh,' came the angry hiss from outside. Florin, realising that his voice had been getting gradually louder, fell silent. He stared back out of the viewing slit, contenting himself with a black look at the nothingness outside. Although Katerina had been close enough to hear him, he couldn't see the slightest trace of her body.

'This,' Lorenzo whispered, 'is madness.'

In spite of his frayed nerves, Florin sniggered. He lowered his head to catch the noise in his hand. When he looked back up, he was punished by a flash of something in the murk outside. Something that could have been anything or nothing.

Not for the first time he thought about the ways in which he might sabotage this effort. To let the monstrous slavers know that Katerina was lethal bait rather than the tasty morsel she appeared to be.

But how could he? And anyway, even if he could, that might make things even worse. They might just kill her outright and then run, disappearing back into the night to deny him even the cold comforts of revenge.

I'd find a way to get them, Florin thought distractedly. Whatever the cost. If they killed her, I'd think of a way to find out where they were, and when I knew that I'd....

He stopped, self-awareness painting a wry smile on his face.

Katerina's madness, it seemed, was contagious.

Before he could find any solace in the thought, Lorenzo gripped his bicep. Florin opened his mouth to complain, before remembering what the signal meant.

Quietly, scarcely daring to breathe as he scooted out of the darkness, he made his way out of the hovel and into the courtyard beyond. He brushed his way down the line of men who waited there, Lorenzo at his heels, and crept towards the sentry who leant against the half-open gate.

The man jumped with surprise when Florin touched him, then relaxed when he realised who it was. Katerina had taken up her station directly opposite the gate, leaning against the wall on the other side of the street like countless other professional women, even though the fog had driven most of them off the streets tonight.

Florin, speaking in a voice that was little louder than a breath, whispered a single word into the guard's ear.

'Anything?'

The man shrugged.

Florin squinted into the night, all of his senses straining. Katerina had agreed to let out a single shriek as she allowed herself to be taken. But there hadn't been so much as a muffled cry or more than a hint of movement in the grey stew of the fog.

Maybe Lorenzo had been mistaken, Florin thought. Maybe he'd just dropped the thread.

Maybe.

In spite of Katerina's strictest instructions, he pushed past the sentry and into the street itself. Nothing moved. The only change that had taken place since darkness had fallen, was the new smell that had insinuated itself into the rotten stench of the street. It was acrid, and curiously inorganic, like the chemicals that wafted around the engravers' district.

Florin held out his hand in front of his face and realised that he couldn't see it.

Ah, to the hells with it, he thought. This *is* madness.

'Katerina,' he called, his voice sounding defiantly loud after the hours of silence.

There was no answer, and Florin silently scolded himself for the twinge of panic that flared in his chest. After all, he'd only been told off by her a few moments ago.

'Katerina!' he repeated, raising his voice as he marched purposefully across the street. 'The fog's too damned thick. We'll try this another night.'

Still no answer.

'You might as well speak up,' Florin said, then paused as his fingers brushed against the wall on the opposite side of the street. The wall she should have been standing against. 'I'm going to keep talking. Why not call me an idiot now and have done with it?'

He tried to keep his voice light as he felt his way along the wall, fingertips trailing along the damp surface.

'Come on, Katerina. I'm serious.'

Silence.

'This isn't funny,' he said, voice sharpening with anger.

He glared around into the darkness, brows furrowed. Then he looked downwards, his gaze drawn by the suggestion of something pale lying on the ground.

He knelt down beside the patch of colour and brushed a fingertip across it. When he realised what it was, that unfamiliar tug of panic returned; the terrifying sense of a world sliding out of control.

The thing on the ground was Katerina's woollen shawl.

'Katerina!'

Florin bellowed out her name. But although he cried out so loudly that something seemed to tear in his throat, the only response as the fog swallowed her name was some distant barking.

Across the street, the gates swung open and the swirling currents of the fog began to glow in the light of a torch. It illuminated both Lorenzo, who carried it, and the crowd of unhappy faces that followed him. The men's heads seemed to float like disembodied apparitions in the liquid sea of fog.

'What's up, boss?' Lorenzo asked, slipping back into the honorific of their first acquaintance.

'She's gone!' Florin wailed, eyes wide in the darkness.

'Which way?'

Florin was about to swear at his comrade for asking such a damn fool question. Then he paused. In the torchlight he could see the timber frame that Katerina had been waiting by. It was perhaps a dozen paces away from where he'd found her shawl, which suggested that she had been taken in that direction.

Katerina had planned to leave a trail of markers, just in case they did lose her, but the shawl wasn't one of them.

Unless, of course, it was.

For one agonised moment, Florin balanced on a razor's edge of indecision. Then he snapped out his judgement.

'I think it's this way. Lorenzo and the first six, you come with me. Butcher, take your lot the other way in case I'm wrong.'

'Shall we douse the torches, like Katerina said?' the Butcher asked, his earnest face shining with moisture.

'No, damn that. In fact, damn all of it. Let's just get her back.'

'Right you are.' The big man nodded happily, and without a further word the two groups pelted off into the murk in desperate search for their missing leader.

Within seconds, Florin came upon a new dilemma, in the shape of a crossroads. Seizing a torch from one of the men, he rushed over to one of the roads and, bent double, started to search the muddy ground for any clue as to which way Katerina's captors had gone.

But despite the slurried condition of the Sump's unpaved roads there was no sign. One footprint looked the same as another, and there were none of the scraps of cloth Katerina had planned to drop.

Florin turned back to where his men waited and cursed. There weren't enough of them as it was, and he knew that if he divided them up again, even if they did find Katerina's captors, they'd be hard pressed to do anything about it.

Once more there was that painful moment of uncertainty. Once more, Florin decided on the least worst course of action.

'Right, there's no sign of her. We're going to split up. You three go left, you three go right, and me and Lorenzo will go forwards. If you see anything, especially if you find one of her markers, start making a noise. We might end up close enough to help each other. All right?'

The men muttered their assent and headed off.

One of them paused before the night swallowed him up to call something back over his shoulder.

'Go with the Lady,' he said, and the call echoed back from the other group.

But Florin didn't hear them. He and Lorenzo had already gone, pelting down the street ahead.

Within moments they came to another junction. Florin wiped a sheen of sweat and mist from his forehead and groaned miserably.

There was no way they'd be able to find anybody in this rat-run. No way at all.

And anyway, who could be sure that the filthy things that had taken Katerina would use the street? They'd shown a horrible cockroach skill in scurrying up to the rooftops. Maybe they were racing from one row of thatch to the next even now, with Katerina's body grasped in their filthy claws, razored teeth slavering at the thought of how sweet her flesh would taste...

No, he told himself. Don't think about that now.

'Lorenzo,' he said, almost pleading. 'what are we going to do?'

'Keep on going,' the older man replied promptly.

'Yes, but where? Every twenty feet there's another road.'

'Just keep going,' Lorenzo said, sounding strangely confident, 'and have faith in the Lady.'

Even in the midst of his panic, Florin felt his mouth drop open in amazement.

'Don't tell me that you've bought all that stuff too?' he asked, not quite believing what his cynical old villain of a friend had just said.

Lorenzo just shrugged. 'What else can we do?' he asked, and led off.

What else indeed, Florin thought, and set off into the darkness after him.

RAFAEL FOLLOWED WALLAF reluctantly back into the tangled streets of the Sump. Not content with vomiting all over the place on the way to the cart, their captive had even soiled himself when they'd finally rolled him over the tailgate.

Despite his good nature, it had all been too much for Rafael. He'd given the dirty swine a good beating before setting out again. The fact that the victim had remained unconscious throughout meant that it had only taken a moment, and that was just as well. As soon as they'd dropped their charge off, Wallaf was itching to be away.

Personally, Rafael couldn't see the point in the rush. They wouldn't get any more gold for carrying more bodies than anybody else. Not that Wallaf had the brains to realise this. Even now, the idiot seemed almost on the verge of breaking into a run.

'Wallaf,' Rafael whispered, catching up with his comrade and laying a hand on his arm.

'What's wrong?'

'Nothing. But let's go a bit slower. I've got something in my boot.'

'All right. I'll wait while you take it out, but hurry up.'

Despite the impatience in his voice the slaver came to a stop and Rafael cursed silently. Now he was going to have to go through the pantomime of removing his boot.

'Just a minute then,' he whispered, trying not to sound too miserable. Leaning against one wall, he fumbled about with his buckle, wondering how long he should draw this out for. But even as Wallaf began to complain about the delay, both men heard the clatter of approaching footsteps.

They didn't need to discuss how to respond. Whoever was coming was obviously both healthy and alert. He wasn't alone, either. Barely a second after the two slavers had heard his footsteps, another set joined them.

Although, thought Rafael as he sidled up against the wall, maybe that wasn't a bad thing. After all, who would run through a blinding night like this? A thief, perhaps, or an assassin.

Whoever he was, he was obviously being chased by the second man.

Rafael laid a hand on Wallaf's arm, his whisper almost inaudible beneath the clattering feet of the approaching men.

'We'll let the first man go past and then grab the one who's following him,' he suggested, his breath warm in Wallaf's ear.

'I don't know...' his comrade said, shaking his head. 'I mean, why bother?'

Rafael almost told the truth, which was that a fresh captive would give them an excuse to go back to the wagon, where they could hang round until the night's work was finished.

But, knowing Wallaf's predilections as he did, he realised that another reason was needed.

'Remember the boss said he'd pay extra for independent captures?'

'Only if they didn't bring any trouble.'

'This won't bring trouble. Anyway, think of what a gold crown would buy at Madame Gourmelon's.'

Wallaf thought. As he did so, the currents of the fog began to glow a muddy orange as the running man's torch came into range. He lowered his eyes and waited in silence as the man stumbled around a pothole and bolted blindly past him.

'All right,' he hissed, reaching a sudden decision. 'We'll take the second one.'

'Good. I'll trip him, and when he's down you give him a whack on the head.'

Wallaf rumbled his assent as the second set of footsteps approached. They were slower than the first, and even through the fog-quilted air, the slavers could hear the painful wheezing of their target's breath.

He sounds exhausted, Rafael thought. Excellent.

And with that he slunk forward to intercept the slowing runner.

He intercepted him sooner than he'd intended to. This one wasn't carrying a torch, so Rafael had nothing to go on but his sense of hearing. Unfortunately, sound was little more reliable than sight in the reeking stew of the fog, and before Rafael could turn to grapple with him, his victim had run into him. The accidental impact knocked Rafael to the ground and tore a cry of pain from his lungs.

Even so he had the presence of mind to grab the runner around the legs as he collapsed. The man cursed as he fell, then yelled something out into the night. When the two of them hit the ground he too called, summoning Wallaf. Somehow, the idiot seemed to have gotten lost in the fog.

A fist clipped his shoulder, a lucky shot that would have knocked him senseless had it connected, and Rafael cried out again.

'Wallaf!'

Even as he called, he heard the sibilant hiss of steel being drawn inches from his ear.

Adrenaline exploded through his system and he snatched upwards. His fingers found scrawny biceps above bony elbows and he tightened his grip, surprised at how small his victim was.

But even though there was no bulge of muscle, his opponent was damnably strong. He twisted and turned, wriggling like a netted eel, and even as Rafael felt his grip loosening, a knee jabbed into his side.

'Wallaf!' he called again, desperation tightening his voice into a scream.

And there, suddenly, was the shape of a saviour. Looming up through the fog he blundered towards the two struggling men, his form a faceless blur in the fog-smeared light of a sodden torch.

Rafael opened his mouth to tell the imbecile to hurry up when he realised that Wallaf didn't carry a torch.

With a sudden burst of energy, he released his would-be victim's arms and kicked him away, scrabbling to his feet as he did so. The flare of a torch swung past his left ear and he sprang away from it, felted boots slipping on the cobbles as he turned to run.

Before he could escape, bony fingers closed around his ankles and yanked them from under him. He shrieked as he fell, Wallaf's name once more on his lips. This time, though, it was more of a curse than a plea.

The filthy coward had obviously deserted him.

Rafael didn't manage to break his fall.

Instead he broke his elbow.

It cracked on a cobblestone, shattering as easily as frost, and he screamed with pain. Tears spilled from his eyes as he rolled onto his back, and unconsciousness hovered nearby, as seductive as a soft bed after a hard day.

He fought the lure of oblivion and scrabbled back to his feet. But it was already too late. Strong hands seized his weakening limbs, and the blur of knuckles ended both his struggles and his pain.

'I THINK THAT he's awake,' Florin said, prodding their captive with the toe of his boot. He lay on the broken cobbles where he had fallen, as still as a corpse apart from the trickle of blood that leaked from his nose.

'I don't know,' Lorenzo frowned and bent down to check the man's bonds. They had used the rope that they'd found coiled around his waist to tie him up. It wasn't until they'd done so that they realised that, concealed beneath the hemp, the slaver had also been carrying three sets of manacles.

Florin toyed with one of them now, the *clink* of the chain links the clearest thing in the murky torch light.

'He's awake. Notice how awkwardly he's lying? If he was unconscious he'd have rolled into a more comfortable position.'

The two men studied Rafael's rigid form suspiciously.

'Perhaps you killed him,' Lorenzo said, and kicked the captive thoughtfully. 'Why did you have to hit him so hard?'

'The thing was,' Florin said, sarcastically, 'that if I'd let him kill you I'd have missed your sunny disposition.'

Lorenzo spat into the fog. 'That's true,' he allowed.

For a moment, the two men stood in contemplative silence, the only sound the clinking of the manacles Florin was toying with.

'Well,' Florin said what both of them had been thinking. 'There's no doubt about him being one of the kidnappers, but I don't see any sign of whiskers or a tail.'

'Maybe the rat-things work in partnership with men?'

'No.' Florin shook his head. 'That wouldn't happen. Who'd trust such revolting creatures?'

Lorenzo grimaced. 'You mean the humans or the monsters?'

Florin glanced at him and winked. 'See what I mean?' he said. 'How would I have survived without such sweet-natured observation? Anyway, we've got no time for this. Let's wake our friend up and ask him some questions.'

'If he's wakeable.'

'Oh, he's wakeable all right,' Florin decided. His face hardened as he got down on his haunches beside the man and, despite the fact that the miserable wretch had probably had a hand in Katerina's disappearance, he had to steel himself for what he was about to do.

'Hey you,' he said, waving the torch back and forth over the man's determinedly shut eyes. 'Wake up.'

Rafael remained still. There was no way he was going to give up his desperate attempt to avoid the unpleasantness that was to come. He was debating whether or not to start snoring when Florin addressed him again.

'Wake up,' he said, 'or I'll cut your ear off.'

The slaver swallowed, then cursed himself for the lapse. Could his captors have seen his adam's apple rise and fall? Would they...

The touch of a knife, the steel as cold as the grave, silenced his thoughts. It rested on the sensitive skin in the fold between ear and scalp, and almost as soon as he was aware of what it was, Rafael could feel the sting of its first, tiny cut.

'Don't hurt me,' he whined, eyes snapping open. Two figures, made large by his terror, loomed over him. He whimpered at the sight of them and his bladder loosened.

The one holding the knife wasn't so bad. It was his comrade. His features, distorted by the torch-lit glow of the fog, seemed scarcely human.

'Please don't let your goblin hurt me either,' Rafael whimpered. The whites of his eyes shone with tears as he gazed at Lorenzo, as petrified as a rat caught in a cobra's glare.

'Charming,' Lorenzo muttered, but Florin wasn't to be distracted.

'You've got something of ours,' he told his captive, his face a careful blank, 'and we want it back.'

'No, I haven't,' Rafael jabbered. 'No. Not me. I'm no thief! I was just out to get some air when your... your friend ran into me. It's all been a mistake. A terrible mis–'

'Be quiet,' Florin told him. 'Just tell us where you've taken the woman you snatched, and I'll let you live.'

A dozen stratagems rushed through Rafael's head, each wilder than the last. Why did things like this always have to happen to him?

'Of course, the longer it takes you to tell me, the less you'll want to live,' said Florin and, with a sudden turn of his wrist, he sliced a strip of flesh from the top of his captive's ear.

Rafael screamed, a surprisingly shrill sound for a man. Then, when he'd finished screaming, he started to sob.

Florin and Lorenzo looked on, unmoved.

'Now then,' Florin said, the calmness of his voice giving no clue to the burning impatience which beat in his chest. 'Tell me where she is.'

'I don't know what you mean,' Rafael blubbered.

Florin ignored the flicker of doubt the man's denial brought. Despite his equipment, he could be telling the truth. Perhaps he wanted the manacles for some other offence, some crime that had nothing to do with Katerina.

But Florin didn't show his doubt any more than he showed his impatience. Innocent or guilty, this snivelling criminal was the only lead they had.

'If you really don't know where she is, then you have my... my commiserations,' he said, selecting the word as carefully as a surgeon selecting a new scalpel. 'Because if you don't tell me where she is I'm going to keep on cutting you until there's nothing left to cut.'

Florin released his captive's ear and placed the glistening edge of his bloodied dagger beneath his running nose.

Rafael's eyes bulged as he tried to look down at the blade.

'Now, where is she?'

The slaver sobbed. What could he do? If he informed on the boss, his punishment would be swift and hideous.

On the other hand, he thought, as the first trickle of blood started from beneath his nose, it couldn't be any worse than what was already happening to him.

'All right,' he said. 'All right. I'll tell you. It wasn't me who took her. It was the others. I didn't even see any women tonight. I always get the stinking ones, the drunks and vagrants. Never the women.'

Even in extremis, the resentment was clear in Rafael's tone.

'That doesn't sound very fair,' Lorenzo offered, and the slaver looked up at him thankfully.

'No, it isn't,' he agreed. 'It isn't at all. I hate working for the bosses. But they, ah, he made me. Yes, that's right. I didn't have any choice.'

'How awful,' Florin said, and wiped his knife on the slaver's tunic.

'Yes, it is. I'm not a bad man. Not really. But I was afraid.'

'Well, let's help each other,' Florin said, hiding his disgust. 'You tell me where these villains took Katerina, and I'll wipe them out for you.'

'Thank you.' Rafael, who'd already realised that if he was going to betray his comrades then the betrayal had better be lethal, quickly agreed. 'But there aren't enough of us. The slavers are at least twenty. They're such damned cowards that they never attack anybody that they don't massively outnumber.'

'Cowards indeed,' Lorenzo muttered.

'Despicable,' Florin agreed. 'Luckily we have the men for it. We'll untie your feet and go and get them now. Oh, and when I untie your feet, remember to run in the same direction as we do. If not…'

Florin grinned mirthlessly as he handed Rafael the tip of his ear back. His eyes were as cold as he meant them to be, and the torchlight lent a bloodstained aspect to his teeth.

'I won't try to run,' Rafael told his new master. 'I want to see those swine killed as much as you do but it will do no good to look for them now.'

'What?'

Rafael cringed. 'I mean, they'll have gone. One of the worthless scum, an idiot called Wallaf, Sigmar curse him, ran away when I attacked your friend. He'll have informed on me by now, the traitorous dog. And the boss always calls off the hunt when things like this happen.'

'Then what's the use of you?' Florin snarled, snatching the dagger back out of its sheath.

'I can show you where the slaves are sold. I'll show you, no problem. We should have plenty of time to get there.'

'Perhaps,' Lorenzo insinuated, 'he's lying.'

'No. No, I'm not. I want you to catch them all. If you don't, then they'll kill me.'

Rafael looked from one of his captors to the other, eyes pleading.

'You must believe me.'

'I suppose that we must.' Florin shrugged his shoulders. 'But remember, betray me and your death will be a long time coming.'

Rafael, who could well believe it, nodded. Florin cut the ropes that bound the slaver's ankles and he struggled to his feet. He wiped the tears and the mucus from his face and tried to ignore the cooling patch of urine that had dampened the inside of his breeches.

Only then did he break the bad news.

'Of course,' he said, swallowing nervously, 'to get to where the slaves are sold we'll need a boat.'

He cringed, expecting a blow, but none came.

'Why a boat?'

'It's in a cove. A hidden cove. I don't know how to get to the tunnel, but I know where it is. Sort of. At least, I think that I can recognise the bit of coastline.'

Florin looked at Lorenzo. Then he shrugged.

'By boat it will be, then. Anything else we need to know? Good. Let's go.'

Rafael stumbled along in front of his new master, silently cursing his fortune. Not that it was his fortune's fault. No, it was Wallaf's. Whatever happened to him, or to any of his erstwhile comrades, was no more than they deserved.

As his new masters drove him into a run, Rafael was amazed to find that, despite the pain and the fear, he was actually looking forward to seeing his fellow slavers wiped out.

It just goes to show, he told himself, what an honourable man I am.

CHAPTER FIFTEEN

Katerina awoke in total darkness. At least, she awoke in total physical darkness. Despite there being no light, a pantheon of multi-coloured swirls danced behind her closed eyelids, moving in time with the agonising pulse that beat in her temples.

She took a deep, shuddering breath, and leaned forward against the fist of nausea that clenched her stomach. As she did so, chains clinked in the darkness. Her chains. She licked the dry skin of her lips nervously and realised for the first time that manacles bound her wrists. They were crude things, heavy bracelets of roughly cast iron linked with a short chain. Another chain passed between them, the length of it disappearing off into the gods alone knew where.

Katerina waited for the wave of nausea to pass, then opened her eyes, willing herself to relax, to observe. The first thing that she noticed was the unforgiving hardness of the granite floor beneath her stiff muscles. Even though her body was still patterned with worrying blotches of total numbness, she could feel how uneven the surface was upon which she lay. How uneven and how wet.

She tried to swallow, her painfully dry tongue rasping against the roof of her desiccated mouth. In the distance she could hear the metronome tap of water plinking down onto stone, an unnecessary reminder of her thirst. Stifling a groan, she rolled up into a sitting position, her chains rattling even as they gave.

The chink of metal was answered by a low growl from the darkness. Katerina froze. Then, realising that her verminous captors would soon be upon her and that she had no time for hesitation, she stumbled into the next stage of the plan. Flexing the numbness out of her fingers, she reached up to bury them deep within the tangled mass of her hair. Anxious not to rattle her chains again, she moved as slowly as melting ice, her fingers sorting through her tresses. They were wild and knotted, which was how she'd arranged them before taking her place in the fog. Now, though, they were also matted with some sticky substance that felt suspiciously like blood.

But that was no problem, Katerina told herself as she sifted through her hair. In fact, it was good. It made it less likely that the copper wire had been spotted. And sure enough, there it was. Her fingertips closed around the cold metallic thread that she'd tied into her tresses, and she smiled with satisfaction.

Another sound floated out of the darkness and Katerina froze again. This time she realised that the noise was no bestial threat. It was just a groan of all too human misery. She pursed her lips thoughtfully and, holding the length of wire between her teeth, twisted her wrists around in the manacles until she could reach one of the keyholes. She brushed the pad of her thumb across it and, judging the width and the depth of the mechanism, started to twist the wire into the right shape. It was finicky work, especially in the darkness, but Lorenzo had taught her well. The locks he'd set her to pick had been finer than these great iron lumps, and he'd had the foresight to complete her tuition with the aid of a blindfold.

More calls started up in the darkness as she slotted the pick into the first lock and set to work. By now, some of them had become recognisably human, slurred words that echoed off the unseen walls of this unlit world.

Katerina tried to remember how she had come to waken down here. She couldn't remember seeing any sign of the vermin that had taken her, nor could she remember any sort of struggle.

She'd been poisoned, she supposed. Like Sergei.

Like Sergei…

She scowled and felt for the bundle of rags that she carried inside her blouse. They were still there, as useless as the embroidery that decorated them. The plan had been for her to drop a trail of them to help Florin and the others to follow her down to this lair.

So, she thought, her chin jutting defiantly. They might not find me.

They probably won't find me.

So what?

As if in reward for her bravado, the first barrel of the locking mechanism clicked back. It was perhaps the most beautiful sound that Katerina had ever heard, and her relieved smile set her teeth glittering in the darkness. Pausing only to rub her wrist, she immediately set to work on the other manacle.

But even as she realised that she would have to twist the wire into a new shape for this one, the first flicker of torchlight danced into sight.

Katerina felt the first pangs of desperation as her piece of wire bent against the mechanism of the second lock. She looked up, eyes widening with fear as the torch-bearer approached. Its form was still hidden by the curve in what she now saw was a natural cave, but its shadow, twisted and monstrous, towered up on one of the walls.

Katerina squinted down at her chains, the metal now a grey blur in the lifting darkness. Then she realised that, in fact, she had no need to worry. Not about her chains, anyway. Now that she had unlocked one of her manacles all she had to do was to take it off and the chain that bound her to the other captives would fall away.

With a flicker of relief, she turned to study her fellow prisoners, watching as the shadows receded from their prone forms. Most of them were now trying to struggle to their feet, but not many of them seemed able to make it. Even as Katerina watched, one man, the tarred horn of his topknot marking him out as a sailor, collapsed back down onto the granite. Something cracked as he fell and his muffled curse was silenced.

Beyond him, somebody else fell to their knees and started to sob, a steady wailing that was punctuated here and there by the splatter of vomit on the unforgiving stone. Katerina felt her own stomach roll in sympathy as the sour smell washed over her.

'Time to wake up,' a voice called out, warm despite the hard consonants of its echo.

Katerina squinted towards the torch and realised for the first time that it was being carried, not by one of the verminous things that she had expected, but by a man.

'Come on,' the slaver called again. 'Don't make us use the whips on you.'

More figures were following him into the cave, each of them swaddled in the same dark robes, and each of their faces obscured by voluminous hoods. Even so, Katerina realised that they were also men, their laughter all too human as they approached their captives.

At their master's mention of whips, they unfurled a selection of the weapons, snapping them in the air as obediently as musicians following their conductor's direction.

There was a scream of pain as they selected their first victims.

'Come on, come on,' the chief slaver said, his good humour evaporating into sudden impatience as he swaggered amongst his captives.

Now that several more torches had been borne into the cave, Katerina could see the raw expanse of it. Its broken granite surfaces glittered beneath a sheen of dripping moisture, shattering the torchlight into a constellation of tiny sparks. The only true darkness left was that which lay within the hungry maws of the tunnels that led to these depths. They gaped open as if in anticipation of the human flesh that writhed so miserably below them.

Katerina was warmed by a fleeting memory of home, but her reminiscences were broken by the cracking of whips and a chorus of high-pitched shrieking.

She closed the unlocked manacle back around her wrist, using the wire to stop the mechanism from locking, and bowed her head.

By the time the slavers had reached her, she was indistinguishable from any other of the cowering people that they had captured. Her head remained bowed. Her shoulders remained slumped. And of the rage that flared within her there was no sign apart from the green fire of her carefully downcast eyes.

Eventually the slavers, content that all was well and already looking forward to spending the Arabyan's gold, dragged the first of the chain gang to his feet and led the way into the darkness below.

CAPTAIN CULVER WASN'T enjoying his beef. Not that it had been badly cooked. Far from it. Within the crust of the roast the flesh was as pink as the first bloom of a rose, and the juices ran as clear and as succulent as a fat man's dream.

Still, despite the fact that he hadn't eaten all day, the excise man barely tasted the meat. Not even the succulent smell that drifted around the wood panelling of his dining room was enough to dissolve the knot in his stomach or the clench of his fists.

The problem wasn't his wife's tongue. Over the years it had grown sharper even as the rest of her had grown fatter, but that no longer bothered Culver. He'd long since learned to ignore both. No, what bothered him tonight was the fact that she'd invited her father over to dinner.

The admiral, who would never dream of letting his son-in-law address him as anything else, wasn't a happy man. At least, he wasn't a conventionally happy man. The flabby contours of his features were red with indignation and above these burning cheeks the man's bulging eyes seemed ready to pop.

Even so, Culver had a sneaking suspicion that, as far as his father-in-law was concerned, this was as good as it got. When it came right down to it, the captain suspected, an evening spent telling his son-in-law that he was nine kinds of fool made the old scrote as happy as a pig in shit. He might scowl and he might bluster but, however outraged the admiral sounded, it never blunted his appetite for his son-in-law's meat.

Or his wine.

Culver tried not to look too annoyed as the admiral waved a forkful of the finest Bretonnian beef at the portrait of his mother and father, whilst complaining about his lack of navigational skills.

'You should never lose a boat in the Bite,' the admiral said, and paused to swallow his meat.

But only briefly.

'No. A good officer should know where all of the snags are. I did!'

'I bet you did, daddy,' said Culver's wife.

Culver tried to ignore her reproachful look and pushed a piece of meat from one side of his plate to the other. Not for the first time did he wonder if he'd be able to roll a body overboard without any of his men mentioning it.

Probably not, he thought miserably as the admiral started to blather on about what he'd have done to some rascal caught smuggling brandy.

'Got to make an example,' he bellowed, even though his son-in-law was sitting no more than an arm's length away. 'Got to string the blighters up.'

'How many did you string up?' Culver snapped, even though he knew that any defiance just made things even worse.

The admiral spluttered like a bomb with a damp fuse, but his daughter, who never had any doubts about whose side she was on, stepped to his defence.

'You know that daddy had to defend the northern reaches,' she scolded her husband. 'He didn't waste his time catching rum runners. Much less letting them go.'

She reached out to squeeze the admiral's hand. He squeezed back.

Culver scowled sourly at this display of intimacy.

'And another thing,' the admiral, who'd washed away his momentary silence with a full glass of wine, continued. 'You should never have accepted quarter from any damned smuggler. I know you'd ruined your ship, but you should have swum instead. Better than the dishonour.'

The admiral glared at his son-in-law until the lure of more beef distracted him.

'You should say thank you to daddy for getting you a new commission,' the old bastard's daughter piped up as her father fought his way though a lump of gristle. For a moment, Culver wondered if it might choke him, but as usual he was disappointed. 'If it wasn't for him we'd have been out on the streets. Oh, I was so embarrassed.'

The admiral grunted his assent and once more Culver's thoughts turned to murder. Perhaps I should do it anyway, he thought as he watched his father-in-law open another bottle of his wine and throw the cork across the room.

'Well?' his wife said expectantly.

'Well what?'

'Say thank you.'

'I already have,' Culver reminded her. 'At least three times every time he comes to visit. Which seems to be every other night.'

'Oh, you're so ungrateful,' she cried, and the admiral took the time out from drinking his son-in-law's wine (two crowns a bottle) to glare at him with even more disapproval than usual.

'See here, sir...' he began, when one of the maids knocked and let herself into the dining room.

'There's somebody to see you, sir,' she said.

'Who?' the admiral asked. 'Tell them we're busy!'

'Uh, no sir. The other sir. The master of the house. Sir.'

Culver grinned, and resolved to double her pay.

'And who is it, my dear?' he asked, smiling even wider as he saw the admiral's cheeks darken from red to puce.

'He wouldn't say, sir. He... oh!'

The maid jumped forward, her mouth opening with shock as the uninvited guest pushed past her. His well-cut clothes combined with the fashionable trim of his hair and the glitter of gold around his neck to suggest wealth. There was a raggedness to him, though, and a dangerous swagger that suggested that he knew well how to use the sword that he wore so easily on his belt.

'Sorry,' Florin said, his wink bringing roses of colour to the maid's cheeks.

'You!' Culver said.

'That's right,' Florin smiled. 'It's me. Remember that time I fished you out of the sea?'

Culver, much to his wife's horror, had the bad taste to laugh. 'I've never been given the opportunity to forget it.'

Lorenzo joined Florin, and leered at the admiral in a most disrespectful way.

'The thing is,' Florin spoke over Culver's father-in-law's apoplectic spluttering, 'we need you to return the favour.'

'How dare you!' the admiral bellowed.

'Get them out of here!' his daughter added.

'Time to return the favour it is,' Culver said and, his appetite having just returned, he grabbed the last slice of beef off the platter and followed Florin out into the safety of battle.

THEY'D BEEN WALKING for almost an hour before Katerina made her first kill.

She had waited this long for many reasons. Partly, her patience came from the fact that her drug-induced numbness had taken a long time to fade. Partly, it was because she needed time to study her enemy, and the subterranean geology of the world through which they moved, before formulating her plan of attack.

Mainly, though, her restraint was due to her unwillingness to admit that she had made a mistake. Although certainly enemies of the Lady, her captors were obviously human. For a while Katerina had wondered if they might be traitors, men so debauched that they were working in league with the verminous horrors she had expected.

Eventually she had concluded that the slavers were no more than they seemed. There were black markets for healthy captives, she knew. She had heard her uncles railing against them, and the bad name they made for the rest of Bordeleaux's traders.

So, Katerina thought, as she had watched the torch carried by the man in front disappear around a twist in the tunnel, they're only men.

She looked over her shoulder to see the slaver who followed her. He was the last in the line, the rear guard of this miserable procession. Behind him there was nothing but darkness, the unlit depths so black that they might never have existed.

The slaver grunted when he saw Katerina watching him and unfurled the whip he carried.

'Look in front of you,' he said, and the foetid air was split by the snap of leather.

The sharp hide tongue wrapped itself around one of Katerina's calves and she fell forward with a cry. There was the snap of flesh against stone as she hit the ground, and then a chorus of clinking chains as the column slowed.

'Get up!' the slaver said, anxious for the first time. He rushed forward, not wanting to be the one who held the chain gang up, and lashed out towards the fallen captive.

This time the blow didn't land. Katerina turned in time to grab the length of knotted leather, letting it twist harmlessly around her hand. Then, before the slaver had any idea of the danger he was in, she had sprung to her feet.

Her movements were no more than a blur in the darkness as she whiplashed around.

A look of almost comical confusion pinched the slaver's face. Open-mouthed, he stumbled backwards, fumbling for words even as he fumbled for the cutlass that he wore at his belt.

Before he could draw either conclusions or steel, the iron mace of Katerina's opened manacle connected with his skull.

There was a short eggshell crunch and the man collapsed onto the ground.

'Keep moving,' Katerina snapped at her fellow captives as she pounced on his body.

But the captives seemed content to stand and stare, their dazed expressions unchanged by the shouts of protest that had started to filter down the stalled line.

Katerina, too busy to waste time in talk, snatched up the whip and cracked it against the floor.

'Move!' she told them, and this time they did.

The last man in the line stumbled past, his powerful shoulders straining against the ragged cloth of a labourer's tunic.

'Here,' Katerina told him, thrusting the torch into his hands. 'Can you carry this?'

'Yes,' he mumbled, and looked at her with an expression that almost seemed horrified.

'Are you…?' he began, but Katerina just cut him off with a sweep of her hand.

'Never mind all that,' she hissed. 'Just keep moving.'

And so, as she stripped the slaver of his cloak and hood, the column clanked away, winding its way ever deeper into the labyrinth.

FLORIN LOOKED DOWN upon his ragtag army and pursed his lips. Even here, hidden by darkness and the cat's cradle of rigging that sprouted up from the deck of Culver's ship, they didn't look like much.

Still, at least they did what they were told. They had waited at the docks for the endless hours it had taken Culver to round up even the skeleton of his crew. Then they had all filed on board the captain's tiny vessel, barely a ripple of complaint coming from them despite the fact that the ship looked about as seaworthy as an apple crate.

Even Florin had been taken aback by Culver's latest command. He had expected another rapier-built cutter, a sister to the one that now lay in pieces amongst the crags of the Bite.

But Culver, it seemed, had not been so fortunate in his new commission. The two masts were square-rigged which, combined with her plump keel, meant that she'd be as slow as a gouty matron.

Whatever this boat had been designed for, it wasn't warfare.

And Florin could guess what she'd been built for. The scent of mouldy ale lingered everywhere. Somehow the smell of rotten hops had woven itself into the very timbers of the ship, quite a feat considering the immaculate condition into which Culver had had her careened.

Now, though, as her captain edged her out of the harbour and into the freshening winds of the open ocean, even that smell was lost beneath the smell of brine and the last ragged tendrils of the lifting fog.

'So, Rafael,' Florin said, putting his men from his mind and lurching back towards the prow of the ship. 'Where did you say this cove was?'

Rafael began to shrug, then stopped himself. Although his captors had been nothing but friendly, he wasn't fool enough to trust in that. Somehow their understanding was even worse than the threats he'd been expecting.

It was just so unnatural.

'Like I said, we go north,' he said, and tried to sound confident.

'How far?'

'I don't know,' Rafael said, then changed his mind. 'I mean, about five miles or so. Maybe more. Or less.'

Florin looked at him.

'Look,' Rafael started to sweat despite the chill of the sea air. 'Just go north until you see a little island with two peaks. It can't be that far.'

'Why don't you know how far it is?'

'I told you,' the slaver whined. 'The capo always led us there. And no, I don't remember the way through the caves.'

'I remember you saying,' Lorenzo nodded with what Rafael thought of as murderous calm.

'I don't remember the way through the caves, I swear it!' he wailed, backing away. 'I never knew the way.'

'Hey, calm down.' Florin wrapped an arm around his shoulder. 'Relax. See, the fog's starting to lift now that we're out of the harbour. Just keep your eyes open and do your best. Can you do that?'

'Yes,' Rafael nodded eagerly. 'Yes, I can do that.'

'Good,' Lorenzo said. 'Because if you don't we'll cut you up.'

Thus motivated, Rafael leaned out over the railings, blinking back his tears as he squinted into the darkness.

Why me, he asked himself bitterly?

I don't deserve this.

Below him the smiling oak of the figurehead glistened with the first specks of spray as the little ship barrelled out to sea and then turned to follow the coastline north.

THE NEXT ONE was more tricky. For some reason, he seemed to speed up every time a useful twist appeared in the passageway. It was almost as though he knew that every time Katerina was out of his sight, she started sprinting after him.

She knew she'd just have to rely on the will of the Lady and whatever stealth and patience she could muster.

Fortunately, when it came to stealth, she could muster a lot.

THE CHILL OF the sea air was doing nothing to cool the fever of Rafael's anxiety. More than once he'd considered throwing himself into the ocean, there to test Manann's mercy rather than Florin's.

But somehow he knew that, the world being as unjust as it was, such a gamble would end in disaster. And anyway the cursed captain of this stinking barrel of a ship insisted on staying half a mile away from the shoreline.

Half a mile!

No wonder he couldn't do what was expected of him.

Even though the fog had thinned to the barest of mists, Rafael didn't see how he could be expected to spot the cove from half a mile away. He couldn't even see the men who swarmed above him, their voices as harsh as the cries of gulls as they moved about in the rigging.

And the moonlight was so dim tonight. The only thing that he could make out was an islet rising up through the spray in front of him. It was impossible to see what shape it was; the black smudge could have had two peaks or it could have had none.

'Are we getting near yet?' Lorenzo asked.

The impatience in his voice plucked on Rafael's nerves. Florin had left Lorenzo to guard their captive whilst he edged his way back off the rolling foredeck to talk to the men, and ever since he'd departed, Lorenzo's pleasant façade had been crumbling.

'I'm not sure,' the slaver whined, and edged away from his grim-faced guard.

Lorenzo followed him. Rafael swallowed and looked away, squinting into the darkness in a pantomime of concentration that did little to dispel Lorenzo's irritation.

'That islet ahead might be the one you can see from the cove,' he offered, and wiped a slick of cold sweat and saltwater from his brow. 'But then again, it might not.'

'Are you mocking me?' Lorenzo growled, and immediately regretted it. He knew that he should be trying to calm this frightened fool down, trying to keep him relaxed and alert.

Even though he knew that, the temptation to unleash his tension on the rat was almost irresistible.

'No,' Rafael wailed, and raised his hands defensively. 'No, I'm not mocking you. Not at all. But I can't see the shape of it from here. Can you see the shape? I can't. Not from here. Not in this dark. It's still foggy!'

'All right,' Lorenzo grumbled. 'All right, all right, all right. Just keep your eyes open.'

'I will,' Rafael said gratefully and turned back to study the islet that loomed up in front of them. It was getting big, and it was getting big fast. Much faster than he would have thought possible considering the mild winds that drove them.

Then he realised why that was.

It wasn't an islet they were heading for – it was another ship.

He wondered if he should point this out, when a hand fell on his shoulder. He jumped, stifling a cry.

'Relax,' Florin told him with a slap on the back and an easy grin. 'Me and Captain Culver were just wondering if you knew anything about that ship up ahead. The one with the black painted hull. And all of its torches out.'

'No,' Rafael's shake of the head turned into a nervous shiver. 'I've never seen it. Our clients usually come in longboats.'

'From where?'

'From Araby. Oh. Oh, I see what you mean. They come from a ship.'

'That ship?'

'I don't know.'

Florin stared at his captive, who backed away until he bumped into Lorenzo.

'Well,' Florin said at last. 'We'll go and find out, then, shall we?'

Rafael's eyes flashed brightly in the moonlight as he tried to think of an answer, anything that might serve to ingratiate himself with his two captors.

As his thoughts disintegrated into a welter of self-pity, he was distracted by the sound that came from the other ship.

The hiss of it was as sibilant as the fall of rain on slate, a sharp contrast to the deeper growl of the sea. Even through his misery, Rafael wondered what it was. He vaguely remembered hearing something like it before.

The angry hiss grew louder and, a split second before the first deaths, the lookout screamed a warning from above.

'Archers!' he cried, his voice as sharp as the steel-tipped cloud that now rained down.

'Archers!'

For some, the warning came too late. Even as the arrows bit into timber and threaded themselves through canvas the first screams rang out from the deck where Florin's men waited.

Rafael threw himself to the deck, and Florin and Lorenzo looked down at him with contempt.

'Looks like we found his mates after all,' Lorenzo offered, and resisted the urge to give the cowering slaver a kick.

Florin just scowled and squinted towards the slaver's ship. Its masts were bare, innocent of any canvas, and for the first time he could see movement amongst its forest of rigging. More ominously, there was also movement amongst the bowmen that he could now see gathered on the foredeck.

'Archers!' a voice bellowed out from above, and he and Lorenzo crouched down as another volley hissed through the spray of the sea.

This time there were fewer cries as the steel bit home. The survivors, it seemed, had had the time to find cover.

Florin waited until the rain of arrows slackened, then sprinted back to the main deck to see what damage had been done.

Before he could reach them, a sailor grabbed him.

'Captain says to get your lads ready,' he shouted into Florin's ear. 'The pig's bladder those monkeys are sailing isn't rigged, not even for tacking! We'll be on her within five minutes.'

Before Florin could ask what the hell the man was talking about, he'd leapt onto a hawser and shinned up into the rigging.

Never mind, Florin told himself as he stumbled back along the forecastle to speak to his men.

Boarding the enemy in five minutes was clear enough.

'Archers!'

Florin cursed as he heard the murderous whisper of the arrows fall, and stumbled over the railing into the deck below just as they started to bite.

'Thank the Lady you're unhurt!' the man beside him exclaimed, and a chorus of agreement murmured out amongst the thunk of steel into wood.

'And you,' Florin called out, trying not to sound as jittery as he felt. 'I just wish I'd thought to bring some bows with us.'

'You weren't to know,' the man, who he now recognised as Butcher, replied. 'And anyway, one of the tars said that we'll be amongst them soon.'

'That we will,' Florin agreed, surprised at how enthusiastic the man sounded.

'We'll get her back,' another man called out, who Florin recognised as Jacques. His voice was tight with pain, and Florin winced at the sight of the arrow which sprouted from his thigh.

'You stay here,' he told him. 'You've done enough already.'

'Don't worry,' the lad said and, incredibly, grinned. 'The Lady will give me strength.'

For the hundredth time, Florin found himself wondering how Katerina had managed to imbue her followers with such a fanaticism. Did they really believe that she was the messenger of their goddess?

'Archers!'

Florin found the warning a welcome distraction from his wandering thoughts. He huddled down, and this time there was hardly any gap between the alarm and the impact of the arrows.

Realising how close the two ships must now be, he scrabbled over to the gunwales. He leant over the side as, with a creak of swinging sails, the ship rolled to starboard.

Barely twenty feet away, her swarming decks lower and longer than those of the Bretonnian ship, the Arabyan vessel wallowed in the swell. Even as Florin watched, the men who'd been struggling to unfurl her sails gave up, leaving their task to slide down the rigging to the decks below.

'Get ready lads,' Florin roared, bellowing against the boom of the waves that were trapped between the two vessels. They surged up, spitting the flecks of their anger high into the air, and Florin felt the cold kiss of brine on his face.

He grinned, a death's head smile playing across his features as he felt the first maddening rush of exhilaration. Behind him, his men huddled closer, the murmur of their prayers filling the agonised seconds that were all that remained between them and battle.

'Thought I'd join you.'

Florin looked across in time to see Lorenzo pushing his way through the waiting men, the gleam of his steel matching that of his eyes.

'How nice of you,' Florin laughed, a hysterical edge to the sound. 'I was just going to–'

'Archers!'

The waiting men ducked as a last flight of arrows hissed above their heads.

And then, with a boom, the two ships met.

Culver's men, well-versed in the art of boarding a ship, sent a score of grappling lines whipping into the other vessel. The great iron claws that weighted them, bit into timber, rigging, flesh.

Before they could secure them, Florin, maddened with adrenaline, led the attack.

'For the Lady!' he screamed as he leapt, vaulting down onto the rolling deck of the slaver's ship.

From behind him, he could hear his call echoing from a score of throats, but already he was immersed in the bloody business of battle.

As the chaos of hot blood and cold steel swallowed him up he could hear prayers, curses, screams of pain. He could also hear laughter, a maniacal sound that he never did realise was his own.

* * *

By the time she got to the seventh man, Katerina had perfected her method.

As methods went, it was simple enough. The slavers' deep hoods meant that they could see little apart from the chained captives who walked ahead of them, the stumbling line becoming more orderly beneath the constant whisper of the slaver's whips.

This was all the advantage that Katerina needed. All she had to worry about was the timing of her sudden, silent rush. Then, once within striking distance, all it took was the twist of a garrotte and that was that.

Easy.

But the problem with the seventh man was that the sudden, silent rush wasn't. Before she had covered even half the distance to him, the water-smoothed rock beneath her feet disintegrated into a shale of sharp-edged pebbles. The rocks bit into her naked soles, the sudden agony tearing a cry from her throat even as it sent her spilling to the ground.

Her target turned to see the cause of the commotion, his wooden torch flaring as he swept it around. In the sudden brightness, he saw Katerina as she scrabbled back to her feet. Her blaze of red hair shone like copper as her hood fell back, and she tossed her cloak aside with an impatient gesture.

'Get him!' she yelled, and even as she raced forward her lurking comrades burst from the shadows to grab the slaver.

The man wasn't eager to be grabbed. Beneath the permanent shadow of his hood, his jaw dropped with surprise, and then he was running, throwing his torch back towards his pursuers as he sprinted through the sliding shale.

'Help!' the slaver screamed as he skidded around a bend in the passageway.

Katerina cursed as she heard a voice raised in answer.

Well, too late to stop now, she thought, and barrelled around the twist in the passageway.

The slaver had stopped running, although not for long. Even as she watched, he abandoned the comrade he'd been warning, and bolted.

His comrade, after a split second of hesitation, turned tail and followed him.

Katerina yelled after them, her voice twisted by the confines of the labyrinth into an inhuman bellow, and their footsteps speeded up.

The two men disappeared around another twist in the tunnel and Katerina bellowed with wild laughter. After all the sneaking about it felt wonderful to be in such hot pursuit.

'Come on,' she encouraged her followers. 'Let's see how far they run!'

As a third slaver joined her enemies in their wild flight, the stone walls began to spread out and the ceiling grew higher. Katerina felt the shale turn to sand beneath her feet, and realised for the first time that she could hear the ocean. It pulsed within the confines of the widening cave, the beat of it like the heart of some great hungry beast.

Ahead, she saw that the slavers were in full flight, cloaks billowing as they kicked their way past the frightened captives and their bewildered comrades.

But as Katerina followed them, the cave ended. The dead blackness of its unseen heights ended in a high arch and, beyond that, the cold spray of stars across the night sky. Mannslieb was high tonight, its pale light bright after the darkness of the depths, and it lit up the beach onto which Katerina emerged.

The slavers paused in their flight as they stumbled out into the sand. Perhaps it was the realisation that there was nowhere left to run that ended their panic. Or perhaps it was the confidence of their leaders, the two men who stood amidst the confusion like a pair of iron pegs driven into frozen earth.

Whatever the reason, the slavers' rout ended as abruptly as it had begun. They lined up on the sand behind their captains, the frightened sounds of their chained captives lending them a fresh reassurance.

Katerina held out an arm to stop her own handful of followers rushing out to meet them. Despite her predation, there was almost a score of the enemy left, and they were well-armed and well-disciplined. For the first time since the exhilaration of the chase, Katerina wished that she had stopped to release more of the captives. Freed, they would have given her the numbers she needed to win this thing. As it was, most of them remained chained and terrified, as useless as a flock of sheep.

The slavers seemed to have already reached the same conclusion. They were moving back onto the offensive, responding to a series of short, efficient orders as they fanned out on the flanks.

'Here,' Katerina said, turning to the first of her men. His eyes looked wide in the dark skin of his face, but at least his hands were steady.

'Take these wires,' Katerina told him. 'And try to release some more of us. The rest of you, stay back in the cave. Come on, back up. That's it. You in the chain, you too. Get back inside and we'll defend you.'

As the chain gang started to shuffle back into the darkness, another voice rang out, clear and sharp.

'Come here,' it ordered, the echoes that followed it adding to the lazy confidence. 'Come here, now.'

The captives paused, confused, until the slavers' leader snapped his whip through the darkness.

Although out of range of the captives, the sound of the whip combined with their confusion to bring them marching obediently out onto the beach.

'Come back!' Katerina cried, appalled at their stupidity, but it was already too late. A pair of the slavers had darted forward to grab the first of their captives and they dragged them mercilessly forward, ignoring their protests as they started to pull the whole chain gang out of the cave as easily as a crow plucking a worm from a hole.

The man Katerina had set to unlocking the chains was dragged past her. She almost turned to give him a hand when she realised it was too late. One of the slavers' leaders was already rushing forward, leading his men into the tangled confusion of captives that now clogged up the mouth of the cave.

Katerina realised that she had only one option left.

'Follow me!' she yelled as, cutlass in one hand and torch in the other, she led her ragged band of followers forward to meet the attack.

CHAPTER SIXTEEN

EMIR FAUZI BANDAR, of the House of Jubail, had been waiting on the beach since his boats had landed that evening. He'd taken advantage of the fog that still remained to have a cooking fire built, and his cook had risen to the occasion most satisfactorily.

After all, although he prided himself on his ability to rough it, the emir could see no reason to take things to extremes.

So it was that whilst his followers had waited in their positions, hungry and unseen, the servant had prepared a supper of roast lamb and stuffed avocados for his master. They were followed by a tray of almond cakes, delightful little confections that glistened like jewels beneath their coating of honey, and some jellied fruits. After he had worked his way through them, the emir had slumped back, lolling onto the divan that had been set up for him beneath the cliffs. There he nibbled on dates and drank an endless succession of tiny cups of tea the cook brought him. The liquid was delicious, as sweet and as hot as an

Estalian girl he had once known, and as the moonlight started to burn its way through the dying fog the emir considered his blessings.

It took him a long time, for they were many. Not the least of them was his bodyguard, who stood as ever in permanent attendance. Bran had been a chance acquisition from a Tilean arena, where he had lost a particularly vicious fight against a pack of orcs. In truth, the emir had bought him for the meat on his bones. The battered muscle and fat on his fallen form would have been just the thing to fatten up a gaggle of skeletal slaves the emir had just bought. But somehow the beast had recovered before the butcher got around to him. Ever since then he'd followed the emir like the world's most hideous puppy, a monster whose loyalty required no more than a daily bellyful of meat.

His mind wandering ever further, the emir toyed with the idea of having the beast taught how to sing. Maybe even how to tell stories. Despite the fact that he hardly ever spoke a word, the emir had come to the conclusion that that was because he had wits, not because he lacked them.

Anyway, when he did speak, Bran had a voice that was as deep and melodious as the ocean. What a baritone he would make!

It was with such peaceful thoughts that the merchant dropped off to sleep. Slumbering beneath the stars of this barbarous northern shore, the emir felt at peace with the world, which was just as well.

He didn't have much longer to enjoy it.

His doom began with the arrival of his business partners. The Bretonnian slavers wailed as they fled out onto the beach, their faces masks of fear in the unsteady light of their lanterns.

Without a single conscious thought, the emir responded to their distress. Vaulting from his divan he pirouetted to hide behind Bran's reassuring bulk. Only then, blinking sleep from his eyes, did he begin to assess the situation.

His first reaction was to make a dash for the boats but as he began to sidle away, he saw the slavers form a line, their panic giving way to renewed discipline. The mob that had been pursuing them hesitated just as the emir had done, evidently surprised at this turnaround. The emir licked his lips thoughtfully, eyes twinkling in the darkness. The crack of a slaver's whip ended his indecision. He watched as most of the captives stumbled obediently forward, and his fat face split open in a cherubic grin. Far from being the battle he had feared, this was obviously no more than some minor scuffle amongst captors and captives. A scuffle which he could, no doubt, turn to his advantage.

'What shall we do, effendi?' his bosun asked, as the slavers began to manoeuvre towards the handful of figures that hid within the shadow of the cave.

The emir pretended to be shocked. 'We'll help our friends, of course,' he said, disapproval furrowing his brow.

'Very well, effendi,' the bosun said and, with a quick bow, started to order his men forward.

'What are you doing?' the emir snapped.

'Helping our friends,' his man replied, suddenly doubtful.

'Not yet, you fool,' the emir sighed and rolled his eyes. 'Wait until they've regained control of the situation. Then we'll help them.'

'Aaaaah yes, effendi. I see.'

The emir shook his head, amazed as always by the stupidity of his subordinates. From along the beach, the discordant symphony of steel against steel rang out, the sound occasionally lost beneath screams and curses. More wailing followed as the chain of captives was dragged down the beach, and more of the slavers poured into the opening of the cave.

Eventually, it seemed that they were fighting no more than a single figure. And then their mysterious attacker was down, tripped by a whip and lost beneath a rush of black-cloaked figures.

'Off you go, then,' the emir told his men.

'And hurry!' he called after them, raising his voice so that it could be heard all the way up the beach. 'Quickly to help our beloved friends!'

By the time his men had reached their beloved friends, the fight was over.

When he was sure the last trace of resistance was over the emir followed them. Picking his way cautiously through the shifting sands, he squinted in the moonlight, trying to make out exactly what had gone on.

Along one side, the chained captives huddled beneath a towering cliff. Their miserable cries mingled with the constant hiss of the slavers' whips, the men taking their revenge for the uprising where they could. Higher up the beach, framed by the gaping maw of the cave, the rest of the victors waited, gathered around their surviving assailant. Although little more than indistinct shadows in the flickering torchlight, the emir could see that many of them had been injured.

As he puffed and wheezed his way nearer, he could see how many had been killed.

'My friends,' the emir called as he approached the survivors. 'Thank the gods we got here in time to save you.'

He tried not to look too smug as, in a sudden flare of torchlight, he recognised the slavers' leader.

'Thank the gods you are all right,' he told him. 'And... oh. This is your captive?'

The emir tried not to look too interested as he studied the girl. Unfortunately, her flawlessly white skin was flawless no longer. Bruises were already blackening on her chin and cheekbones. Her clothes hardly showed her curves to their best advantage either. They were little more than a collection of rags, the torn and bloodied cloth rumpled around the grimy chains that the slavers had heaped upon her. But the glistening, autumnal fire of her hair, that was still clear to see. The emir watched the lustre of it as it shifted in the lamplight, a cascade of living embers.

Then Katerina looked up. A feral fury glistened within her emerald eyes, the animal brightness a match for any cat's, and in that instant the emir knew that he must buy her. There were caliphs that he knew, men of certain dispositions, who would pay almost anything for such exotic beauty.

Almost anything at all.

'Ugly thing, isn't she?' he grimaced carefully and looked away.

'Oh, shut up,' his business partner snapped, his face hardening beneath his hood.

The emir didn't have to pretend to be offended. 'What a way to talk to me,' he spluttered, but before he could continue, the Bretonnian gestured him into silence.

'I said shut up. This silly little floozy is my niece.'

'No need for talk like that, Gilles,' his brother cut in.

Gilles just snorted and glared down at Katerina. 'You're as bad as your bitch of a mother.'

Katerina glared back up at him and, despite the weight of chains that were wrapped around her, managed to struggle to her feet.

'You're even worse than her,' she hissed at her uncle, shoving her face towards him. 'You're a disgrace to our family. You have no honour.'

Gilles shoved her away, cursing as she collapsed back into the sand but his brother didn't share his anger. Quite the opposite. Bouillon seemed to find the whole thing most amusing.

'She's Franz's daughter all right,' he chuckled. 'Remember how he used to go on about honour?'

'Yes,' Gilles grunted, and scratched his chin thoughtfully. 'Funny how it always seemed to work for him.'

'If it had worked that well,' Bouillon reminded him, 'then Franz would still be here and we wouldn't have this dilemma.'

'She's certainly a most remarkable dilemma,' the emir ventured, his eyes flitting across the black-cloaked corpses that lay behind her. Somehow, even without the bloody clues that soaked Katerina, he knew that most of them had been her doing.

'Isn't she just?' Bouillon agreed.

'What shall we do?' Gilles grumbled. 'I don't fancy killing her. She's Franz's, after all. On the other hand, will she keep quiet?'

'Would you?' Bouillon asked his niece, but her only reply was a look of absolute contempt.

'No,' he sighed. 'Thought not.'

'Perhaps I can help,' the emir said. 'You know that I have many businesses, and many clients. Some of my slaves go to the fields, others to the salt mines.'

'Yes, and others to whorehouses,' Gilles snapped. 'You can forget about that. She's our blood, when all's said and done. I'd sooner kill her now than have her doing that.'

'Let me finish, my friend, let me finish. I should be angry that you would even accuse me of having such thoughts, but no matter. I know how upset you are.'

'Get to the point,' Gilles told him.

'The point is that there are many palaces full of many women. Women with nothing to do. A young lady such as your niece here would do very well in such a place. She could teach them her tongue and perhaps learn how to sew. As well as being comfortable she would be absolutely safe.'

'It's our absolute safety I'm more interested in,' Bouillon muttered. 'What if she escapes? If you knew her as well as we do, then I wouldn't put it past her.'

'Nobody escapes the caliph's harem,' the emir said, and for once his words had the ring of truth about them.

'What do you think?' Bouillon asked Katerina. 'Fancy learning to sew?'

But Katerina was no longer paying attention to him. Instead she was staring at the emir's bodyguard, her eyes alive with sudden calculation. Ignoring her uncle's repeated question she started to speak. Her voice grew guttural as she did so, hoarsening into an alien accent that made her words almost unintelligible.

The emir smiled nastily. He'd seen many a brave soul reduced to a gibbering wreck by the sight of Bran.

'Ah, she's noticed my bodyguard,' he gloated. 'See how thoughtful she becomes. Bran had that effect on my prisoners, doesn't he? Here, Bran. Step forward. Let the girl see what will happen if she causes any trouble.'

'Remember,' Gilles warned him as the ogre thudded forward into the torchlight. 'She's our niece.'

'No problem. It's just a demonstration. Bran, show her your teeth.'

For once, Bran seemed not to understand. Instead of threatening the girl he just looked at her, the beaten expanse of his face as expressionless as always.

Katerina jabbered some more.

'Yes.'

The sudden volume of the beast's voice sent the men around him jumping back with alarm. Once more, the emir misunderstood.

'Yes, well, go on then. Show her your teeth,' he said, his podgy hand fluttering towards the beast's mouth like a fat moth towards a flame.

Bran turned to his master and snarled. The saliva that coated his teeth gleamed in the torchlight with a reddish, bloodied sheen, and the abattoir stench of his breath washed over his master. The emir scowled, embarrassed by the beast's stupidity.

'Not me, her,' he scolded the thing that loomed above him. The other men, both Arabyan and Bretonnian, backed away, uncomfortably aware of just how big the slab of a creature was. The top of the emir's turbaned head barely reached the grotesque swelling of its midriff but the emir stood his ground. Even now it hadn't occurred to him just how delicate a thing Bran's loyalty might be.

The beast turned back to the girl and looked at her, its head lolling to one side. She winked up at the smashed meat of his face, a gesture the emir put down to a spasm of terror.

'Bran,' he said, hands on his hips as he scolded the ogre like a fishwife with an errant son. 'I told you to show her your teeth.'

Bran looked at him blankly, nothing on his face but an expression of drooling stupidity.

'You've lost your touch,' Gilles jeered from a safe distance, and the emir's temper snapped.

'Show her what you can do,' he yelled and, in a fit of pique, reached up to slap the bulge of Bran's gut.

The ogre's response was instantaneous and, to anybody who knew anything about his race, utterly predictable. With a roar of pure, uncontrolled rage he leapt forward, the vast hams of his fists closing around the soft meat of its master's shoulders.

The emir squeaked with disbelief as his feet left the ground. He realised that he must be dreaming. He must be. Why, only moments before he had been thinking about teaching this beast, this huge beast, how to sing. As he struggled to understand what was happening, Bran opened his mouth and, with a roar that wouldn't have shamed the best baritone in Tilea, tore off the emir's head.

His followers watched in stunned disbelief as Bran bit down on the morsel, crunching down on the skull as the emir's blood splattered over him. Then, his face black with his master's blood, Bran hurled the body to one side and turned to face them.

The bosun, taking charge of the situation, led his comrades in a sprinting retreat. Gilles and Bouillon exchanged a single glance before following them, their cloaks flapping behind them as they raced for a place on the long boats.

Katerina watched them flee, a look of feline satisfaction playing across her blood-spattered face. Then she looked at Bran as he lost interest in the running men and began to feast on the emir's headless corpse.

As the chewing and slurping grew louder, Katerina lay back down on the sand and thought about what she had told him. It wouldn't have worked. He had been interested to hear her speaking his dialect, that was all. And ogres didn't stay surprised for long.

Then his master had had the temerity, the insanity, to hit his gut.

And that had been that.

Katerina started to laugh as she remembered the emir's face when Bran had turned upon him. It was a jagged, humourless sound and as it echoed back out of the cave it hardly seemed human. The Lady, she decided in the midst of her hysteria, moves in mysterious ways.

And with that thought her laughter turned to sobbing.

'HOW MANY LEFT?' Florin shouted, blinking at the sting of blood in his eyes. He hadn't even felt the scalp wound when it had been inflicted, but now that the first clash of combat was over the bleeding was impossible to ignore.

'How many of who left?' Lorenzo shouted back, and ducked as an arrow zipped overhead.

'The enemy,' Florin snapped, and waved the dark-stained blade of his sword towards a fleeing Arabyan. He scurried up the ladder that led up the timber wall of the ship's forecastle, and Florin looked past him to the cluster of retreating sailors and busy archers who held it. The sibilant accents of their leaders ricocheted around the ship, a harsh tongue for a harsh job.

Mere seconds before, Florin had thought that the battle was over. He had thought that the coppery taste of his own blood had been the taste of victory, and the man he'd just slaughtered his last but he had been wrong. True, the Arabyans had baulked at the ferocious charge of his men, their lack of training of no consequence amongst the tangled rigging and rolling deck.

Unfortunately, although the Arabyans had run from the ferocity of their attackers, they had not run far. Even as the first Bretonnian victory cries rang out, the slavers were crowding into the stern deck and the forecastle, twin strong points that loomed over the mid-deck like a hammer and anvil.

'Clever bastards,' Florin spat disgustedly and watched as one of his men tried to follow the last fleeing Arabyan onto the forecastle. His bravery was rewarded with two arrows, the thrust of a cutlass and an axe stroke that cleaved his skull in two. Florin winced and looked back to study the stern deck, but things were no better there. The single narrow ladder that led up to it was guarded by a knot of Arabyan swordsmen, their faces grim beneath their turbans.

He swore again and, wiping the slick of blood from his forehead, cast an eye over his men. Some of them were still fighting, stumbling around the fallen tackle and ropes that cluttered the deck as they finished off their opponents. Others remained slumped on the blood-soaked planking, clutching their wounds or lying still and unmoving. The rest seemed to have realised their predicament just as Florin had. A few of them, goaded by the hum of arrows, tried to rush the stern deck, but the blaze of steel that awaited at the top of the ladder sent them crashing back down.

Florin ground his teeth with frustration and glared about him. Even now his men outnumbered the Arabyans. The slavers had hardly been more than a skeleton crew. But what good were numbers if they remained stuck on the mid-deck, hemmed in like cattle in an abattoir? An arrow, its feathers ghost-white in the darkness, flashed past him. The length of ash punched straight through the neck of one of Culver's men, sliding home as easily as a skewer through offal. The man fell back with a gurgling shriek.

'What shall we do?' Lorenzo demanded, and Florin saw the question reflected in the drawn faces of the men who huddled around him.

What could they do? Their victory had proved as fleeting as a fistful of dew. This deck, paid for with their blood, had become a killing ground, a perfect trap that left them exposed to the archers on the two higher decks.

There was the bark of an Arabyan command and the air hissed as another volley fell amongst the Bretonnians.

A chorus of screams rang out from around him. It was all too much for Florin.

'Follow me!' he roared, waving his bloodied cutlass towards the forecastle. 'Follow me!'

He raced towards the ladder that led up from the deck, all the while screaming vain defiance at the men who waited at the top of it. But even as they prepared to hack him down, Florin stopped, hurled his cutlass towards them, and pirouetted around to thump his back into the timber wall of the bulwark.

He crouched down and made a saddle of his hands.

'Come on, then,' he told Lorenzo. 'What are you waiting for?'

The older man's face worked as he tried to yell three separate expletives at once. But then the half-seen blur of an arrow drove everything from his mind except for a single thought, that the only way out of here was up.

He planted one booted foot in Florin's hands and, with a wild yell, leapt upwards, his cutlass a blur as he rolled into the packed ranks of the Arabyans.

Florin looked up in time to see him disappear over the railing, then gestured to the next man to follow. He boosted him up, and then somebody else, and then, when two other men took his place, he snatched an axe from the deck and barrelled up the ladder.

This time the only figure waiting at the top of the ladder was Lorenzo.

Florin grinned with relief and pushed past him, axe flashing down towards the nearest turbaned head. Already, the remaining slavers were dropping their weapons and raising their hands, offering them up as if in prayer to their uselessly furled sails. Now that their advantage was gone, they had more sense than to fight. Florin could see how few of them there were.

How few and how frightened.

A pair of his men, still snarling with the madness of battle, rushed forward, but Florin leapt in front of them, holding them back with an outstretched arm.

'Do you surrender?' he asked the Arabyans. They shuffled nervously, glancing back over the rail at the churning waves below but the sea looked too hungry to be inviting.

'Yes, effendi,' one of them said, looking back from the dark ocean. 'Oh yes, we surrender.'

'Then tell us where the slaves are.'

For a moment the Arabyan hesitated.

'Where are they?' Florin repeated, hefting his axe.

'They are still on the beach, effendi. My master hasn't brought them back yet.'

'What beach?' Florin demanded, but suddenly he knew. His gaze slipped past the slaver and onto the dark shoreline beyond.

Except that it wasn't dark any more. At least, not entirely. Bright orange sparks wove in and out of the blackness, and although they were no bigger than fireflies, Florin knew torches when he saw them.

'You say that your master has gone to fetch them?' Florin asked, and stood aside as his men hastened forward to seize their captives.

'Yes, effendi.' The leader of the Arabyans sidled closer to Florin. 'Look. Can you see their torches?'

'Yes,' Florin said. He licked the dry skin of his lips and leant over the side as though he might somehow be able to see Katerina through the darkness. Before he could see anything there was a shouted warning, an explosion of agony on the back of his head, and a darkness deeper than any Bretonnian night.

CHAPTER SEVENTEEN

'Stop malingering,' a voice said through the pain. 'I know you're awake.'

Florin groaned and covered his eyes against the sharp stab of sunlight. His face felt sticky and begrimed, but what really bothered him was the ache in the back of his skull.

'What were we drinking last night?' he asked Lorenzo, who barked with laughter.

Florin winced at the sudden noise. Gradually, as the grogginess faded, he started to remember the events of last night. The fog and the bloodshed seemed unreal in the painfully bright light of day, as though it had all been nothing more than a nightmare. Then, with a jolt of horrible realisation, he remembered what had started off the nightmare.

'Katerina!' he shouted, and sat bolt upright. Squinting in the daylight, he looked at the sheets of canvas which snapped and bulged overhead, and the figures that moved amongst them. The ship rolled to one side and his stomach rolled with it, but suddenly his own misery seemed unimportant.

'Where's Katerina?' Florin asked, grabbing Lorenzo by the arm.

'On the other ship,' Lorenzo told him.

'What? Then we have to go back. We can track them.'

He tried to get to his feet but Lorenzo pushed him back down against the gunwale.

'No. The other ship's ours too. We won it, remember?'

Florin's brows furrowed beneath their caking of blood.

'All I remember is getting hit by someone.'

'And the someone in question paid the price.' Lorenzo nodded, his eyes wrinkling into lines of grim satisfaction. 'Typical Arabyan, making a truce then attacking someone from behind.'

'What about the rest of them?'

'Oh, they all came quietly enough. They're in the slave holds now. See how they like it.'

Florin looked over the gunwale to see the black lines of the slavers' ship, the stained canvas of her sails billowing in a following wind. His eyes slid over her dark lines then stopped, caught by a tiny figure with flaming red hair that stood in the stern. Even from this distance, Florin could recognise her, and a surge of relief washed away all his other symptoms. He blinked back a wash of tears and blamed the wind for them. Then he turned back to Lorenzo.

'I'm confused,' he said.

Lorenzo just grunted.

'You said the man who hit me was a typical Arabyan.'

'Damned right.'

'Then why was he the only one to try it on?'

Lorenzo opened his mouth, then closed it again.

'I mean, if he was typical...'

'Try to rest,' Lorenzo told him. 'You're obviously still concussed. It's a shame. I was going to tell you who else we captured last night,'

'Who?'

Lorenzo managed to hold out for almost five whole minutes.

ALL OF BORDELEAUX'S merchants agreed that the Hansebourgs' trial was the highlight of the year. Duke Alberic himself, resplendent in a suit of armour that shone like silver, presided over the event, which was held in the marketplace so that all could see.

Some were surprised that the city's ruler deigned to attend the trial of the two Hansebourgs. After all, despite their fortune they were still no better than commoners.

Although some were surprised, the cognoscenti were not. They knew that the first penalty for selling Bretonnians to masters other than their own was the forfeiture of all possessions. And as rumours of the Hansebourgs' wealth had grown every day since their capture, the duke was no doubt keen to see that their possessions were appropriated by the right person.

The right person, of course, being himself.

His justice was unsurprisingly swift, although not unmerciful. He could have had the two men beheaded or impaled. Or even, if he'd been more old-fashioned, torn into quarters by bulls in the arena. As it was he just had them branded, along with the captured Arabyans, and sent off to live out their lives as two more serfs on his estate.

Bordeleaux, being what it was, was delighted by the judgement. The townsfolk turned out in full force to see the two men as they were dragged away, lining the twisting streets to cheer and jeer and to hurl both mud and abuse. Even the comtesse came to watch, arriving on foot now that her carriage and horses had been taken. And when she attacked her brothers-in-law, screaming like a fishwife despite the single set of fine clothes she'd managed to keep, the crowd had roared its delight.

It was one of the last things the comtesse did before leaving Bordeleaux. Less than a week later she sailed away to the warmth of Tilea. There she lived out her days, content to hide both her shame and the dwindling supply of coin she'd managed to hide from the duke's bailiffs. Although she thought of her daughter often, she was somehow never saddened by her absence.

By the time winter blew into Bordeleaux, Katerina was almost penniless. Considering the share of the captured ship she'd received, that was an achievement all by itself.

Although penniless, she was far from poor. The collection of hovels that had surrounded the patch of muddy yard were gone now, replaced by an agglomeration of wooden houses, surrounded by a rough but serviceable stone wall. It was a miniature urban fortress that dominated the streets around. And within this fortress lived her tribe.

With her coin, and with the Lady's blessings, they had become a prosperous and successful tribe. From Butcher, who had rebuilt his shop, to the labourers who toiled in the docks, her folk bore little resemblance to the starving vagabonds she had first come across.

Nor did Bran seem quite the monster he had been on the beach. Content with a steady diet of offal and beer, the ogre spent his days dozing in the lower half of Katerina's own house, and his nights dozing in the corner of Florin and Lorenzo's inn. His very presence was enough to deter the most troublesome of men, and for a while he was even something of a celebrity, his part in Katerina's tale exaggerated until it was big enough to fit Bran himself.

But the greatest of Katerina's treasures was still little more than a dream, a silent promise of the joy that was to come.

It was this that led her once more to the Lady's great temple, there to make the same dizzying climb that she had made after Sergei's death. This time she moved more easily up the masonry of the temple, for she was strong and well rested but even though the breeze blew chill beneath the icy blue autumn sky she was sheened with sweat by the time she reached the top of the spire, and brushed her fingertips against the goddess's.

This time there was no trace of the Lady herself. There was just the chipped gold and frozen features of her statue, its gaze inscrutable as it peered out across Bordeleaux and into the ocean beyond.

Katerina didn't mind. She had come here to offer thanks, that was all, and somehow she knew that wherever she whispered the Lady would hear. Her lips moved as she looked down once more onto the city below, the tangled maze through which countless thousands of lives threaded their way. One of them was Florin's, and she smiled as she thought of him. Since their return to Bordeleaux they had grown ever closer.

Katerina smiled happily as she thought about just how close, and she put her hand over her belly. There was hardly any sign yet; beneath her tunic her stomach was still as flat and smooth as ever.

It wouldn't be long until the bump started to show, though. Her smile grew broader as she realised that, for the first time since her father had died, she would have a real family. And so would Florin.

EPILOGUE

THE MONEYLENDER MUTTERED into his beard as he counted, the coins glittering in the light of the single candle. The rest of the counting chamber was lost in shadows, a dark void within which only the gold, the guttering flame and the angles of his sharp face were visible.

Apart from the clink of metal and the low, insistent murmuring of the man counting, the room was silent. It always was. No matter what was happening in the world outside, the chamber's walls were thick enough to silence it. So were the two iron bound doors, each of which was as thick as Mordicio's bony old chest.

The silence was part of what made this the old man's favourite sanctuary, but only a small part. After all, this was where his gold, the very stuff of his life, was kept, and the sight and feel of it always soothed his soul.

Right now, his soul did need soothing. The creature Skrit had failed to either do his job or answer his summons. The thing must have been closer to the madness the green stone brought than he'd realised. In the past that hadn't mattered, because another assassin had always appeared to take his fallen leader's place. This time, however, there had been no sign of any of them, leaders or not.

Mordicio tried to cheer himself up with the thought of how much gold he'd save on the stone, but it was no good. The rat-folk had been the perfect, the ultimate assassins. Apart from anything else it would have been impossible for anyone to have linked them back to him.

He sighed and, finishing a pile of twenty coins, he pushed it to one side. He leant back on his hard wooden stool and pressed his thumbs into the small of his back.

That was when he saw it.

Or rather, he saw the shape of it, a patch of darkness that was even blacker than the shadows which surrounded it. Mordicio felt his heart race, pattering within his narrow chest like a rat in a cage.

'Hello, my boy,' he smiled. 'You gave me quite a fright. I thought that I was alone in here.'

The shape said nothing as it scuttled forward, its claws clicking on the slate floor. Steel gleamed in its paws, the weapon indistinct in the darkness, and Mordicio knew that his death was upon him.

'Take a seat,' he invited, as easily as if the horror were any other invited guest.

To his surprise, the thing did take a seat. Or rather, it leapt upon the empty stool and perched upon it, as easily as a raven on a skull. Its hood had fallen back far enough for Mordicio to recognise the furred snout and chiselled teeth of its cursed kind, but even in the midst of his terror he was sharp enough to see that this wasn't Skrit. Apart from anything else, it only had one eye.

'I am surprised that Skrit didn't come to see me himself,' he ventured, his fingers disappearing into the sleeves of his robe.

Mordicio's visitor shivered at the mention of the name, and for the first time it spoke.

'Skrit won't be seeing you any more,' it shrilled, and its tail flicked back and forth with delight.

'I see,' Mordicio said with an avuncular nod. 'Well, thank you for telling me, my boy. It's nice to know these things.'

'Skrit,' his visitor continued, 'was a weakling. A fool.'

'I can't say that I ever knew him well enough to say,' Mordicio observed carefully. 'I'm still waiting for him to finish a little job he was doing for me.'

'You paid him in the stone.' His visitor got straight to the point. 'You owe him some more. Give it to me.'

Mordicio smiled and bowed his head.

'Of course I will,' he soothed. 'Of course I will. When the job is done.'

'Give it to me *now*,' the creature hissed, and thrust its misshapen snout over the table. Mordicio watched the thing's snout wrinkle, and sighed as he thought about all the guards that were waiting so uselessly out of earshot.

'I don't know about that, my boy,' he lied, and leaned back away from the creature. It snarled and leaned closer towards him.

Mordicio waited until it began to speak before he struck.

For an old man he moved with an incredible speed. His left hand closed around a fistful of slimy snout and razored teeth whilst his right flashed from within his sleeve. The stiletto he wielded was aimed straight at his assailant's remaining eye.

There was a shriek of rage and an explosion of darkness as the candle was swept to the floor. Then a shriek of triumph, inhuman and high-pitched.

And then nothing.

ABOUT THE AUTHOR

Robert Earl graduated from Keele University in 1994, after which he started a career in sales. Three years later though, he'd had more than enough of that and since then he has been working, living and travelling in the Balkans and the Middle East.

Robert is currently back in the UK with his Romanian wife (who is still giving him hell for using her brothers' names in the *Inferno!* story *'The Vampire Hunters'*). *Savage City* is his third Warhammer novel.

READ TILL YOU BLEED
DO YOU HAVE THEM ALL?

1. Trollslayer – William King
2. First & Only – Dan Abnett
3. Skavenslayer – William King
4. Into the Maelstrom – Ed. Marc Gascoigne & Andy Jones
5. Daemonslayer – William King
6. Eye of Terror – Barrington J Bayley

7. Space Wolf – William King
8. Realm of Chaos – Ed. Marc Gas-coigne & Andy Jones
9. Ghostmaker – Dan Abnett
10. Hammers of Ulric – Dan Abnett, Nik Vincent & James Wallis
11. Ragnar's Claw – William King
12. Status: Deadzone – Ed. Marc Gascoigne & Andy Jones
13. Dragonslayer – William King
14. The Wine of Dreams – Brian Craig
15. Necropolis – Dan Abnett
16. 13th Legion – Gav Thorpe
17. Dark Imperium – Ed. Marc Gascoigne & Andy Jones
18. Beastslayer – William King
19. Gilead's Blood – Abnett & Vincent
20. Pawns of Chaos – Brian Craig
21. Xenos – Dan Abnett
22. Lords of Valour – Ed. Marc Gascoigne & Christian Dunn
23. Execution Hour – Gordon Rennie
24. Honour Guard – Dan Abnett
25. Vampireslayer – William King
26. Kill Team – Gav Thorpe
27. Drachenfels – Jack Yeovil
28. Deathwing – Ed. David Pringle & Neil Jones
29. Zavant – Gordon Rennie
30. Malleus – Dan Abnett
31. Konrad – David Ferring
32. Nightbringer – Graham McNeill
33. Genevieve Undead – Jack Yeovil
34. Grey Hunter – William King
35. Shadowbreed – David Ferring
36. Words of Blood – Ed. Marc Gascoigne & Christian Dunn
37. Zaragoz – Brian Craig
38. The Guns of Tanith – Dan Abnett
39. Warblade – David Ferring
40. Farseer – William King
41. Beasts in Velvet – Jack Yeovil
42. Hereticus – Dan Abnett
43. The Laughter of Dark Gods – Ed. David Pringle
44. Plague Daemon – Brian Craig
45. Storm of Iron – Graham McNeill
46. The Claws of Chaos – Gav Thorpe
47. Draco – Ian Watson
48. Silver Nails – Jack Yeovil
49. Soul Drinker – Ben Counter
50. Harlequin – Ian Watson
51. Storm Warriors – Brian Craig
52. Straight Silver – Dan Abnett
53. Star of Erengrad – Neil McIntosh
54. Chaos Child – Ian Watson
55. The Dead & the Damned – Jonathan Green

WWW.BLACKLIBRARY.COM

- 56 Shadow Point – Gordon Rennie
- 57 Blood Money – C L Werner
- 58 Angels of Darkness – Gav Thorpe
- 59 Mark of Damnation – James Wallis
- 60 Warriors of Ultramar – Graham McNeill
- 61 Riders of the Dead – Dan Abnett
- 62 Daemon World – Ben Counter
- 63 Giantslayer – William King
- 64 Crucible of War – Ed. Marc Gascoigne & Christian Dunn
- 65 Honour of the Grave – Robin D Laws
- 66 Crossfire – Matthew Farrer
- 67 Blood & Steel – C L Werner
- 68 Crusade for Armageddon – Jonathan Green
- 69 Way of the Dead – Ed. Marc Gascoigne & Christian Dunn
- 70 Sabbat Martyr – Dan Abnett
- 71 Taint of Evil – Neil McIntosh

- 72 Fire Warrior – Simon Spurrier
- 73 The Blades of Chaos – Gav Thorpe
- 74 Gotrek and Felix Omnibus 1 – William King
- 75 Gaunt's Ghosts: The Founding – Dan Abnett
- 76 Wolfblade – William King
- 77 Mark of Heresy – James Wallis
- 78 For the Emperor – Sandy Mitchell
- 79 The Ambassador – Graham McNeill
- 80 The Bleeding Chalice – Ben Counter
- 81 Caves of Ice – Sandy Mitchell
- 82 Witch Hunter – C L Werner
- 83 Ravenor – Dan Abnett
- 84 Magestorm – Jonathan Green
- 85 Annihilation Squad – Gav Thorpe
- 86 Ursun's Teeth – Graham McNeill
- 87 What Price Victory – Ed. Marc Gascoigne & Christian Dunn
- 88 The Burning Shore – Robert Earl
- 89 Grey Knights – Ben Counter
- 90 Swords of the Empire – Ed. Marc Gascoigne & Christian Dunn
- 91 Double Eagle – Dan Abnett
- 92 Sacred Flesh – Robin D Laws
- 93 Legacy – Matthew Farrer
- 94 Iron Hands – Jonathan Green
- 95 The Inquisition War – Ian Watson
- 96 Blood of the Dragon – C L Werner
- 97 Traitor General – Dan Abnett
- 98 The Heart of Chaos – Gav Thorpe
- 99 Dead Sky, Black Sun – Graham McNeill
- 100 Wild Kingdoms – Robert Earl
- 101 Gotrek & Felix Omnibus 2 – William King
- 102 Gaunt's Ghosts: The Saint – Dan Abnett
- 103 Dawn of War – CS Goto
- 104 Forged in Battle – Justin Hunter
- 105 Blood Angels: Deus Encarmine – James Swallow
- 106 Eisenhorn – Dan Abnett
- 107 Valnir's Bane – Nathan Long
- 108 Lord of the Night – Simon Spurrier
- 109 Necromancer – Jonathan Green
- 110 Crimson Tears – Ben Counter
- 111 Witch Finder – C L Werner
- 112 Ravenor Returned – Dan Abnett
- 113 Death's Messenger – Sandy Mitchell
- 114 Blood Angels: Deus Sanguinus – James Swallow
- 115 Keepers of the Flame – Neil McIntosh
- 116 The Konrad Saga – David Ferring
- 117 The Traitor's Hand – Sandy Mitchell
- 118 Darkblade: The Daemon's Curse – Dan Abnett & Mike Lee
- 119 Survival Instinct – Andy Chambers
- 120 Salvation – CS Goto
- 121 Fifteen Hours – Mitchel Scanlon
- 122 Grudge Bearer – Gav Thorpe